Buying The Farm

by

Rhonda Hanson

Buying The Farm

by

Rhonda Hanson

ISBN 978-0-9703817-5-0

Copyright 2024

by

Grace Under Pressure Publishing
P.O. Box 337
Bell Buckle, TN 37020

*All rights reserved. No reproduction of any kind
without expressed written consent from
Grace Under Pressure Publishing*

graceunderpressure.com

Dedication

To all those who very kindly took the time to read my other books and who made me feel loved and appreciated. I expect I will write fewer and fewer books in the coming years, but this is a story I wanted to tell. Thank you for taking the time to read it.

Rhonda Hanson

Buying The Farm

It was getting dark. She knew she should get up to go inside, draw the curtains, and turn on the lights but she felt she just needed a few more minutes to work up the motivation. It had been a long day with nothing to show for it, other than the animals being fed... what few there were left. She had to sell most of them over the past few days to pay some bills. There were a few chickens and a couple of goats left, and one old horse that was probably nearing the end of his life.

She still had Nip, though. She reached a hand down to scratch the Australian cattle dog's head. All his cattle were gone and poor Nip didn't know quite what to do with himself, so he stayed close to his owner's side, eagerly waiting for her to let him know.

As she pushed herself up from her rocker, he jumped to attention and then began to encourage her to go in, once he saw that was her intention, by giving her little nudges with his nose on the back of her leg.

She smiled down at him, and let the efficient dog think he was doing his job. "Let's call it a night, Nip," she said in her low, quiet way.

Nip knew that meant supper and picked up the pace, leading her to his dish for some fresh kibble. She poured it out for him, then returned to the front room to close the front curtains and turn on the lamps.

She had intended to sit and try to get her mind off things by doing a little reading, but she rubbed her eyes and changed her mind, deciding to turn the lights back off and just end this very long day. She checked the locks and then stopped on her way upstairs to bed, remembering the stack of mail by the door.

She let out a tired sigh. Ignoring it wasn't going to make it go away. She picked up the bundle and leafed through it, wondering what she could leave until morning and what needed immediate attention.

"Iris Anderson. Mr. and Mrs. Glenn Anderson. Iris Foster Anderson. Mrs. Iris Anderson." She read the addresses silently and drew a grimace, telling herself that regardless of how many variations of her name there were, there still wasn't enough of her left to make one good Iris.

The bulk of the mail was addressed to Glenn Anderson. She would have to be the one to open all those, as well.

"Bills, bills, bills," she muttered. "What am I supposed to pay them with, my looks?"

Iris Anderson said this out loud with convincing sarcasm, completely unaware that some might consider her looks worth enough to settle several times what she owed. She stood looking vacantly at her collection of windowed envelopes with the weight of what they represented bearing down on her.

"Not tonight," she breathed wearily. "I can't do this tonight. I'm going to bed."

Nip heard a phrase he recognized and climbed the stairs behind her to make sure she didn't get distracted and actually turned in, so that he could circle his own bed several times and then lie down to sleep off his supper.

Iris removed several pillows from her bed and turned down the covers, before heading into the bathroom for a quick shower. She towel-dried her long, ginger hair roughly until her loose curls began to form again, then stood staring at her reflection as if she were seeing a stranger in the mirror. Her light blue eyes, that her tenth grade art teacher had once informed her were arctic blue, stared back at her in a disinterested, apathetic manner. She decided that she looked as tired as she felt.

She wasn't exactly counting the hours until tomorrow's meeting with the bank manager, but she knew that lying awake all night and dreading it wasn't going to change the outcome.

"I'm done," she said glumly and crawled into bed. "In more ways than one, I'm done."

Iris had trouble getting comfortable. Her neck was stiff and she'd begun a headache. She punched her pillow a few times until she was finally able to cradle her neck in it more comfortably, then opened her eyes after a bit to stare blankly up at the dark gray ceiling above her.

She already knew what John Mabry was going to tell her, although she also knew that the kind, concerned bank manager wasn't going to enjoy it anymore than she was.

Iris realized that he had gone above and beyond, in the hopes of being able to help her keep the farm but the long, drawn out illness of her late husband, Glenn, had taken a toll on their finances, even though this was hardly what put Iris in the heartbreaking position of losing the farm after his passing.

Thinking of this now caused the typical bitter awareness of her resentment to surface. She struggled to come up with at least some measure of shame for being angry with her late husband, who had never revealed to her the shocking extent of their indebtedness, apparently exerting all his efforts at hiding it rather than dealing with it.

Iris had thought that things were on a fairly even course, since these windowed envelopes had never made an appearance in the mailbox before recently. She had no way of knowing that her late husband had been keeping their existence to himself and had allowed her to believe that the farm was making money.

In the meantime, creditors had begun closing in on Glenn Anderson and he had chosen to cope by simply drinking more. He'd developed cirrhosis and his liver eventually failed, due to his doubling down on the same behavior he had falsely sworn to his young wife that he had abandoned.

The last year of his life was spent in pain, and periods of incoherent ramblings until at last, as a final gesture that in his clouded mind, may have been intended as a kindness to Iris, he chose to put the both of them out of his misery by swallowing the entire bottle of his newly refilled pain medication and chasing it down with alcohol.

Iris lifted her arm to rest it on her forehead and let out a heavy sigh, as she once again observed that allowing his wife to come into the room with a loaded breakfast tray and not only find him dead, but forcing her to realize that she had lain in ignorance all night long, next to a man who was not sleeping but dying, was anything but a kindness.

She had tried to tell herself that he had probably meant well and had maybe been hoping that his life insurance would take care of everything for her, but she soon discarded that hope when the insurance's monthly premium turned out to be just another bill that he had stopped paying. She made herself face the fact that he had deliberately left her with the aftermath of his actions.

Iris blinked back tears in the darkness, overwhelmed with all of it, thinking that surely she was too young to have already found herself in such dire straits.

She was only in her late twenties, having married Glenn Anderson immediately after she graduated high school, and she felt that she had aged more in the past two years than she had in all the years she'd lived before then.

She'd had such dreams of the life that she and the dashing young football player were going to build together after their exciting elopement, especially when Glenn's grandmother left her old farm to him and told him to make what he could of it. If only he'd had parents around to instruct him in the management of his grandmother's farm, maybe things would have worked out differently but he had been raised by his grandmother and after she passed, he was essentially on his own.

Of course, the same could be said for Iris, who had come up through the foster care system until she turned eighteen and went from that stretch of various experiences to becoming a wife. Iris had drawn a lot of teasing in high school for having the last name Foster, as if it had determined her lot in life, but she'd developed a thick skin early on and found it amusing, herself.

She was so ready for a change of status that she jumped into marriage with no reservations, determined to have a happy ending, after all. She'd hoped for a child at the beginning of their marriage to love and to care for in a way she had never known, but it wasn't meant to be, so she had contented herself with learning what she could about farm supervision and had come to love it and began to feel that they could turn it into a profitable venture.

Yet another thing that wasn't meant to be, she reflected with regret. She continued to try to corral her rambling thoughts until the wee hours of the morning, when she was finally able to fall asleep, if only fitfully and out of mental exhaustion.

Morning came too soon but it did come, and Iris dutifully pulled herself out of bed and flashed a dour look at the restless Nip, who had important things to do outside.

"Just hang on there," she advised dryly, heading into the bathroom to wash the sleep from her eyes and pull on a pair of jeans for now, until she had to prepare for her trip into town.

Nip led the way downstairs and stood waiting impatiently for her to open the kitchen door, then bounded out of it like a rocket that was headed straight for the two goats, who saw him coming and prepared to defend themselves.

Iris managed a faint smile of amusement and busied herself getting coffee started, then brought the pile of mail she'd given up on the night before to the kitchen table to try to decide what was the highest priority.

The more she tried to categorize and prioritize, the more hopeless it seemed. A moment of frustration caused her to slam her fist down on the pile of mail and then sending it flying onto the floor with a sweep of her slender arm. She rested her forehead in her hands and allowed a few tears of desperation to escape.

The simple truth was that she had nowhere to go. She had no family and no close friends that she felt comfortable enough with to ask about possibly renting a room from, even if she had the money to pay rent.

She already knew that John Mabry was going to tell her that she had to sell the farm and she also knew that the money from the sale would barely be enough to pay off the debts, and that was if she was lucky. She was literally going to be homeless soon.

She couldn't even blame the shameful way the government treated farmers in general for her own predicament. The fault lay squarely on the shoulders of poor financial management.

She tried to imagine where she could find a job that might pay her enough to at least secure temporary lodging, but she couldn't even follow that trail of thought without staring hard at nothing and shaking her head in defeat.

She finally shoved back from the table and downed a quick cup of black coffee, then headed back upstairs to get dressed for her dreaded trip into town. She might as well get it over with.

She pulled a light, simple summer dress from the hanger and slipped it over her head, then stepped into a pair of sandals before standing in front of her bathroom mirror and inspecting her face and hair critically. There wasn't much she could do for her beautiful but unruly, long, copper hair but tie it back, so she just bent down toward the floor and shook it out with her fingers, then threw it back before applying the barest essential bit of color to her cheeks.

She reminded herself that it didn't matter what she looked like today, since it wouldn't change anything. What was coming was coming and not even Aphrodite, herself could stop it, let alone Iris Anderson.

She exhaled in resignation, then picked up her truck keys to get this over with. All too soon, she pulled in to park in front of the small town bank and sat still for a moment, taking in a few deep breaths before making her way inside.

Mr. John Mabry stood as she was shown into his office, and came around his desk to take her hand in greeting.

"Have a seat, Iris," he invited.

She settled into the chair nearest his desk and quietly declined his offer of coffee.

He eyed her with a kind, but frank expression. "I'm sure that if anything had changed with your situation since our last talk, you would have notified me so it's probably safe to assume that we're exactly where we thought we would be today."

She nodded but made no reply, other than to offer him a weak smile of agreement that he returned sympathetically.

"Iris, I'm not sure what we could get for your farm by selling it, especially since most of the livestock has already been sold, but you do still have some equipment. Is that right?"

"Yes, but none of it is in the best condition," she admitted sadly. "Of course, some guy might whip out a wrench and prove me wrong, but I think most of it is in need of repair."

He nodded, thinking that she probably wasn't wrong about that. Glenn Anderson had not been known for his mechanical skills, and most things had just found their way to the back of the property line, to become overgrown with vines and weeds and eventually rust away.

Mr. Mabry pulled a folder over and laid it in front of him, before looking up at Iris with genuine disappointment.

"I was so hoping to turn this thing around," he told her and she looked down at her hands, feeling the embarrassment that rightfully belonged to her late husband and quietly despising him for it.

The banker seemed to be able to read her thoughts. "It's not fair for you to have been left with all this," he observed flatly, reaching for his reading glasses and opening the file to glance over the figures he'd been compiling for the past few days to discuss with Iris Anderson.

"Your total indebtedness includes such things as of course, the farm itself, some of the equipment, credit card balances..."

He paused when he saw Iris look up at him quickly in confusion.

"What credit cards?" she asked tightly. "I don't have any credit cards." She immediately answered her own question. "But I suppose Glenn did."

"They're in his name," Mr. Mabry confirmed.

"I expect that it's not possible to know what he charged on them. You just have balances, I guess."

"If you have copies of his death certificate, the credit card companies may be willing to give you a copy of the last statement.

Normally, a credit card company doesn't go after the surviving spouse for payment, but will more than likely insist that they have a claim staked in the proceeds that occur from the sale of your property."

He shook his head in disapproval. "They don't seem to know when to quit."

John Mabry glanced up at her curiously. "Have you not received any credit card bills since Glenn passed?"

"To be honest, I don't know," Iris admitted. "I can hear exactly how irresponsible that sounds, but I haven't opened all the envelopes that keep coming in the mail, because I can't do anything about them until the farm is sold. It's just something else to keep me up all night.

"I've sold almost all the livestock to pay for the balances we had at the feed store and for a few of the bigger pieces of equipment, but I hardly think that the few chickens and a couple of goats that are still there will do much to lessen the impact of the rest of all those bills. But sooner or later, they'll have to go as well," she finished, with the weight of all this evident on her slim shoulders.

She raised her beautiful blue, teary eyes to the banker and her complete humiliation tugged at his fatherly heart. "Mr. John, is there any way that we can avoid a public auction?"

He knew exactly what prompted her question and couldn't blame her for asking. The last thing she needed, on top of everything else her late husband had left her with, was for the entire town to stand around, witnessing her shame.

Of course, most people in their little town liked Iris Anderson and they realized that it was Glenn, not Iris, who should be blamed, but that didn't stop tongues from wagging and not everyone could be counted on to be tactful, or to keep their opinions to themselves.

"That's something I wanted to talk to you about today, Iris," he answered, sliding his folder to one side. He saw no point in continuing to verbalize every single item of debt. She simply couldn't do anything about any of it, other than give up her home, her land, her life, and she was doing all that without protest.

"I've been approached by a couple of interested parties, who are expressing a desire to purchase your farm but I've held off on mentioning them to you, because I have enough inside knowledge to have become aware that both of them are developers and have no interest in keeping the land intact.

"They both simply want to parcel it up and build cheap, cookie-cutter homes on it."

He saw her bleak dismay and hurried to continue.

"I did reach out to a man who I'm personally acquainted with. I feel he would be the best buyer for you, provided he's interested. His family have all been farmers for generations and he has several large successful farms, himself. He has roots in this town and would certainly want to maintain your land's identity as a working farm, provided he does end up purchasing it. That is what we should hope for."

She seemed to exhibit some relief in that possibility and Mr. Mabry decided that he would focus all his efforts on convincing the potential buyer to seriously consider buying the Anderson farm or at the very least, come take a look at it.

"I have a call in to him," he advised her, with a smile of encouragement. "Let's not give up hope. He just may be interested and if he is, he would definitely be the kind of buyer you'd want to deal with. He won't try to make any low-ball offers to you.

"Of course, he'll either be interested or he won't. He's not a man to be talked into anything. But I expect he'll at least be willing to see your farm."

Iris sensed that this was as far as their meeting was going today. She smiled up at Mr. Mabry and stood, as he seemed to be about to do so, himself.

He walked with her through the bank and stood with her on the sidewalk for a moment, resting a hand of reassurance on her shoulder and doing his best to encourage her.

"As soon as I know something, Iris, I'll call you right away and let you know. In the meantime, you might take a drive around your place and try to see it through the eyes of a potential buyer who's not afraid of hard work."

The kind man reached into his lapel pocket and pulled out a folded piece of paper.

"Don't be afraid to take a look at this. It's what we need to get for your farm in order to settle your debts, but the good news is that once that happens, you can breathe easier.

"You're young and this sort of thing will fall off your credit report in a few years, and you can hopefully begin again."

She nodded, taking the paper from him but not looking at it just yet. She needed a little time and he understood.

He patted her arm with a kind smile. "It'll be alright, Iris. I know it doesn't seem like it just now, but it will be."

Chapter Two

Barrett Webb sat in his vehicle and looked at the less than impressive rickety sign that announced to anyone who might wonder, that the road to his left would lead to the Anderson farm.

He drew in a deep breath and admitted to himself that nothing about what he was seeing so far, seemed to have any connection to anything like a farm but Barrett was a disciplined and realistic man and after agreeing to meet with John Mabry, he realized that the widow who was forced to sell the farm could hardly be expected to maintain it to any real degree.

Although John Mabry wasn't the type to engage in gossip, or divulge personal details about his clients, he made an exception in this case because he wanted Barrett Webb to have all the facts, hoping that they might sway him to be willing to purchase the farm from Iris. If not, the developers were waiting in the wings like a pair of vultures, to insult her with their low offers and remind her that she was up against the wall. If it was in John Mabry's power to stop them and to prevent the property from going to public auction, he certainly intended to try, even if it meant sharing personal facts about Iris Anderson that he would normally protect.

The man who was now about to turn his truck down the road to the Anderson farm knew from what John Mabry had told him, that Mrs. Anderson had been blindsided by the manifestation of overwhelming debt that had been concealed from her.

He knew that she had singlehandedly been trying to do what she could to hang onto her livestock and to keep things running, but had finally been forced to admit defeat and face the consequences of her late husband's actions.

A scowl of displeasure washed over Barrett Webb's face, as he wondered what kind of man would allow this sort of needless misfortune to occur and worse yet, live and die in such a way as to abandon his wife by making her a widow and causing her to have to deal with the repercussions alone?

Barrett suspected that the answer was a selfish, immature, careless man or perhaps not a man at all, but a boy. He drew in a deep breath and cautioned himself to not draw conclusions about matters he had only been told about, but had no personal knowledge of.

John Mabry had also confided to him that once the farm was sold, Iris Anderson had nowhere to go. She had been raised in foster homes and had no family that she knew of. He'd mentioned that he and the local minister were planning to look into what options might be available to her, but that they weren't intending to discuss it with her until they felt they had found a solution, not wanting to give her false hope.

Barrett began driving down the road toward the farmhouse, which he had been told would be about a half mile down at the end of the road. If all the land he had seen so far belonged to Iris Anderson, and the road to her house was a half mile long, Barrett suspected that the tract consisted of enough acreage to at least peak his interest.

He wasn't concerned about the rundown state of things that John Mabry had warned him about. The Webb family had plenty of people on the payroll who would be ideal for such a challenge and Barrett reasoned that if he, himself had no interest in buying the farm, he'd at least give his father a chance to entertain the idea of adding it to his own holdings.

Of course, Barrett was aware that his father had other issues to be concerned over today, so he would more than likely try to avoid passing something as mundane as the purchase of a farm on to him. The senior member of the Webb family had an elderly aunt living in this area. Aunt Sadie was blind and her feeble, vulnerable condition caused her to constantly need close supervision.

She was a resident of a nursing home in an adjoining county, and he had asked Barrett to check on her today before heading back to determine what sort of condition he would find her in, if he were to suddenly appear unannounced at the facility.

Barrett had felt his father was being overly concerned, but he had humored him and stopped by the nursing home without first making an appointment to see Great-Aunt Sadie, and was appalled to find her slumped down in a wheel chair, not in her room but out in the hallway, confused and waving her arm around but not speaking. Whatever she had last tried to eat, was on her clothes and had dried on her chin.

After restraining himself from expressing his anger out loud and startling her, he first knelt down in front of her and told her who he was. She immediately broke into a sweet smile and lifted her shaky hand to touch his face and fuss over him. Barrett stopped an aide in the hall, no longer bothering to hide his anger, and demanded to know who had left Aunt Sadie sitting out in the hall in this undignified manner. He demanded to speak to the administrator and the flustered aide hurried away to let him know that Miss Sadie Webb's family member was here asking for him.

As Barrett expected, suddenly all sorts of available personnel appeared, fawning and expressing concern over Miss Sadie. She was taken back into her room, her bed linens changed, and the bath that she should have had that morning was finally given to her, while Barrett had a few choice words with the administrator.

Thinking of this now caused a stern frown to rest on his handsome face and he was still wearing it when he stopped his truck in front of the farmhouse and stepped out to look around.

Iris was in the chicken pen, trying to see if there were any more eggs besides the few she'd found earlier in the morning, since the day was growing hot and the hens seemed to be off their laying.

She had obviously been doing odd chores around the property, as her jeans were dirty and the cropped, sleeveless top she'd put on to try to stay cool was streaked with soil stains and something that looked suspiciously like grease.

Barrett saw the flash of her long coppery hair, as the sun bore down on her and lit it up. He was surprised that she hadn't pulled her hair back or pinned it up in this heat, but was secretly glad that she hadn't. She made quite a picture, standing in the midst of the fussing, frantic hens with her beautiful cattle dog doing what he could to keep them all together.

She had turned on a faucet and was filling the trough for the chickens to get a drink, then let her dog drink from the end of it as she laughed at him, and whipped the stream of water over his hot coat. She finally turned the hose on herself, washing the evidence of chickens off her bare feet and letting the water run down her hot neck as she held her hair up and out of the way.

Barrett wondered if she was perhaps the daughter of the widow and smiled wryly to himself, as he also wondered if someone as beautiful as she certainly was had to endure an endless supply of "farmer's daughter" jokes from the locals. He expected she had heard it all.

Apparently, the loud, indignant chickens had made enough noise to drown out the sound of Barrett's truck as he had driven it very slowly down the road, looking all around him. As Iris turned off the faucet and straightened up, she saw him standing next to it and was clearly startled.

She looked down at herself in quiet panic. It had been her intention to finish up in time to grab a quick shower and change before the man John Mabry was sending arrived. She looked up at the sun and back at him, telling herself that he was early. He confirmed this.

"I'm terribly sorry to arrive ahead of time. I had an errand to attend on my way here and I'm afraid I was done earlier than I'd expected, and drove on out to look at things from the main road. I hope you'll forgive me."

Iris hurried to dismiss the look of irritation she certainly must be wearing and replaced it with a quiet smile, stepping through the gate to the chicken pen and locking it before approaching him.

"I'm Barrett Webb. John Mabry invited me to take a look at your property."

He offered his hand and Iris looked down at her own filthy ones and glanced back up at him with a look of apology in her striking, blue eyes.

"I'm sorry for not shaking your hand," she said in her soft voice that had a slight husky quality to it. She lifted both her hands to show him that she meant well and he smiled.

"That's quite alright. Chickens are notoriously messy."

She nodded and turned to look back at them with disappointment.

"They're starting to go off their laying. I've checked them for mites and worms, and I keep their coop fairly clean. They're not very old so I'm beginning to think it's the heat."

"It very well could be," Barrett agreed.

He watched her train her eyes on them for another moment before she turned and looked back at him with a little shrug and a self-conscious laugh.

"I don't know why I'm letting myself get all involved. I'll soon be finding new homes for them, anyway."

Barrett looked at her with surprise that he couldn't hide, and she tilted her head and studied him.

"You did say that Mr. John sent you?"

"He did, but..." He was baffled. "Surely, you're not Mrs. Anderson?"

"Somebody has to be," she said with a sigh. "I guess I'm the lucky one. "

"This is your farm?" Barrett just wanted to be sure.

"What's left of it," she replied with a dismissive wave of her hand. "Such as it is, it's mine for now."

Barrett wasn't usually at a loss but he was clearly mystified. Surely this young woman wasn't the recently widowed Iris Anderson? He stood looking at her with such focus, that she began to wonder if her face was as dirty as the rest of her.

"If you don't mind," she said, beginning to feel more and more embarrassed over her appearance, "I'll just run inside and wash up and put on some clean clothes. Please have a look around and make yourself at home."

"Certainly," he returned softly, watching her hurry indoors with bewilderment still apparent on his face. Had John Mabry deliberately not told him that Mrs. Anderson was so young?

Barrett reasoned that the man probably hadn't thought that it was an important detail and he couldn't understand why he was now letting it become one.

He forced himself to concentrate on the business at hand and walked along the pasture fence, gazing across the way and noting with approval that a stream cut through the field and appeared to be running. He hoped it was spring fed and made a mental note to ask, before continuing to look around.

His warm, chestnut brown eyes wandered over the landscape. He was able to see beyond the old, broken down equipment and fields badly in need of haying, and suspected that there was potential. Someone had more than likely put a great deal of time and effort into the farm many years earlier and in spite of its neglected and dilapidated state, he could see what was obviously once an orchard off in the distance, and enough fence still standing to indicate where separate pastures had been.

He was still taking it all in, when he heard the screen door close and turned to see her coming down the steps with clean jeans and a sleeveless top, the exact color of her light blue eyes. She stopped to slide on some sandals that had been left on the porch before approaching him.

"Do you have any questions?" she asked, letting her eyes wander around the fields, trying to look at it as John Mabry had suggested and hoping that the man could see something worth salvaging.

"How many acres are included?" He looked down at a small pad that he had scribbled some things down on when he'd been sitting in his truck on the main road earlier, and wanted to make sure he didn't forget to ask.

"Six hundred eighteen," she answered and he raised a brow in silent appreciation and made a note of it.

"Mrs. Anderson..."

"Just Iris," she corrected blandly. "I'm feeling old enough as it is lately, so let's not make it worse."

He smiled at her remark.

"Only if I'm allowed to be just Barrett," he agreed. He glanced out toward the direction of the stream.

"Have you had any recent rains?"

"No," she sighed. "I wish I could have done some kind of rain dance before you got here so you'd think it rained all the time here but if I had the power to do that, I wouldn't be in this mess."

He almost laughed but checked himself. Perhaps she didn't mean to be funny. He gestured toward the stream.

"I noticed that in spite of it not raining recently, the stream is actually flowing."

"It's spring fed," she said, her face brightening as she was able to point out something positive about the place. "There are a couple of wells on the property. It's good water."

He nodded and then took another look around. "Is there road access to much of the property?"

"There is," she said. "There's a farm track that runs around the perimeter and a few lanes, cutting through. I have an aerial map in the house, if you'd like to take that with you. I'm afraid a lot of fence is in need of repair. We had cattle on some of the land and the fence took a lot of maintenance. I'm afraid I dropped the ball on that."

She grinned regretfully and he drew his brows and looked at her curiously.

"Surely, you didn't try to deal with that yourself?"

"For a while. But that's a long story." She cut herself off with a little laugh. "There used to be an old orchard that way."

She pointed to the place he'd noticed earlier. "I expect some of the trees still drop a few apples but they're pretty old, so I'm not sure how good the apples are. The birds and deer could tell you, though."

Barrett moved slowly toward the pasture fence and stood in thought. Iris watched him, wishing that she could read his mind. The wind seemed to be playing with his dark curls, as he rested his hands on his hips and weighed everything out.

An idea was trying to form in his mind but it was so out of the blue and unexpected, that he told himself that he needed to be alone to think it through.

He finally turned around and saw Iris down on her knees, roughing up the coat on her cattle dog and speaking to him in a low, corrective voice.

"Australian?" Barrett asked, and she glanced up at him with a smile.

"He is. This is Nip," she added and Barrett walked over and presented the back of his hand to the herd animal before reaching to give his ears a scratch.

"He's very handsome," he observed. "You mentioned having had cattle. I imagine that was Nip's job, then?"

"It was and he's a brilliant herd dog," Iris bragged, giving the dog a pat as if he could understand her. "I'm not sure what to do with him," she added, standing as something shadowed her pretty face. "But I guess I'll cross that bridge when I get to it."

"He wouldn't stay with the farm?" Barrett asked, watching her consider that.

"Well... if it remains a farm, he could. But if a developer ends up getting it, I'll need to find him a home."

"Let's hope it doesn't come to that," he replied with a smile and Iris had to make an effort to not allow what was probably a polite comment to generate false hope.

"Did you want to see the farmhouse, or would you probably just knock it down?"

"I try not to show up with a wrecking ball if it can be avoided," he said lightly, a grin lighting up his handsome face. "I wish I had time to see it today but I'm afraid I didn't carve out the amount of time I should have."

Iris looked down at the ground, wondering if this meant he wasn't interested then glanced back up hopefully when she heard him ask her if she minded if he returned on Saturday.

"No, that would be fine," she assured him. "Do you want that map of the property lines?"

"If it wouldn't be too much trouble," Barrett said. He really did need to know exactly what he was looking at.

He watched as Iris stepped lightly up the steps, her long hair catching the breeze and tumbling back to rest just above her waist. She reached inside the door and turned around with the map in one hand, coming back down to look up at him while she held it out. He reached for it without looking down at it, returning her brief gaze and silently appraising her before he made himself glance down at the map and thank her.

"Would ten Saturday morning work for you?" he asked her. "I don't want to eat up your day."

"That'll be fine. I'll try to hold back the hoards of potential buyers until then," she laughed and he grinned.

"Whatever you do, don't sell it before Saturday," he admonished her.

Iris watched him drive away with the hope she'd felt earlier begin to stir again.

Barrett watched her in the mirror, as he was leaving, and wondered if the idea that was beginning to present itself was really that ridiculous, after all.

Chapter Three

Stuart Webb cradled his coffee cup in his hands and looked over it at his son, a sober demeanor resting on his face. He had listened to Barrett's account of the condition he had found Aunt Sadie in and realized that she had to be removed from that facility.

The problem was that so much front work had gone into choosing the nursing home that they had eventually allowed to care for their aged relative, and at the time it seemed to be deserving of its high rating. Sadly, it was the best of the contenders.

A new administrator had been hired and there was a large turnover of staff. Barrett had also informed his father that it was obvious that the nursing home was overcrowded, with some rooms housing three and four residents.

He sat his cup down and folded his arms, considering the state of things.

"Well, Son, you know that Aunt Sadie absolutely would not agree to moving in with us although I never could understand why, exactly. All she would say is that she'd rather be a burden to strangers than to her own family and none of us could convince her that she wasn't a burden to anyone. I wouldn't be surprised if she were to put that same argument to you, now."

Barrett nodded thoughtfully but still felt that what he was suggesting had some merit, if he could bring everyone onto the same page with him. His father's voice cut into his thoughts.

"Would you purchase this farm, whether or not the seller agreed with your proposal, or is that the only reason you'd be interested in buying it?"

"No, even though it's in a state of neglect, it's very nice property. Over six hundred acres, with spring-fed water sources and good road access. I've purchased much less desirable farms, so I suspect I'll make an offer on this one. I'm going back in the morning to see more of it, since I didn't have a lot of time, yesterday."

Both men looked up, as Mrs. Patricia Webb came into the kitchen with a smile. She stopped beside her son's chair and gently clasped the back of his head, gathering his full, dark curls that trailed down to his collar in a loose grip, as she often did in order to tease him.

"When are you going to a barber, Barrett?"

He grinned up at her and she gave him a little wink, before stopping to pat her husband on the shoulder and make her way to the coffee pot.

"I heard you men talking about Aunt Sadie," Mrs. Webb said, bringing her coffee over to the table. "Barrett, how did you find her, yesterday?"

"Not good, Mother," he admitted. "There seems to be a great deal of neglect where she's concerned. It looks as if we need to step in and make new arrangements."

Patricia Webb's face reflected her worry. She looked over at her husband. "Do you think there's any point in trying again to get her to move in with us? I do think we should at least try."

"Barrett is working on that," his father replied.

"Yes, and hopefully it will solve more than just one problem," he commented cryptically, rising from the table and reaching over for the weathered Stetson hat he'd removed when he arrived. "I need to run back over to my place to pick up some barbed wire and then take that out to Morton's men. They're probably waiting on me, which is never a good thing."

He grinned, causing his shadowed expression to suddenly give way to a charming lightness. "That's all I need, to be scolded by my own men."

His parents laughed and returned his gentle embraces, as he took his leave and went about his business, still mulling over what he would do if Iris Anderson didn't seem to want to agree to what he suggested.

His parents watched him go with fondness, although Stuart Webb's reaction to Barrett's report about his aunt managed to leave its mark on his face.

"Poor Aunt Sadie," he sighed. "Just as stubborn..."

"As you are," his wife interjected with a little laugh. "So, I guess you come by it honestly."

He smiled down at his cup. "Barrett's looking to buy a farm not too far from here and if he does, he may end up spending more time over there than at his own place. For a while," he added.

His wife nodded. "I guess he's done that with pretty much every piece of property he's ever bought. You know who's not going to like that, right?"

Her husband scowled. "I just wish the farm was a lot further away. Maybe then, Blanche Hollis would decide it's not worth her trouble to chase off after him."

Mrs. Webb agreed with her silent nod.

Blanche Hollis sat polishing her nails, turning them into a vivid red, and reflecting on the fact that Barrett Webb had still not called her, as she'd asked him to.

She put the cap back on her nail polish with a frown, and sat waving her hands through the air, wondering what it was that was keeping him so busy lately. Not only had he not called her, but the last time she did manage to talk to him, he declined her invitation to join her and some of her friends for a pool party. He offered no explanation, whatsoever. He simply said he couldn't make it and told her that he had to hurry to a meeting.

As soon as she thought her nails were dry enough, she grabbed her phone and tried calling him again then hung up when the call went to voicemail with a petulant expression, pursing her lips and crossing her arms.

Of course, Blanche knew that Webb Enterprises was a hugely successful operation for Barrett, as well as for his father, but she still couldn't understand why he couldn't devote at least some time to a personal life. It went without saying that by personal life, Blanche meant herself.

She stood up to look around for her keys, deciding that if she couldn't get in touch with him by phone, she would simply show up at his place and get some answers.

Moments later, she hopped into her convertible, as red as her nails, and headed off to locate the handsome farm investor and do her best to lure him away from whatever it was that was making him unavailable to her.

She intended to tell him that she wouldn't be neglected forever, and that if he didn't pay more attention to her, there were plenty of other men around who would.

Unfortunately for Blanche, Barrett Webb was no more reachable at his home than he had been by phone. The housekeeper who came to the door simply informed her that he wasn't in and that she hadn't been told when to expect him.

A peeved and fuming Blanche Hollis sped her little car down the driveway, her blonde hair flying around in the wind, and headed toward town, deciding that even though she'd been unable to deliver her ultimatum, she still knew how to make good on it. Besides, a little jealousy was good for a man.

Iris couldn't figure out what was going on with her truck but whatever it was, she was going to have to figure it out, herself. She certainly didn't have the money to pay a mechanic.

When she started to make a quick run to the store, believing that she had plenty of time to get back before ten, she got no further than halfway down her road before the truck began misfiring and didn't seem to want to accelerate.

She backed it all the way to the house, although it didn't seem to want to do that either. Once she got it parked under a tree, she sat in it for a while, trying to remember if she'd ever had an issue like this with any other vehicle.

Of course, the truck was old, so maybe it was just ready for the salvage yard. Iris smiled sadly at the thought. She loved the old truck and would never let that happen.

She headed off to the old shed behind the house and eventually returned with a small toolbox. If she'd been keeping up with the time, she probably wouldn't have begun the project of trying to determine what was wrong with the old Apache but since she hadn't actually gone anywhere, it seemed to Iris that it was much earlier than it really was.

It was because of this, that Barrett Webb slowed his vehicle down as he rounded the circle drive of the property and drew his brows in confusion at the sight of two legs with pretty, bare feet that appeared to be sticking out of a truck motor.

He parked his own truck and got out, with a slow grin finding its way across his face. He suppressed a laugh when he heard Iris Anderson actually talking to the old motor, calling it "sweetie" and trying to convince it to "open up and say ah."

He hesitated to call out to her, not wishing for her to be startled and end up bumping her head on the underside of the hood, so he leaned back against the side of his truck and decided to wait until she finally emerged.

When she did, it was with a happy smile of satisfaction. She had slowly been checking each sparkplug, removing and replacing one wire at a time, since she wouldn't remember the firing order and had nothing handy to write it down on.

It hadn't taken her long to discover one plug that was absolutely corroded and she was hoping that this was the culprit, since the truck had been running fine until today.

As she pulled herself out of the motor and stepped down, she caught a glimpse of Barrett out of the corner of her eye and looked at him in surprise and confusion.

"Is it ten o' clock, already?" Iris looked up at the sky then around, as if she were a bit disoriented.

"Only just," Barrett replied with a smile. "What seems to be the issue?"

"Well, it's old, for one thing," she laughed. "But it started misfiring and got pretty sluggish about halfway down the road, so I brought it back and just thought I'd have a look at the plugs.

I had an old riding mower that acted that way once, and that's what it turned out to be. I'm just hoping that's all it is this time. I can't make room in the budget for a mechanic, just now."

He came closer with a look of appreciation for the old classic truck, then glanced over at its owner. "Fifty-eight?"

"It is," Iris admitted, with a note of affection for it. "And from the looks of this plug, it must have come with the truck."

She smiled to let him know that she didn't really believe that, then pulled an emery board from her jeans pocket and began filing away at the layer of white corrosion on it.

"I don't have to ask you if I have grease on my face," she said, grinning down at her work. "I can feel it. In fact, I can almost taste it."

She lifted her stunning, pale blue eyes to rest them on him with a self-deprecating grimace. "By the time I turn in at night, I usually have grease and everything else all over me. It takes a while to actually get clean enough to get in the bed, and if grease ends up in my hair, then I may have to pull an all-nighter."

He silently appraised her lovely, long, russet hair and smiled at that, watching her deft hands work to get the spark plug almost pristine before she felt she was ready to reinsert it and put its wire back on.

"Would you let me do that for you, or have I just insulted you by asking?" Barrett wondered.

She answered him by holding the plug up along with a feeler gauge, as if they were rare gems, and presenting them to him with a flourish.

He gave her a teasing look. "Aren't you going to tell me what the proper gap is?"

She took the gauge from him and selected the right blade before handing it back.

"Sure about that?" he challenged with a grin.

"I've never claimed to be sure about one single thing in my entire life and it has served me well. For the most part," she added dryly, with a little sigh that didn't get past him. "But I do think .035 is right. If not, I guess we'll know soon enough," she warned him, with a charming little smirk.

When the faithful old truck thanked them both by firing up right away and idling smoothly, Barrett lifted his hand to receive the high five that Iris instinctively aimed at him.

She reached inside the truck and brought out a canister of hand wipes for the both of them. "I keep these around, just in case," she told him. "Not that the truck breaks down often but I do take it when I go fishing, which is why I keep these inside."

"Do you like fishing?" Barrett asked in surprise.

"I do. The stream doesn't have anything in it big enough to fool with, but I've always suspected there's an underground source on a special part of this land and I used to dream about having it dug out to make a large pond or a small lake. I like to dream big. It's free and it doesn't hurt anyone," she told him with a grin. "But for now, I just drive to a place not far from here and make a day of it. Or, I used to," she amended, with just the hint of a frown.

She reached for his used hand wipes to put in a makeshift trash bag in the truck and looked up at him, not realizing that when she gazed at most people in that childlike, simple manner, they were captivated by her.

"Thanks for helping," she said lightly before seeming to remember why he was here. "Did you want to see more of the property first or start with the house or... you tell me," she finished with a little laugh. "Or maybe you drove all the way out here to let me down easy," she added, smiling faintly.

"I didn't come to let you down," he hurried to reassure her, watching her face light up with hope. "But I would like to drive around and take a better look. Would you agree to come with, and be my navigator-slash-tour guide?"

"Sure. I've not been out on much of the property in a while, so it'll be nice seeing it again."

He opened the door to his truck for her to hop in, then came around and looked over at her with a question in his eyes. "Do I go back out to the main road?"

"No, just drive around along that fence toward the back yard and there's a gate we can go through. That'll give you a better look at things up close."

When they reached the wide, metal gate, she jumped out and unchained it then put one foot up on the bottom rail and pushed off with the other, riding it inward like a kid and causing Barrett to laugh softly to himself.

He pulled through and she closed it behind them, purely from habit, then stood looking at it with an odd expression before opening it again and letting it swing back.

"There's no point in closing it, I guess," she explained as she got back into his truck. "All Nip's cattle are gone."

She looked out the window, blinking back a few rogue tears then back at him with a smile when she heard him quietly tell her that he was sorry about that.

"Well, it is what it is," she observed without bitterness. "It's not like they were pets."

He drew in a deep breath, regretting the situation this beautiful young woman found herself in and hoped that he could somehow work things out to give her a much better outcome than she'd been able to hope for.

He followed her directions, stopping every now and then to get a better look at some feature that seemed especially promising. The old orchard surprised the both of them, being in much better shape than Iris had supposed. The trees appeared as if they could use a bit of dead limb removal and topping off, but they were still bearing nice looking fruit.

Iris stood looking at them with a feeling of remorse, thinking that she could have been selling these apples but also knowing that it wouldn't have brought in enough money to even dent the amount of debt owed to her creditors. She shook her head and looked away and Barrett could only imagine that she was second-guessing herself about something, as she seemed prone to do.

They continued on around the acreage and it wasn't hard for Barrett to spot the part of the property that Iris had envisioned for a pond. It seemed as if that's what it had been intended for.

"This is your place," he said quietly.

"Yes." She sat looking out on it then opened the truck door and stepped out, walking toward it with her fingers tucked into the back pockets of her faded jeans and her long, loose curls whipping in the breeze.

Barrett watched her go, letting out a sigh and wishing the woman would simply let him pay off her debts and have a happy life but he knew she would never agree to that. He also knew that even if he told her that she could stay, she wouldn't. He would have to somehow make her think that she would be helping him by staying. It's not so much that she was proud, but she seemed to have an ethical quality to her that made her unwilling to just have anything handed to her that she didn't earn, herself.

He gave her a few moments alone, knowing that she was standing there taking a good hard look at her reality and wondering what was to become of her. He had intended to sit down with her in the farmhouse and talk to her about his idea, but now he decided not to wait.

Iris turned around when she sensed him close by, then flashed him a little smile as he came to a stop beside her to share the view of what was certainly a beautiful parcel of land.

He looked over at her curiously. "Why did you say that you suspected an underground water source here?"

"I'm a water witch," she said, trying to keep a straight face but failing miserably, once she saw his reaction. She rippled out a little laugh and he visibly relaxed.

"You're too easy," she told him, looking around at the field with eyes that reflected both the sunlight and her affection for this part of the property she had decided was special.

She leaned toward him and pointed ahead. "See how that strip of grass is greener that anything on either side of it? Look, it runs on that way for a good bit."

Barrett was very aware of her nearness to him, as he followed where she was indicating and thought about what she was saying.

"You might be onto something," he admitted quietly. "The ground there seems to be depressed a bit more."

"It's actually more so now than it used to be," Iris agreed. "But whenever it does rain, this is one of the last places to dry out so I've pretty much ruled out a sinkhole."

He was impressed by her deductive reasoning and silently decided that he would pursue attempting to discover whether her suspicions were correct.

"Iris..." He stopped and she glanced over, wondering what made him not finish whatever it was he'd been about to say. She didn't ask, though. She simply let him follow his thoughts without prompting him.

After a moment, he gestured for her to follow him back to the truck and stopped to let the tailgate down.

"Can we sit?"

She sensed that he was about to let her know if he intended to buy the farm from her or not, so she nimbly hoisted herself up and came to rest on the tailgate as gracefully as if she were a bird lighting on a branch. Barrett had intended to help her, but she was too quick for him.

He settled down next to her and was quiet for a long moment. Iris glanced over at him, noting his solemn profile and taking in his thick dark curls that clustered around his collar and the stubble beard that he managed to keep from becoming untidy. She had already approved of his very nice brown eyes that weren't too dark, allowing his emotions to be detected.

Iris privately acknowledged that Barrett Webb was an incredibly handsome man who seemed to fit right in with his surroundings. She had seen his hat lying on the truck seat and it was easy to imagine him wearing it.

She realistically admitted to herself that any man who looked like him had to have a wife or a girlfriend at home, so she had wisely stopped her admiration of him at a purely superficial level and forced herself to simply wait in silence for him to tell her what he'd decided.

When he finally did, she was stunned.

Chapter Four

Iris sat perfectly still, being careful not to interrupt and trying hard to focus on Barrett's first words, which were to inform her that he would purchase the farm, commit to keeping it a working farm, and pay whatever she needed to have for it.

It was when he paused then looked at her and added, "Iris, I'd like to talk to you about the possibility of your staying here," that she drew in a quick breath, unwilling to even hope that he'd really just said that to her.

Her joy was quickly replaced by a less pleasing emotion however, as she reluctantly began to suspect what he might actually mean and held up one hand to keep him from finishing.

He stopped and looked at her closely, trying to determine what it was he was seeing in her eyes. She seemed upset with him but made no effort to tell him why.

"I'm not sure how I've offended you, but I can clearly see that I have. I'm so sorry," he offered softly.

Iris wiped away the first suggestion of tears and stared down at the ground under their feet as they sat next to each other on the tailgate.

She looked back up at him now with a question in her eyes, always believing that most misunderstandings in life came from making assumptions. She was prone to do that, but she didn't want to be guilty of doing it, now. She hoped he was too much of a gentleman to be suggesting what she thought.

"You're not..." She wasn't sure she could make herself ask. "You don't mean that you want me to stay here as your..."

He suddenly realized what she was thinking and hurried to reassure her. "No, Iris, I don't mean anything like that!"

The relief that washed over her was impossible to miss.

He rested his eyes on her, and thought about how many women might actually hope that he would mean something like that and a sense of admiration for her began to stir inside him.

"I would never ask you to do anything indecent. There are no strings attached to my offer," Barrett said with quiet firmness. "I want you to understand that. I simply know a good business opportunity when I see one and my purchase of this property is based on the merits of the property, itself. I mean that, Iris," he added, allowing her to read him carefully.

She nodded and suddenly felt embarrassed for letting him know that she thought he was asking her to remain at the farm for his own personal pleasure.

He saw her flush of color and smiled then gave her a little wave of his fingers to dismiss the entire thing.

"Whether you choose to stay or not has no effect on my decision to purchase the farm. I need for you to know that. I do want to ask a favor, but it's completely respectable and it would be an immense help to me and to my family."

She bit her bottom lip before making herself ask the question. "Your wife and children?"

"I'm afraid I've never slowed down enough to manage having either of those," he laughed. "No, I mean my parents. Webb Enterprises is a joint effort between my father and myself and we work closely together on many things, although not this particular acquisition. But we have a situation in our family that you may be able to help with."

Her confusion was evident. "I can't imagine how, but try me, I guess. As long as you don't need me to work on any of your vehicles. I'm pretty much tapped out after spark plugs, air filters, and thermostats."

He looked down at the ground with a faint smile, appreciating her effortless humor. He felt her eyes on him but rather than meet her gaze, he leaned forward, resting his elbows on his thighs, and let himself stare out over the land that spread before them. Finally, he straightened back up and glanced over to find her still studying him but patiently waiting.

"My father has an aunt, so naturally my great-aunt. Sadie." Another little smile played around his mouth, as he thought about the woman he had always found fascinating, even as a small boy.

"She's in a nursing home about a half-hour from here," he continued. "That's the first stop I made Thursday before driving on out here. My father wanted me to check on her without letting anyone there know that I was coming, and the conditions I found her in were deplorable."

Iris could understand the dark, stern frown that settled on his face. She had always had a soft spot for elderly persons and hated to think that someone would mistreat them, but she knew that it did happen.

She laid a hand on his arm, without being conscious of doing it. "Is she okay, though?"

Barrett looked down at her hand and marveled at the simple comfort her touch brought him.

"She is, as far as not being in any immediate danger but she's a helpless individual with needs that are being ignored. She can't do anything for herself."

Barrett noticed the way Iris slowly realized she had her hand on his arm and now removed it.

"How can I help?" she asked softly.

"Well, I want you to know all the facts first," he answered. "Aunt Sadie is blind. She hasn't always been," he added. "But she has been for many years. That's why I was so angry when I found her just parked out in the hallway in her wheelchair, without her even knowing where she was. She was feeling around in the air but was being careful not to speak. I imagine she was afraid."

Tears sprang into Iris's expressive eyes and she rested her hand against her throat. Barrett saw her genuine reaction and felt immensely gratified.

"I'm afraid I blew a gasket," he admitted.

He expelled a breath and looked directly at Iris with complete transparency. "If this would not be something you'd want to be involved in Iris, I completely understand but I wondered if you might be willing, at least temporarily, to stay here after I purchase the farm and help me with Aunt Sadie?"

"Help you?" She was puzzled for a moment. "Oh, are you thinking of bringing her here to live?"

Barrett could tell that she didn't seem to be bothered by the thought. She was only curious.

"I admit I have been," he replied. "Once I saw how she was simply parked out of everybody's way and left with her food drying on her face and her clothes, all I could think about was taking her out of that place.

"My family has urged Aunt Sadie for years to live with them, but she has steadfastly refused. She said she'd rather be a bother to strangers. She has to know how much we love her but apparently, that's how she feels."

Iris nodded, completely understanding. "Do you think she'd even be willing to come here then, since she feels that way?"

"I certainly do hope so," he said, although not with a great deal of optimism. "I'm going to make a more concentrated effort to try to talk her into it."

"If she does decide to come, does she need any sort of specific medical care? I'm not a nurse, although I did serve as one for my late husband."

Nothing even remotely emotional connected itself to either her demeanor or her tone, when she said this. Barrett felt that she could have been talking about a stranger, for all the effect it had on her. He longed to know why but then told himself that what John Mabry had shared with him about her troubles would certainly contribute to her ambivalence about her late husband.

"She would only need basic things, such as taking her vitals, that sort of thing. I'm not completely aware of what sort of prescriptions she has but I intend to meet with her doctor to determine that. Mostly, Iris, she just needs help with going to the bathroom, getting put to bed, feeding, bathing."

He stopped and furrowed his brow. "Actually, now that I'm saying all of that it seems to be a great deal. I'm not sure that's something I should be asking you to take on."

"No, that's nothing too difficult. As I said, I had to do all that for my late husband, Glenn. I should be fine taking care of your aunt. Is she in the chair because she can't walk, or is that mainly due to safety concerns because of her blindness?"

"I think she's still able to walk, but she chooses to remain in the chair. I'm sure it's the fear of falling or something along those lines, that convinces her to stay in it."

Barrett stopped and looked at Iris so steadily, that she began to feel self-conscious.

"Are you even considering this, Iris?"

"I really don't have a choice," she sighed. "I don't mean for that to sound as if that's the only reason I would help you and I'm sure it does sound like that, but it's the simple truth so I won't bother to pretend that it's not."

She let her pretty eyes move aimlessly around the pasture without really seeing it.

Barrett could see that she was processing a thought, and waited. Finally she lifted her gaze to his.

"In the interest of full disclosure, since you are purchasing not only the farm but the house, I feel I should tell you that my late husband died in it, upstairs."

John Mabry had only told Barrett that she was a widow, but hadn't provided any details. He had wondered about it a few times over the past couple of days.

"I probably shouldn't tell you that just after you asked me to take care of your aunt," she added with a quick flash of wit, after she realized the timing of her revelation. "But it wasn't anything I did. That was all him."

"Suicide?" Barrett made himself ask and she nodded slowly, the ghost of anger washing over her beautiful face.

"That's a discussion for another day," she finally said, a little too brightly. "I don't really want to muck around in all that. But I did want you to know in case it mattered to you."

"It doesn't," he assured her quietly. "But I am really very sorry for the situation you find yourself left with."

"Well, that didn't become the state of things simply because he died. That was a long time coming, as I recently discovered," Iris observed, as her trace of anger settled down into nothing more than mere candor.

"At the end of the day, I try not to camp out around things like that. Sometimes, you just have to cut your losses and ride off." She grinned up at him unexpectedly. "That's cowboy talk."

She made him laugh. "You're a natural."

Barrett glanced around, wondering what else they needed to discuss then realized that he'd neglected to tell her about his own intentions.

"Iris, if you don't want me to do this I won't, but I think you should know that anytime I purchase a property that includes a house, I move in temporarily and use it as a sort of headquarters while I assess what needs to happen around the property, how many workers I need to bring in, and organize priorities. How many bedrooms are in the house?"

"There are three upstairs and one downstairs. There are two bathrooms and one of those is downstairs."

He pressed his lips together and seemed to be processing that information.

"First things first," he finally said. "None of that matters, if I can't convince Aunt Sadie to come live here.

"But entertaining the notion that she may, I guess you and I need to figure out whether she would need to be downstairs or whether, since she makes no effort to be ambulatory, she might do well upstairs so that you both can be on the same level. But we'll work it all out," he added with a kind smile.

He glanced back at her. "If you're not okay with any of this you have only to tell me. I don't want you to be uncomfortable."

"It's your house," she quipped and he smiled faintly.

"It's yours as well, hopefully. I should know something from Aunt Sadie soon. But Iris..." Barrett broke off and compelled her to look at him before he continued.

"If Aunt Sadie decides not to come here, then I insist on augmenting the sale price of the property so that you can be able to provide yourself with a place to live. That's non-negotiable," he added with a firm tone as he detected the beginnings of protest. "Regardless of how things work out, you will have a place to live. I'll see to that."

She felt a tear splash down onto her hand and looked away. "Thank you, Barrett."

"It's my privilege," he returned quietly.

He looked down at the truck's tailgate they were sitting on. "I don't know about you, but this thing is getting a little warm for me."

She immediately sprang off of it, glad to know that he finally realized they were slowly being grilled in the hot sun.

"I was hoping you'd notice," she confessed.

Barrett grinned and slid off the tailgate, then pushed it up to latch. He stood a moment, resting his elbow on the top edge of it and allowed himself to take a long, appreciative look at the land around them.

"I expect your banker will provide me with a detailed history of this property but I can't help but wonder what it was like at its peak. Despite it's falling into disuse over the years, it's really beautiful."

"For the most part," Iris agreed. "If you don't look too hard at all the broken down equipment, but if you give it long enough, the Virginia creeper and trumpet vines will take care of all that."

Barrett didn't miss the slight expression of remorse that came with her words but he knew she was placing too much blame on herself for not maintaining the property. She was essentially left alone to do what it would take a full-time crew to accomplish.

"We'll turn it around," he assured her. He continued to survey the area as she watched him, wondering about his process and longing to know where he would begin.

Iris had tried to learn what she could about farm management early on and had been fascinated by the subject but eventually had to abandon the hope of being able to utilize what she was learning, since she had to spend all her time taking care of her late husband. Her buyer seemed to know what she was thinking.

"The grass is good and full," Barrett decided. "I actually have some cattle that could use it, since they've just about eaten their pastures clean. After I close on the purchase, I'll send some men out here to get the fences repaired and then move the cows on out to get them started feeding."

He looked over at Iris with a smile hiding in his eyes. "Does Nip work cheap?"

"You may not think so, when you see how much kibble he can put away," she laughed. "But he's a good cattle dog, Barrett, and I'd love it if he could be useful to you. There are two goats still here and he makes them crazy, trying to herd them and contain them all day long."

Barrett laughed at that and rested his hands on his hips, looking around and still seeming to make silent decisions about the future of the farm.

"Just the goats and chickens here, then?"

"There's a horse here. He's old and very sweet and gentle. I haven't had the heart to get rid of him because he seems happy here. But I've been planning to see who might take him."

"Let's go see him," Barrett proposed, coming around to open her door. She lifted herself to sit and he closed the door behind her, looking directly into her eyes for the briefest moment before coming around to get behind the wheel.

Iris guided him on around the fields so that he could see what they'd not driven past, before showing him the way to the little pasture near the house where the stream ran.

When they stopped the truck, she walked over to a wooden gate and lifted herself up to lean over it, giving a sharp whistle then waiting patiently.

"He's slow, but he gets here eventually," she explained to Barrett, who had come to join her at the gate.

As the old horse rounded the corner of the little stable and moved to greet his owner, Barrett raised a brow in surprise.

"You've got a nice Morgan," he observed, and Iris nodded.

"He has a few years on him, but I suspect he could still thrive a little longer," he mused quietly. "I'll send our vet out to take a look at him and see what he needs."

Iris reached her hand to stroke her horse's velvety nose and breathed a whisper to him. "You hear that, Howie?"

Barrett was leaning against the gate next to Iris and now turned to look closely at her with the light of teasing in his eyes.

"Howie the horse?" he demanded. "That's terrible."

"It's short for Howitzer," she informed him and he laughed.

"Of course it is. How did I miss that?"

She frogged him lightly in the arm, twisting her lips into a little grimace. "Stop, it's a Civil War thing. A lot of soldiers rode Morgans, then."

He actually knew that, but he was surprised that she did.

"Just a suggestion," he said lightly, making himself look back at Howie instead of into her eyes. "Whenever the goats get tired of Nip chasing them around all day, you might consider closing them up in here with Howie. Horses actually love company and it might lift his spirits a bit to have some friends."

She seemed both surprised and disappointed that she had never thought of that.

"It shall be done," she replied, comically serious.

Barrett reluctantly moved back from their casual position at the gate with a sigh. "I suppose since I'm in the area, I should head on now and check on Aunt Sadie, and see if I can talk her into coming here. She's notoriously set in her ways, so you may want to pray for me."

Iris looked around with a little smile, thinking that he was joking. "If I could pray, I'd have tried that by now," she replied wistfully.

"Why can't you pray?" He searched her face to determine if she was teasing him since she seemed to enjoy doing that, but she appeared to be completely serious.

She shrugged, but offered no explanation and he didn't press her but purposed to pray, himself.

It was difficult to believe that this fascinating, beautiful woman had endured all that she had without ever having talked to God about it. This caused a feeling of sorrow to begin to stir in Barrett's heart but he knew it was proper for it to be there, and allowed it.

He drove them back through the gate they'd started from and stopped in front of the house, getting out to come around and open the door for Iris.

She looked up at him after she got out, and wondered if he was coming into the house.

"I'll have to come back again to see how we can arrange things in the house," he told her. "But right now, I'll just check on Aunt Sadie and head back home. I've got a few stops to make and I'll run out of time, if I don't keep moving."

"Barrett, thank you," Iris said impulsively. She seemed close to tears, realizing that she would soon be out from under the weight her late husband had left on her shoulders. "Thank you so much."

He smiled down at her and stroked her cheek with his thumb, then grinned and showed her the bit of grease he'd just removed.

"You're so welcome, Iris," he returned, softly. "We'll talk soon."

She stood watching him drive away, thinking that she never could have prayed for anything more wonderful than today.

Chapter Five

Stuart and Patricia Webb stood looking around at their son's newly acquired property, both of them checking the time occasionally and wondering where Barrett was.

When they'd been told that Aunt Sadie not only agreed to come live with Barrett on this farm, but actually seemed relieved and happy about it, they were overjoyed and asked him if they could come out to greet her and help her get settled in.

They'd both been curious to know how Barrett thought he'd be able to set up his operations here, manage a crew, and still be able to give Aunt Sadie the attention she needed and were glad to hear that he had full-time, live-in care arranged for her. He'd told them that her caregiver would be going with him to get Aunt Sadie and that they'd be able to meet her and ask her any questions or voice any concerns.

Stuart Webb spotted Howie and his goat friends and made his way through the yard toward the side pasture to get a closer look. He didn't see a gate nearby, so he simply swung his long legs over the fence as he probably would have done, even with a gate right in front of him.

"I'll just wait right here," his wife laughed. "I can see the horse just fine without ending up in traction."

Mr. Webb turned back to grin at her, then approached the horse calmly, pausing at the corral gate and speaking gently, stretching out his hand for the horse to come smell.

"He's a Morgan," he called out to Barrett's mother in approval. "He's an old man," he added with a sympathetic laugh. "I know how you feel, Old Timer." He gave Howie's nose a gentle stroke.

Howie looked at him with intelligent eyes, seeming to understand what he was saying and gave his hand a soft nudge, as if recognizing a friend.

Mr. Webb glanced back at his wife with a grin. "He's got a heart of gold."

"How can you tell that?" she demanded, watching the two of them with enjoyment.

"Because he has the ability to be aggressive, but he chooses to be meek," her husband replied in a soft voice.

"Are you sure he's not choosing to be old?" Patricia Webb challenged with a little laugh.

"Don't listen to her," Barrett's father advised the old Morgan, continuing to caress his jaw and administer light pats. "She's not a good judge of horse flesh."

"This may be them," his wife alerted. "I can hear a car."

Stuart Webb gave the horse another pat, then made his way back to step over the fence and join her as Barrett's large sedan pulled around the circle and stopped in front of the house.

Their son got out and gave them both a quick hug before opening the rear door to allow Iris and Aunt Sadie to exit. He had popped the trunk and now motioned to his father.

"Dad, can you lift Aunt Sadie's chair out of there?"

Iris hadn't yet emerged, because Aunt Sadie had clung to her hand all the way and was gripping it now, as if it were a lifeline.

Iris leaned over to speak softly into her ear. "We're home, Aunt Sadie. Barrett's parents are here to visit with you."

The old lady smiled in delight, still clinging to Iris while her chair was unfolded and locked into position.

"Iris, Dad and I will help Aunt Sadie get into her chair, if you want to step out," Barrett suggested with a soft smile.

She lifted their interlocked hands and looked up at him with a helpless grin. He laughed and reached in to gently lift Aunt Sadie's fingers from around her hand.

"It's okay, Aunt Sadie," he reassured her. "Iris isn't leaving, she's just getting out of the car and you can have her hand again, as soon as we get you inside."

When Barrett moved back and Iris lifted herself out of the back seat and stood next to the car, Patricia Webb drew in a quick breath and stared in spite of herself, at the beautiful creature in front of her, taking in her tall, slender build, her flowing, long, dark ginger curls and unbelievable blue eyes.

"My goodness, sweetheart, you are absolutely lovely!" she exclaimed, surprising herself as well as Iris.

She quickly moved to gather her into a light embrace.

"I'm Barrett's mother, Patricia," she happily informed her. "I don't know what we were expecting when Barrett told us that Aunt Sadie has a caregiver, but it wasn't you!

"That's actually a compliment," she hurried to add with a reassuring little laugh.

"Thank you. It's really nice to meet you," Iris said, smiling sweetly at her. "I'm Iris Anderson."

"Anderson? Did Barrett buy this farm from you, then?"

"He did."

"Well, he never found anything like you at any of his other farms," she teased.

Iris could have been a little embarrassed, but Mrs. Webb was so friendly and welcoming that she was touched, instead.

They both stood watching as Barrett and his father placed Aunt Sadie gently into her chair and tucked her lap blanket securely around her before rolling her to the porch, then stopping to lift her chair easily up the wide, shallow steps.

Mrs. Webb still had her arm resting on Iris's slim shoulder, and her happy relief was in her eyes.

"We've been waiting for years for Aunt Sadie to be willing to leave that place," she confided quietly to Iris.

Iris gave her a comforting smile and the two of them began to gather Aunt Sadie's things from the trunk and bring them over to the porch, until they were sure they had it all.

"Just leave that please, Iris," Barrett said from the door. "Dad and I will get it in a few moments, but Aunt Sadie is asking for you and she wants to give Mom a kiss, she said."

"Thank you," he whispered softly to her, as she moved past him to see how she could help Aunt Sadie.

She looked up at him with tender eyes, then knelt down so that Aunt Sadie could let her know what she needed.

Barrett's parents noticed their brief interaction with approval.

Aunt Sadie seemed to be lifting her fingers, searching for something.

"What do you need, Aunt Sadie?" Patricia Webb leaned down to ask with concern.

"My flower girl," she said with a little smile.

"She means Iris," Barrett informed his mother. "Aunt Sadie christened her as 'My Flower Girl' as soon as I introduced them."

Iris slipped her hand into Aunt Sadie's searching fingers and she immediately took hold of it and relaxed.

"Are you ready to go to bed for a little while, Aunt Sadie?" she asked, resting her eyes on the elderly woman's face and attempting to assess her condition after the drive.

"I think so," she agreed. "I'm a little tired."

"Barrett and his father will help me take you up to your room and then I'll help you get in bed," Iris explained, feeling that it was important to always let someone like Aunt Sadie, who was completely at the mercy of others, know exactly what to expect. "The room is upstairs but you have two big strong men, so it'll be really easy for them to help you. Will that be okay?"

"That'll be fine," Aunt Sadie replied, reaching up a shaky hand to find her face and caress it.

"I'll come up with you," Iris assured her.

Barrett and his parents were standing nearby to watch Iris with Aunt Sadie and when they were sure that she understood what Iris had told her, Barrett reached down and lifted the frail, petite woman up into his arms, as if she were a child.

"Aunt Sadie, we're going to have to fatten you up," he teased as his father began folding her chair to follow them upstairs. "You don't weigh enough to stuff a pillow with."

"Oh, stop," she laughed.

He continued to make her laugh with his lighthearted comments as he carried her up to her room.

Iris looked around for the bag she had put some of Aunt Sadie's immediate needs in and reached down to pick it up.

Patricia Webb laid a hand on her arm as she moved to follow them. "Thank you, sweetheart, for doing this for our family. It's hard to imagine someone as young and beautiful as you are being willing to make this kind of commitment to our aunt. We just can't thank you enough."

Iris gave her a gentle smile. "I'm happy to help."

Mrs. Webb watched her carry Aunt Sadie's travel bag up the stairs and raised her hands up to dab at the corners of her eyes. She silently sent up a prayer of thanks to God for Iris.

She looked around the farmhouse, realizing that its cozy warmth was the result of Iris's efforts.

She found it completely charming, in spite of its simple decor. She could see little touches here and there that would brighten a corner or cheer up something that would ordinarily be unattractive, such as the old cast-iron wood stove in the corner that Iris had managed to turn into a showpiece, simply by making the corner a stone backdrop, using rocks she had collected from around the property, and adding an old kettle, fireplace tools, and a metal bin filled with aromatic cedar.

She was still taking it all in when Barrett and his father came back down the stairs.

"Iris got the percolator in the kitchen ready before we left, Mother, if you and Dad would like some coffee," her son offered.

They were always ready for coffee and followed him gladly into Iris's homey, neat kitchen. Barrett plugged the coffeepot in and began to pull cups from the cabinet, as if he knew where they were kept.

He set them down then came back to the table and pulled out a chair to join his parents.

"She told me where to look," he confessed with a grin. "I've only been inside the house once, and that was just before we left to go pick up Aunt Sadie.

"We helped get her into bed, and Iris is just sitting with her and making small talk until she relaxes enough to fall asleep."

"Would anyone be able to hear Aunt Sadie from down here?" Stuart Webb wondered. "She's not very loud."

"There's a monitor next to her bed. You're not hearing them right now because Iris is wearing the receiver on a string around her neck. She'll turn it on when she comes back downstairs and she'll be able to hear every sound Aunt Sadie makes and if she needs to, she can also see her with it."

"That's brilliant," Patricia Webb breathed.

"Her idea," her son informed her. "She had to care for her late husband and it enabled her to go about doing her chores and still be able to hear him."

"She seems so young to be a widow," his mother said, shaking her head.

"She is," Barrett agreed. "From what John Mabry told me, she's around twenty-eight."

Mrs. Webb looked back toward the door before speaking again then leaned forward to proclaim in a loud whisper, "That is the most beautiful girl I think I have ever seen, Barrett Webb!"

He completely agreed but didn't say so. Instead, he and his father exchanged knowing grins and Stuart Webb reached over to lay his hand on hers.

"Back 'er down, Patty. The boy's not blind."

She laughed and swatted at him while Barrett hopped up to check on the coffee.

Mr. Webb took his cup from Barrett and gestured in the direction of the side pasture. "What's the horse's name?"

His question made Barrett smile, as he remembered Iris introducing him to her old Morgan.

He lifted his brown eyes to his father's to see his reaction when he answered. "Howie."

The older man laughed. "Howie the horse?"

"That's exactly what I said," Barrett replied. "Apparently, Howie is short for Howitzer."

His father raised his brows, impressed. "Well now, that's pretty clever."

Patricia Webb wrinkled her brow, trying to figure out what was clever about Howie being short for Howitzer.

"Morgan horses were used quite a bit during the Civil War," her husband explained. "So were Howitzers, although most people wouldn't know that. I guess I'm just surprised that Iris did."

"I bet she knows all sorts of things," Patricia declared, already a fan of the girl who was becoming such a blessing to their family.

"She's had to fend for herself, so I expect she does," Barrett said mildly, toying with the handle of his coffee cup. "She knows how to keep her old truck running."

"That Apache?" his father asked.

"That's the one. It's a fifty-eight. I came to finish seeing the place last Saturday and as I was pulling around the drive, I saw a pair of legs sticking out from under the hood. She was looking for a bad plug.

"She found it too, and whipped out a file and cleaned it up. She even knew the proper gap for the plugs on a V8 short block engine, Dad. It fired right up, and purred like a kitten."

He laughed quietly, thinking about her pretty face streaked with grease and her impulsive high five when the truck responded favorably to her efforts.

Mr. Webb continued to look impressed, while Patricia Webb reached over to clasp her son's arm firmly and fix him with a no-nonsense, motherly look of warning.

"Barrett Webb, if you let that girl get away, I may never speak to you again!"

He rested his amused eyes on his mother's face. "I don't have her, to let her get away, Mother."

"Well, what's the problem?" she demanded. "You'd better not drag your feet and have some other guy snatch her up, or you and I are gonna have a Come-To-Jesus meeting!"

He laughed and looked over at his father in appeal. "Isn't it Mother's nap time?"

He grinned and reached over to give his wife a caress on her shoulder. "Better let the two of them just get on with each day as it comes, Patty. Barrett's got a lot on his plate, trying to get this farm back in the black and Aunt Sadie may end up being a bigger job than Iris signed up for. We'd better just see how things go."

"I hate it when you make sense," she grumbled, managing to give in to a smile when both men burst out laughing at her.

Barrett nodded toward the living room to indicate that Iris was coming down the stairs and while she was moving into the kitchen and looking down to make sure the monitor was on and turned up loud enough for her to hear, he got up and poured some coffee for her and pulled out a chair.

She glanced up and noticed and gave him a grateful smile.

"She's sleeping pretty good," Iris said in her gentle, husky way, studying the video screen a moment before switching to audio. "I think she's worn out, but she seems fine. Her vitals are actually good."

She sat down and cradled her coffee cup, looking around the table, suddenly shy.

Stuart Webb fixed that when he leaned forward and made her look at him, then asked, "Howie the horse? Really?"

"Stop!" Patricia said, laughing.

Iris fixed Barrett with a deadpan look before giving in to a reluctant smile.

"Actually, Dad got it right away," he remarked with a grin. "He didn't need an explanation."

"Howie's actually a rescue," Iris told them. "I was trying to keep him from being put down. Barrett thinks he may not be that bad off. I'm hoping," she finished.

"He doesn't look that far gone to me," his father agreed. "We should get Abner out here to take a look at him."

"That's what I was thinking," his son replied.

Iris smiled down into her coffee, overcome with a sense of wellbeing that she'd not known for many years.

Chapter Six

Barrett stood looking out the kitchen's screen door, watching Iris with Aunt Sadie. It was an unusually nice day, with enough of a gentle breeze to keep it from feeling too humid, and Aunt Sadie seemed overjoyed when Iris asked her if she'd like to spend a little time outdoors.

She confided to Iris that she couldn't even remember the last time she'd been able to do anything like that, and Barrett was more than willing to bring her chair outside and then transfer Aunt Sadie to the shade of a sugar maple tree in the backyard.

Iris was reading to her and Barrett knew Aunt Sadie was probably paying more attention to the soothing, musical sound of Iris's unusual soft raspy tone, than her actual words.

Barrett actually needed to get out to the fields, since the fence around the best grass had been repaired and he had a trailer of cattle arriving soon. He allowed himself a few more moments to enjoy seeing his great-aunt living a much better life than the one he'd recently found her trapped in.

He looked down at his ringing phone and frowned, annoyed to see Blanche Hollis continuing to try to get in touch with him, probably for some silly party. Barrett sighed and pressed the button to mute the ring for that call and put his phone away.

He couldn't figure out, for the life of him, why Blanche Hollis thought he had any interest at all in her. He'd certainly never gone out of his way to interact with her.

Blanche's father was a livestock dealer and owned a couple of large auction houses, so Blanche had managed to make his acquaintance when she happened to be at one of the auctions Barrett had attended.

She normally wouldn't be caught dead around what she called "stinky cows" but that particular auction was being held offsite as part of an all-day event that featured a carnival, several contests, and vendor kiosks.

Blanche was there with her loud friends for those less objectionable activities but soon wandered away from her group of cronies, when she spied the handsome Barrett Webb walking by with his father, on their way to check for a couple of nice Brahmans they were considering breeding with their Herefords.

She began leisurely strolling along behind them and was able to eventually position herself close enough to stand by him, as he and his father leaned against the rails of the pen, waiting for the bulls to be brought through.

She wasted no time telling the men that her father, Lester Hollis, was in charge of this auction and that he owned both local auction houses. This was, of course, something the Webb men knew but Barrett politely acknowledged her information as if it were news. This was all Blanche needed for encouragement.

She had managed to convince him to accompany her to a couple of dances over the past few months, convincing herself that it was the opportunity to spend time with her that made him agree. She would have been mortified to learn that Barrett would have attended such an event without any date at all, since he enjoyed seeing his friends at social gatherings and never had any trouble finding someone who wanted to dance.

As her efforts to reel him in began to wear on Barrett, he had considered simply blocking her number on his phone but after she had driven to his home a couple of times, he knew that would hardly stop her from continuing to wage her campaign to make him yield to her charms. Barrett found her to be petty and shallow, rather than charming.

A flash of irritation swept across his handsome face, as he told himself that she was probably not going to stop until she had forced him to become rude.

His scowl was still on his face as he opened the door and approached Iris and Aunt Sadie.

Iris glanced up and noted his expression with a look of curiosity. He winked faintly at her and gave her a slight shake of his head to let her know that it was nothing important.

"I'm sorry to interrupt you beautiful ladies," he said, coming over to rest his hand on his Aunt Sadie's shoulder.

She reached up her thin hand to caress his and smiled. "My flower girl is reading the Psalms to me."

Barrett allowed a quiet look of approval to settle on his face. "You always loved them, Aunt Sadie."

"I still do," she laughed.

Barrett rested his eyes on Iris's lovely face and she returned his gaze only briefly before looking down with a slight flush. He smiled to himself, thinking of how different she was from the annoying Blanche Hollis.

"The cows are coming," he said lightly, certain that finding out that Nip was about to have cattle to boss around again would cause her to look back up at him and smile. She didn't disappoint him.

"Are they on their way?" she asked.

"Yes, and I'd better be on my way also, I suppose. I want to put them through the chutes, so that we can drench them and give a few shots before we turn them loose."

He wondered why she was looking at him so intently, then realized she had never seen him wearing a hat before. He touched the brim of it.

"I'm afraid it's a necessary accessory when I'm outdoors all day," he laughed.

"It's nice. You wear it well," she replied.

He lifted it slightly as an implied greeting and made her laugh. "I didn't see Nip out front. Does he roam around the property much?"

"He's probably out keeping an eye on Howie and the goats," Iris speculated.

"I'm sure you're right." Barrett paused before heading off to find his new cattle dog. "How long do you think you and Aunt Sadie will be outside, Iris? I want to be here to help when you're ready to go back in. "

"I'm in no hurry," Aunt Sadie informed him, grinning with contentment.

Barrett gave her shoulder a little pat, then raised his brows for Iris to weigh in.

"Are you feeling good enough for another hour, Aunt Sadie?" she asked, looking closely at her for any sign of fatigue.

"I'm feeling very well, honey," she insisted. "Let's keep going."

"You heard her," Iris said with a little grin.

"I'll come back in about an hour then and check on you." Barrett looked at her thoughtfully. "Iris, where's your phone?"

She searched around blankly. "I think I last had it when I made coffee."

"Let me get that for you," he offered.

He wasted no time locating her phone and bringing it back out to her.

"I want you to always be able to reach me," he said quietly, laying it in her hands and giving her a soft smile. "Please call, if you need anything at all."

She returned his smile and watched him walk away toward the side pasture to whistle for Nip, still staring after him as she realized that Aunt Sadie was patiently waiting for her to carry on reading to her.

<hr />

Blanche Hollis sat at the kitchen counter listlessly passing her spoon back and forth through her cereal in a bored fashion. She'd slept in until after ten o' clock, too late for breakfast and too early for lunch, which was her typical custom.

She looked up as her older brother came into the kitchen and began rummaging around in the fridge for something to drink. He looked as if he'd already been out and about, so Blanche just assumed he'd made a pit stop at their house, rather than drive all the way out to his own place.

"Hey, B." He greeted her absentmindedly, continuing to search for something cold that appealed to him and finally spotting some bottled tea. He claimed one for himself.

"Hey," she returned sullenly.

He came over to roost on a stool and glanced her way, while he removed the cap from his drink.

"Are you just now getting up?" he demanded, a little surprised.

"Don't start," she sighed, moving her cereal to one side and resting her chin in her hands. She looked at him curiously. "Are you just in the neighborhood, or what?"

"I'm helping Dad today. He's trying to purchase some cattle and saw a trailer full of them being moved from one of Barrett Webb's pastures so he wanted me to flag the driver down and find out if Barrett was thinking of selling them."

Blanche perked up when she heard Barrett's name. "So, is he selling them?" She suspected that this might give her an excuse to suddenly show up during her father's transaction.

Tobey Hollis took a long drink then shook his head. "No, Barrett was having them transported to a farm he just bought. Dad will have to look somewhere else."

Blanche wondered if it was buying a new piece of property that was keeping Barrett Webb so busy rather than the possibility that he was avoiding her and brightened up at the thought.

"I guess the driver didn't say where the farm was?" she asked, as if she were simply making small talk.

"Said he was heading out toward Fairfield to the old Anderson farm," her unsuspecting brother replied, getting up and shoving his stool back under the edge of the counter.

He stopped to toss his empty bottle into the kitchen trash.

"If Dad drops in for lunch, tell him that I might have a lead on another herd that Barrett's driver told me about. I'll call him later and let him know."

He tossed a wave to his sister, who wasn't listening and only nodded as he went back out to his truck.

She sat smiling down at her cereal spoon as a plan began to formulate for getting to see Barrett Webb, after all.

Probably not today, she decided. Tobey said a load of cattle was being moved to the new farm and if that was anything like it was when cattle arrived for her father, she could safely assume that Barrett would be out in the pastures working with his men.

She had no idea how long dealing with cattle took, but if she wanted his undivided attention when she stopped by his new property to congratulate him, she decided that she'd have a better chance if she waited another day or so when he wasn't so distracted, fooling around with his silly cows.

Blanche reached for her phone and tapped until she found a photo of Barrett she'd taken while he wasn't paying attention. She spread her fingers to enlarge it and a smile of satisfaction appeared, as she studied his handsome face, taking in his thick, dark curls, his brown eyes and nice brows, and his thinly groomed beard.

She had decided long ago that Barrett Webb was the best looking man she had ever seen and she had no intention of letting him slip through her fingers. Whatever it took, she would have him and that's all there was to it.

※

Iris came down the stairs after thinking she'd heard someone at the door and was surprised to see Patricia Webb standing out on the porch. She hurried to open the screen door to let her into what was now her son's home.

"I'm so sorry," she apologized softly. "I was upstairs with Aunt Sadie and I didn't realize anyone was here. I hope you haven't been waiting long, Mrs. Webb."

Barrett's mother beamed at her and gently corrected her. "Patricia or Patty, sweetheart. I consider you family."

Iris smiled, as she held the door open to let her come in.

"How's Aunt Sadie today, Iris?" She looked around and indicated the couch and Iris was quick to apologize again and ask her to sit.

"She's had a good day, today, Mrs..." She stopped and grinned at her silent rebuke. "Patricia. Barrett helped me take her outside for a while this morning and I read to her. She seemed to enjoy the breeze and hearing the sounds going on around her, especially the chickens, I think."

Patricia Webb smiled faintly at that. "Is she sleeping, now, after being a little more active?"

"She just fell asleep a few moments before I came downstairs," Iris answered, touching the receiver she always kept with her. "I'm still trying to become more familiar with her habits so that I can keep her on some kind of schedule, but it's only been a few days. I did try talking to her about the way things worked at the nursing home, but she really didn't seem to know much about it."

"I'm not surprised," Patricia said dryly. "Their schedule seemed to be to get them out of bed, put them in a chair, and park them out of everybody's way."

She looked over at Iris with a look of regret. "You'll have to pardon my cynicism, Iris. Stuart and I have just been so upset with the shape Barrett found Aunt Sadie in. There's really no excuse for that."

"I agree," she offered sadly.

Patricia reached over and touched Iris's hand gently. "Honey, Barrett asked me to go see Dr. Reese, who has been Aunt Sadie's doctor for several years now, and see if there were any prescriptions due. I thought I'd just be stopping by the front window and picking them up, so I was surprised when the girl asked me to wait and then came around to the door and told me that he wanted to see me."

She stopped and looked at Iris questioningly. "Were you told much about Aunt Sadie's medical problems, Iris?"

She shook her head. "Barrett just said that she didn't require a lot of actual medical care, other than giving her regular meds and keeping up with her vitals."

Patricia Webb leaned back against the couch and nodded. "Well, I imagine that's all the information he had. He was hoping to get to talk to Dr. Reese himself, but once he found out the cattle were on the way, he asked me if I could step in.

"Aunt Sadie's blindness occurred when she was in her fifties, so over thirty years ago, when Barrett was just a boy. She had a type of meningitis that everyone seemed to think she couldn't possibly recover from, but she's a fighter. It did take her quite a number of years to become as stable as she seems to be now, but Dr. Reese was concerned with her last results, after his lab tech stopped by the nursing home and drew Aunt Sadie's blood. That's how Dr. Reese does things, with nursing home residents.

"He generally sends a lab tech to them, rather than have them brought in for a visit and then, if there's cause for concern, he either asks the family to bring the patient in, or he makes a visit to the facility.

"He wasn't aware that Aunt Sadie had left the nursing home, which is one of the reasons he wanted to talk to me, today. But in addition to that, he wanted to talk about her last test results."

Iris was looking so intently at Patricia Webb with a sort of dread in her eyes, that she stopped and reached over to give her hand another reassuring pat.

"Aunt Sadie's in her late eighties, Iris."

She nodded slowly and waited.

"Dr. Reese seems to feel that Aunt Sadie is showing signs of renal failure and at her age and with her medical history, he's not giving us any hope that it can be treated."

Iris looked down at the floor as she felt tears began to well up in her eyes, and didn't want Patricia Webb to see.

"I've been thinking that she had become dehydrated at the nursing home and thought that might explain why she didn't seem to have much output," she said quietly. "I'm afraid I've been encouraging her to drink more and she didn't want it, but she wanted to please me, I guess."

When Iris heard herself admit this, her tears furiously escaped despite her efforts to contain them, just as Barrett opened the screen door and stepped into the room. He had seen his mother's car in front of the house and had come to see if she'd spoken to Aunt Sadie's doctor.

Patricia had moved over close to Iris and had her arms around her, gently soothing her. "You can't let yourself think like that. You didn't know, honey."

"What's going on?" Barrett demanded. He came around to Iris's other side and knelt beside her, before looking up at his mother with an expression of bewilderment.

"What's happened to upset her, like this?"

Patricia slowly released Iris and found a tissue for her. She pressed it into Iris's hand before sitting back down and trying to answer her son, without further upsetting her.

"Dr. Reese gave me some bad news about Aunt Sadie's last blood work. He says that she appears to be in renal failure. He offered to test further when I asked him if he was sure, but he also said there's really no point, and that it would only be for the family's sake. Iris is just distressed by it, Barrett, and feeling guilty for something that she couldn't possibly have known."

Barrett looked at his mother with quiet alarm, then put his arm around Iris when she very faintly said, "I shouldn't have been trying to get her to drink more. That's the worse thing I could have done."

He pulled her closer and reached a hand to his mother for another tissue.

She gave it to him then decided to walk into the kitchen, to give them a moment alone.

Iris seemed to be heartbroken over just the thought that she might have done any harm to Aunt Sadie. She rested her head on Barrett's shoulder and he spoke quietly, stroking back her hair from her face, urging her to listen to him.

"Iris, I believed like you did, that she was dehydrated. There was simply no apparent reason to suspect anything else. Aunt Sadie was obviously being neglected at the nursing home, so it was reasonable to suspect that she wasn't getting enough food or water. She weighs no more than a child."

Barrett continued to comfort her, slowly coaxing her to take a deep breath and to not only hear him, but to consider what he was telling her.

She finally wiped her eyes and let out a cleansing breath. "I'm so sorry," she offered softly.

"You have nothing to be sorry for," he assured her, with so much kindness that Iris felt tears threatening again.

Barrett touched her chin to persuade her to look at him.

"We'll just do what we can for her to give her the best life possible. We'll find out the best way to treat her, and when God does call her Home, we'll just pray for her passing to be sweet and peaceful. That's all we can do, Iris."

He held her gaze with his, and she finally nodded and tried to give him a shaky smile.

"Okay?" he asked, smiling back at her.

She nodded again. "Okay," she whispered.

He stroked her cheek and looked up as his mother cautiously and silently made her way back into the living room.

"We're okay," he said, looking up at her and motioning for her to come join them.

Iris suddenly looked surprised and fumbled with the monitor, trying to get the volume turned up. After a moment, she looked up at Barrett in wonder.

"She's singing!"

Barrett and his mother leaned in to listen with her.

Patricia Webb flashed her son a bittersweet smile.

"Peace In The Valley."

When Iris made a move to stand, Barrett rose to his feet and offered her his hand. She let him help her then turned off the receiver.

"I'm just gonna go up to see how she's doing," she said, looking up at Barrett with beautiful, but sad eyes.

She headed upstairs and the two of them watched her go, before Barrett turned to ask his mother the question she had been waiting for.

She slipped her arm around him and breathed out a sigh. "Not long, Son. Months, at the most."

Chapter Seven

"Did you know I was a nurse, back in the day?"

Iris glanced over at Aunt Sadie in surprise, trying to determine if she was being serious, teasing or beginning to experience the dementia that Dr. Reese had warned them not to be anxious about if it should manifest, since it was consistent with advanced renal failure in someone her age.

She looked at Patricia Webb with the question in her eyes and Barrett's mother reached to give Aunt Sadie a light caress on her slender arm.

"She sure was," she confirmed, to Iris's relief. "And not only that, Aunt Sadie was an Army nurse."

The elderly Miss Webb smiled at that. "That's where I met my true love," she said, with a touching look of bittersweet recollection. "Malcomb Howard."

She laughed softly and waved a hand toward Iris. "Now, doesn't that sound like two first names to you?"

Iris took her hand and gave it a gentle squeeze. "It does."

"And I told him that," Aunt Sadie replied. "He always got a kick out of me pretending to be upset and asking him why he wouldn't tell me his last name."

Iris and Patricia Webb shared a smile.

"He was a handsome man, wasn't he, Aunt Sadie?" Patricia asked, knowing what her response would be.

"Oh my, yes!" She grew quiet for a moment and Patricia knew she was looking at him in her heart, and remembering.

"He had curly red hair."

"Iris has hair like that, Aunt Sadie," her niece informed her. "It's long with loose curls, almost to her waist and the color of a new copper penny."

Aunt Sadie seemed delighted. "Does she?"

She released Iris's hand and raised her own upward. Iris seemed to know what she wanted and leaned close so that Aunt Sadie could touch her hair.

She ran her fingers through it and then gave her face a stroke with her fingertip. "Now, you know I can see your hair, because I remember Malcomb's hair so clearly. So I just have to think of his hair, but longer and on a pretty girl."

"She's very pretty, Aunt Sadie," Patricia Webb confirmed. "And she has sweet blue eyes, like those hydrangeas you used to have outside your kitchen window."

"So did my Malcomb," the old lady said softly. "That's why I planted those flowers, you know."

"I remember," Patricia said, sitting back in her chair and smiling faintly.

"We were to be married," Aunt Sadie revealed with a touch of sadness. "But Malcomb never came back. When I looked out my window, and saw his mother and father coming up my walkway and Mrs. Howard wiping her eyes, I knew what they'd come to tell me."

"Aunt Sadie, I'm so sorry," Iris said, and her compassion was very real.

"I know, sweetheart. I'm sorry, too."

There was a lengthy silence for a few moments before Aunt Sadie lifted her hand.

"Somewhere in my things, there used to be a picture of Malcomb in a little frame. Of course, I can't see it now, but I like to hold on to it. If you ever get a chance, do you think you could try to find it?"

"I did find it, when I unpacked all your things," Iris was relieved to be able to tell her. "I didn't know who it was, so I just put it in your top drawer. Would you like it now?"

Aunt Sadie's face lit up with joy. "Oh, yes, please!"

Iris crossed over to the chest of drawers and lifted the small silver framed picture out, then studied the young, happy man looking back at her, with a pang of sympathy. The photo was black and white, but she could imagine that his hair was red, as Aunt Sadie had told her.

"You're right, Aunt Sadie," she said, as she brought the picture back to her bedside and placed her fingers around the frame. "He was very handsome."

Aunt Sadie clasped the picture to her chest and smiled at that. "Yes. I'll see him again. I wonder if we'll both be young and beautiful, or if he'll be young and I'll be an old lady that he won't even recognize?"

"You'll be young and beautiful forever, Aunt Sadie," Patricia Webb assured her.

"Won't that be something?" her aunt breathed.

"Yes."

The women sat quietly, each in her own thoughts before Aunt Sadie spoke again.

"Being a nurse has its good points and its bad. It's good to know things, when someone needs your help. But it's not good to know things when you're the one who needs the help, because you don't even have the luxury of ignorance."

Iris and Patricia looked at each other with shared dread, as they realized what she was saying.

"I knew when I was diagnosed with meningitis and then lost my vision, what my last days would probably be like. I just thought my last days would have come a long time ago," she added with a little laugh.

"I'm glad for Iris's sake that God let us keep you, or she never would have been able to meet you." Patricia flashed a kind smile to her.

"Yes," Aunt Sadie agreed placidly. "My little flower girl, who reads the Psalms to me. Maybe when my spirit begins to leave this tired, old body, I'll be able to see her, just for a second. That would be lovely!"

Iris began to feel overwhelmed with emotion, and couldn't understand why she cried so easily these past few days. At one time, she had been so in control of her emotions that others began to wonder if she even had any.

She never cried when Glenn killed himself. The only emotion she'd felt when she found him was anger, which only grew worse in the weeks and months that followed, as she discovered the truth about his attempt to hide the fact that they were facing foreclosure, and all because he'd decided to drink up what little money they had.

It seemed to Iris that the more kindness she discovered in people, the more she struggled to cover up her feelings, and tears had begun to embarrass her with more frequency. It took so little for this wonderful woman, who hovered between life and death, to reduce her to tears. In such a short time, Iris had begun to love her as she'd never been able to love a mother or a grandmother and now she was losing her.

She laid a gentle hand on her thin shoulder then impulsively leaned over and kissed her forehead. "I love you, Aunt Sadie," she whispered, causing similar tears to puddle in the old lady's eyes.

"I love you, too, Flower Girl," she replied quietly.

The two women sat with her, as she drifted into a nap, clinging to the photograph of her Malcomb and smiling her way into some sweet dream of the two of them.

Patricia stood and came around to rest her hand on Iris's shoulder. "I'm going to head back home, sweetie. Are you going to be okay here? I imagine it may be dark before Barrett comes back. They're separating the pregnant cows from the rest of the herd and he got a late start."

Iris stood up to move toward the stairs with her and held up her receiver. "I'll be fine. I'll probably go down with you and see if there's anything I can put on the stove for his supper, and then come back up here for a while."

She followed Barrett's mother downstairs and walked her to the door. "Thank you for coming."

Patricia wrapped her up in a squeeze. "Thank you, honey, for everything you do. Our family sure loves you."

Iris smiled shyly and stood watching her make her way to the car, returning her wave.

She checked her receiver before going into the kitchen to see what she could come up with for Barrett to eat. She put together a stew that could simmer on the back burner, then stopped to listen for what sounded like a knock at the front door.

⌘

Iris could see the young woman through the screen, as she hurried to the door, wiping her hands on her apron and wondering if this was someone who had made a wrong turn and was asking for directions.

The screen door was latched and Iris simply stopped to speak to the woman from inside the house, without opening it.

"May I help you?" she asked softly, not missing the look of surprise and displeasure that instantly appeared in the stranger's countenance.

"Who are you?" the woman demanded bluntly.

As gentle and polite as Iris was prone to be, she never catered to rudeness.

"Who are you looking for?" she countered evenly.

"I'm looking for Barrett," Blanche Hollis snapped. "Tell him that Blanche is here."

"I'm afraid Barrett is out working cattle," Iris said, feeling a little disappointed that Barrett Webb even knew someone this offensive and annoying. "Would you like to leave a message?"

"What are you doing in his house?" Blanche asked, not bothering to mask her irritation.

"Is that your message?" Iris returned with maddening control and patience.

"That's my question to you!" the blonde woman fired back, with an unattractive red scowl on her face.

"You ask the question as if I owe you a response," Iris stated quietly. "You are a stranger. I owe you nothing."

Blanche stood looking at Iris with a rush of thoughts all pelting her at once, but was able to work out that if she wanted to make any progress at all, she'd better change her tactics.

"You're right, of course," she said unexpectedly. "I'm a stranger, and you don't have to answer any of my questions.

"You'll have to forgive me," she continued. "You see, Barrett and I date, so when I knocked on the door and a strange woman appeared, I was thrown off by that. I'm sorry," Blanche added hastily, noting the brief flash of regret that swept over the beautiful woman's face when she learned that Barrett Webb was taken.

"I'm not sure which pasture Barrett is working in," Iris replied, choosing not to acknowledge the insincere apology. "I do know that Patricia said it might be after dark before he returns."

Blanche was startled to hear this tall, slender, stunning woman refer to Barrett Webb's mother by her first name, as if they were close. This further enraged her but she exerted all her efforts into suppressing an angry response, although she couldn't resist another question.

"Do you live here?"

Iris only stood regarding her with fascinating, but completely unreadable eyes and Blanche abandoned the question when she realized that whoever this person was, she was obviously very comfortable inside Barrett Webb's house and would not be pressured into satisfying her curiosity.

"Please tell him that Blanche stopped by and that I'll call him later to see if we're still going to the dance that we talked about."

The silent, reserved Iris Anderson was unnerving Blanche Hollis without even being aware of it.

Blanche turned to flounce back out to her little red convertible with what was intended to be dignity, but only managed to rise to the level of petulance.

Iris stood looking after her, as the little red car threw up a cloud of dust until it was out of sight, then glanced upstairs, wondering if Aunt Sadie had been disturbed, even though she'd made no sound.

She quietly climbed the stairs and looked in on her, coming over to lay a hand on her brow and determining that she was sleeping soundly and in no discomfort.

Iris made her way back down to the kitchen to check on Barrett's supper, then stood looking down at the simmering pot with a feeling of sadness stealing over her.

Of course, someone like Barrett was in a relationship! She reminded herself that she had already believed that this would surely be the case, so why was she surprised when the woman he was seeing showed up at his new property?

She became aware of a tightness in her throat that usually preceded crying and quickly drew in a deep breath, letting it out slowly and forcing herself to realize that it hadn't been tenderness that Barrett Webb had been expressing to her over the past few weeks, but mere kindness.

She had been misreading his light touches, as he'd rest a hand on her shoulder to explain something to her, or lift a strand of hair off her cheek.

Iris began to feel foolish and pulled out a chair to sit down at the kitchen table, where she'd been forced over the years to sit and take herself to task and gain some perspective.

As much as Iris hated to think about it, she knew that Aunt Sadie's days were all too quickly coming to an end and there would be no further need for her to remain here. She needed to begin to plan for where she might be able to go.

Barrett had insisted on paying her for her help with Aunt Sadie, but she had steadfastly refused to accept it. However, she'd heard him tell his mother that he'd included an amount in his purchase of the farm that would allow her to be able to have a home, when the time came for her to leave.

So he had always planned for her to leave then and had even made provision for it, Iris told herself. Of course, Barrett didn't live here either. He'd be returning to his home, which was a half hour away and either rent out the farmhouse, or maybe even tear it down and use the extra land. But it was unlikely that he'd rent it to her, just to have someone living in it.

Besides, if she were to remain here that would mean she'd have occasion to see Barrett from time to time and if he ended up marrying the woman who'd come to the door today, it would be too awkward. Iris was a strict realist and she knew that this Blanche would immediately insist that he ask her to leave.

She didn't want him to have to ask her, she decided. She'd just begin to look for other possibilities and slowly begin to get her things together so that when the time came, she could leave quickly and not drag things out. She supposed the first thing to do would be to check with John Mabry and find out if there really had been extra money after the house and all the indebtedness had been paid and if so, how much was in her account.

The banker had handled everything for her and had satisfied all the creditors after the mortgage was paid, but she hasn't spoken to him since the sale was final. She just knew that the windowed envelopes no longer arrived. She decided that she at least needed the facts, so that she would know what she could afford and where she might be able to settle.

Iris thought she heard a faint sound over the receiver and hurried up the stairs to check on Aunt Sadie.

She had only been turning slightly, but still continued to sleep. Iris came over and sat down beside the bed, watching her with loving eyes that insisted on crying, despite her best efforts.

She leaned forward and rested her forehead in her hands and allowed a few tears before she began to wipe her cheeks.

She leaned back in the chair and crossed her arms, looking off toward the window next to the bed. The late afternoon sun reflected in her eyes, and tinted her hair an even richer hue of auburn. She pressed her lips together and stared at nothing, wondering once again what was to become of her.

She must have sat there for almost an hour, putting her thoughts into order and removing her emotions from the equation as she had learned to do when her husband was still alive. Aunt Sadie had stirred once, and smiled in her sleep. Iris wondered if she was dreaming of her Malcomb.

She checked the time and felt she should wake her, so that she could assess her condition. She leaned over her and called her name quietly. She had to repeat her name several times and touch her cheek before Aunt Sadie finally responded.

Iris felt sharp dismay, as she realized that she was sleeping more and more and that her condition was worsening. Only hours before, Aunt Sadie had been talking very lucidly and recalling her Malcomb with clarity. Iris was surprised to have such difficulty getting her to rouse now but she answered Iris and told her that she felt alright, although she kept moving one hand across her chest.

Tears quickly found their way down Iris's cheeks when Aunt Sadie asked who she was and when she told her, didn't seem to remember her, even when Iris told her that she was her "flower girl".

Iris counted her breaths and noted that they were shallow. She lifted her up to add a pillow and tried to make her more comfortable. It seemed to provide some relief for now, but Iris recognized that the symptoms she had been advised to look for were beginning to manifest.

Once Aunt Sadie was resting comfortably, she came back down to the kitchen to call Patricia Webb but laid the phone back on the table when the back door opened and Barrett came in a little earlier than his mother had supposed.

She stood looking down at her phone instead of at him, and he drew his brows and came over to look closely at her.

"Is something wrong?" he asked quietly.

"I left some stew on the stove, if you're hungry," Iris told him, moving away and going over to check it.

He watched her walk away without even glancing at him. He said nothing for a moment but continued to study her, puzzled. This morning she had been her lovely self and had looked up at him with sweet, trusting eyes, but she was almost cold now and was consciously avoiding him.

He approached her again, deliberately blocking her from being able to simply move away.

"Iris, what is it?"

He fixed his soft brown eyes on her face and made no effort to hide his confusion. "Why won't you look at me?"

"Are you hungry?" she asked. "I think it's probably cooked long enough."

"Iris, stop!"

Barrett took the soup ladle out of her hands and placed it on the stovetop, then gently gripped her shoulders and turned her to face him.

"Talk to me," he urged, searching her expression carefully. "Is it Aunt Sadie?"

She was feeling that she was surely about to begin crying in front of him if Barrett continued looking at her so intently and speaking to her so tenderly. Now, as he asked about Aunt Sadie, it gave her tears permission to flow without exposing her.

"I think it may be time to discuss hospice," she answered brokenly.

He stood regarding her soberly, reaching a finger to wipe her tears from her cheek and coaxing her to look up at him by lifting her chin. "Is she beginning to be in pain, Iris?"

"I think her chest is hurting her," she answered. "Her breathing is a little thin. And..."

She stopped, and her lips began to quiver.

"And what?" Barrett waited for only a moment. "And what, Iris?"

"She didn't know me." Her efforts to hold back her tears were in vain, and she began crying with real grief as she heard herself tell him that.

Barrett immediately pulled her into his arms and held onto her, letting her cry on his shoulder and stroking her hair. He closed his eyes and felt dangerously close to tears himself, as he realized that Aunt Sadie would probably leave them much sooner than they'd believed.

Chapter Eight

Patricia Webb looked out of the window next to Aunt Sadie's bed and could see Iris sitting on the rocks by the stream, seeming to stare blankly into the water. She had taken Patricia Webb's advice and gone out of the house while hospice workers bathed Aunt Sadie and got her bed changed.

Patricia felt that Iris needed to get some fresh air and a change of scenery anytime someone else was available to be with Aunt Sadie, since she would never leave her side otherwise.

Barrett's mother had noticed that Iris was becoming pale and withdrawn and thought at first that she was just having difficulty seeing Aunt Sadie begin to struggle with the end stages of her condition. She was sure that was true, to a great extent. But she'd also noticed Iris's body language around her son and felt that she was purposely distancing herself from him.

Patricia Webb had been more than a little put out when that tiresome Blanche Hollis arrived uninvited earlier in the day, acting as if she had a right to just show up whenever she felt like it. She couldn't understand where she'd gotten that idea.

Patricia had positioned herself at the front door and advised the girl that not only was Barrett not around, but that the family was dealing with a close relative's illness and suggested that she call before driving all that way again.

Blanche feigned deep concern, offering profuse apologies and asking Barrett's mother to please call her if she could help in any way, then returned to her car to leave but not before looking past her at Iris, who had come out of the kitchen with a pan that the hospice nurse had asked for.

It was impossible for Patricia to miss the way Blanche literally glared at Iris and pursed her lips in anger, before leaving.

If Iris was aware of Blanche's presence, she didn't react, but simply continued up the stairs.

Patricia Webb had witnessed Blanche's open hostility with a thoughtful expression, and somehow felt that she had known in advance that Iris would be there.

She wondered if this had anything to do with the change she'd noticed in Iris's demeanor around Barrett lately, and began to consider whether she should speak to him about it. If Blanche had been rude to Iris, he would certainly want to know.

She pulled herself away from the window and smiled at the nurse's aide who had finished bathing Aunt Sadie and was preparing to have another worker help her make the occupied bed. When Patricia asked her, she said they would probably be another twenty minutes or so. She decided to walk out to the stream and check on Iris.

Iris looked up as she approached and raised herself to stand, thinking she might need her to return.

"Oh honey, I didn't come to make you get up," Patricia told her. "The hospice workers have just finished with Aunt Sadie's bath and they're going to make the bed and then get her vitals. They'll be a while, yet."

She came over to stand next to her and looked down at the rippling stream that was dancing over the rocks.

"I love the sound of running water," she informed Iris, with a little smile. "It's very spiritual, I think."

Iris smiled down at the stream, but made no reply.

Patricia turned to look at her with the same gentle brown eyes that her son inherited. "Iris, what's wrong, honey? Can't you tell me? I don't mean to get into your business, sweetheart, but I can see that you're troubled. I get the feeling that it's not simply about Aunt Sadie."

Iris looked straight ahead and Patricia could see that she was struggling, but she drew in a breath and controlled her emotions. "I'm alright. It's hard to watch Aunt Sadie hurting, though."

"Well, Iris, hospice is helping her with that and even though they've chosen not to suction her, she seems to be breathing a little better, for now."

Iris nodded, continuing to look out into the trees, saying nothing.

Patricia decided to be more intentional and reached over to touch her hand. "You saw Blanche at the door, today." It wasn't a question. Iris looked down but didn't comment.

"She was here before, wasn't she?" Patricia squeezed her hand. "Iris, it's pretty obvious from the way she looked at you today, that she's seen you before."

"She came by one day last week," Iris finally admitted.

Patricia's face was grim, as she found out her suspicions were correct. "Does Barrett know?"

Iris shook her head. "I was supposed to give him a message, but by the time I remembered, too much time had passed and I just didn't. I'm sorry," she added.

"What was the message?" his mother prodded, trying to read her face.

"She wanted to know if they were still going to a dance together. I suppose that's why she came back today. I forgot to tell him," she confessed in a dull voice.

Patricia wrinkled her brow. "Why did she think they were going to a dance together? Barrett doesn't have time for any of that nonsense!"

Iris expelled a heavy breath but didn't speculate.

"Is hospice saying how much longer Aunt Sadie can stay with us?" she asked unexpectedly.

"Not long, sweetheart. We're probably looking at days, maybe a week."

Both women were silent for a while, each thinking of the dear, elderly woman and already feeling the loss.

"She doesn't know me, anymore," Iris whispered.

"That's okay, darling," Patricia soothed. "You know her, and that's what comforts her. She can feel your love. I see her relax when you put your hand on hers. She may not remember any of our names, but she knows she's with people who love her and that's made all the difference to her, these past few months."

Iris nodded, and wiped away a tear, then crossed her arms to hug herself, feeling too many emotions today.

"I need to be thinking about where I'll go, soon."

She hadn't intended to say those words out loud, but she had said them and Patricia was looking at her, clearly disturbed.

"Barrett hasn't asked you to leave," she said gently.

"I can't stay here."

"But Barrett won't be here, Iris. When Aunt Sadie passes, he'll return to his own home. Why can't you stay here?"

She just looked down and shook her head. She didn't want to have to see Barrett anytime he might happen to come out to the farm and just drop by. She knew that sooner or later, Blanche would ask if she was still living here, and demand that he ask her to leave. She didn't want to stay until he found himself in that position.

"I'll have to go," she insisted, almost too softly to be heard. She looked up at Patricia and managed a faint smile. "I think I'll go check on Aunt Sadie, now. They should be about done and might be needing to leave."

She stepped past her and began making her way to the house, with Patricia staring after her, feel dangerously close to tears herself, but hers were more from anger than any other emotion. She had no idea what Blanche Hollis had said to Iris, but she was going to make it her business to find out.

<hr>

Iris sat across from John Mabry and waited while he accessed her account. Finally, he looked up at her and informed her that she had just over a hundred thousand dollars in her balance. His words stunned Iris and she just sat staring at him.

"Now, Iris," he was quick to point out, "all you were trying to get for your farm was enough to pay off the mortgage and your outstanding debts. That amount may have been a lot, but it was far below what your farm appraised for.

"Barrett Webb wanted to purchase it for full appraisal value, but he also knew that you had been made aware of the amount you actually needed, and he was sure you wouldn't accept much more than that.

"Adding this much over the asking price still didn't equal the appraisal, so try not to feel that he was just doing you a favor. He still bought your farm for below the appraised value, even expanding the sales price."

The banker looked at Iris with curiosity when she still seemed to be undecided about accepting the money.

"Barrett told me that he'd informed you that he intended to increase the price, so that you would be able to find a place to live," he said mildly. "I'm not clear as to why you seem surprised."

"I thought that was just if I decided not to stay and take care of his Aunt Sadie," she explained quietly. "I didn't understand him to mean regardless."

"Well, before you start thinking that he's just being nice, remember that he's not only a good business man, but he's a decent person. He knew that you were practically forced out of your home through no action on your part, and the last thing he wanted to do was practically steal it from you. He still felt that the amount he added wasn't enough, but he and I both knew you'd balk at the hundred thousand, let alone more."

She sat silently and tried to feel better about taking the money, but it was going to take time. She knew that John Mabry was being completely honest with her and that what he was saying made sense, but she felt embarrassed about the amount being so large.

"Iris, try to hear me," he said kindly. "You could have perhaps received more money from one of the developers who wanted the property, but I knew you didn't want it split into tracts for cheap housing, and that was their intention.

"Your farm is worth far more than Barrett Webb paid for it. He knew it and I knew it. You were given a copy of the appraisal, so you should have known it, as well. You're actually owed more money than he gave you, if fair is fair, and he would still give it to you in an instant, if he thought you'd take it."

She nodded slowly. "I suppose."

John Mabry looked relieved. "When the time comes that you have need of it, come see me Iris, and in the meantime, I'll be looking around for a place you might consider moving into."

She stood up and reached for his hand. "I will. Thank you, Mr. John."

She walked out of his office and climbed into her truck, still trying to digest what she'd been told. It was a far greater amount of money than she'd even thought about.

A feeling of relief washed over her, as she realized that she should be able to find a place and get a job, somewhere.

She drove back to the farm, intent on not leaving Stuart and Patricia Webb on duty too long. They had both been very gracious and insistent about sitting with their aunt so that she could run a quick errand and had urged her to not rush, but to spend some time relaxing.

Iris suspected that if they'd known the reason for her trip to town, they might not have been so accommodating.

She pulled around the drive and parked her truck off to one side to leave the driveway clear, then made her way into the house, still mulling over what John Mabry had told her.

Iris came up the stairs to check on Aunt Sadie and was surprised to see Barrett sitting with her. She looked around the room with a blank expression.

"You must have come straight up," Barrett said quietly.

She nodded, then came over to lay one hand on Aunt Sadie's forehead to check for a fever, and the other on her chest, to feel her breathing.

"Dad and Mother are in the kitchen making coffee," he offered, watching Iris's gentle way with Aunt Sadie and noting the solemn shadow on her face.

He saw a change in Aunt Sadie's expression when Iris touched her. "She knows your hands," he told her softly.

She looked at her face, and wondered if that was true. She did seem to relax. Iris smiled down at her, even though she couldn't see the smile or return it.

After a few minutes, she looked at Barrett with nothing in her once expressive eyes but politeness. "If you want to go have coffee with your parents, I can sit with her."

Barrett looked steadily at her, wondering what had happened between them. He'd thought, or maybe just imagined, that they were at least friends. After the night she made him stew and he'd held her in his arms to comfort her when she told him that it was time for hospice, she'd changed toward him.

She wasn't exactly cold, or even hostile. She was simply aloof, as if they were strangers. He'd felt that they'd shared a few close moments and exchanged looks that meant something, but it was clear that Iris didn't think of him in the way he'd hoped she was beginning to.

He stood now and leaned down to kiss his aunt's forehead and whisper something in her ear, then straightened up and looked at Iris with a question in his eyes.

When she looked away, he tightened the muscles around his mouth and quietly left the room.

He made his way down to the kitchen and poured himself some coffee before joining his parents at the table.

"Iris came back and went straight up," he explained, when they seemed surprised to see him.

"She wasn't gone very long," his father observed. They both looked at Patricia, while she stared down at her cup, very obviously deep in thought.

"Are you okay, Mother?" Barrett finally asked. He knew that Aunt Sadie's time was close according to hospice, and felt that this might be what she was thinking about.

She ran her hand through her hair absently and let out a sigh. "I'm fine. Just a lot to think about."

She didn't elaborate, so her husband tried again.

"You're not still making arrangements for Aunt Sadie's service, are you, Patty?"

"No. That's all pretty much done. The funeral home gave me some forms to fill out a few days ago, in case I wanted to keep them with me and do most of that in advance, rather than having to rush through it, later.

"I've managed to fill in most of the family information." She said, rubbing her eyes. "All the 'preceded in death by' and 'survived by' and dates, et cetera."

She stopped and looked at Stuart with emotional eyes. "I included Malcomb."

"What did you say?" he asked tenderly.

"Preceded in death by the one great love of her life, Malcomb Howard, First Sergeant, United States Army."

Her husband smiled and reached over to touch her cheek. "That's perfect, Patty. Thank you for thinking of that."

"Actually, it was Iris who thought of is," she admitted. "Aunt Sadie told her all about Malcomb and it seemed to affect her in some way. She asked me if I thought it might be nice to add him, and then of course, began to apologize furiously, in true Iris fashion, for speaking out of turn."

Patricia smiled, as she thought about the way Iris had immediately felt that she had overstepped her bounds. "It's hard to believe she's not a Christian. I've never known anyone as truly sweet and humble as Iris is."

Barrett looked up at her with disappointment. "Why do you say she's not a Christian, Mother? Did she tell you that?"

"She did," his mother admitted, regretfully. "She said it wasn't that she didn't want to be. She just never really understood it. Hospice arrived while we were talking and we never did get back to discussing it."

He looked down and considered her words sadly. Of course, he wasn't sure he was the person to try to talk to her about eternity. Whatever it was that had come between them, it had caused her to distance herself from him. At one time, Barrett would have felt confident about sharing his faith with her, but now he felt she wouldn't listen to him.

Patricia watched him, and seemed to know what he was thinking. "Barrett, Iris is looking for a place to move into."

He looked up quickly at her, and was stunned. Stuart frowned and settled back in his chair, waiting for his wife to continue, but she seemed to be finished.

"Why, Mother?"

Patricia's heart was stung by the desolation in her son's eyes. She leaned forward to lay her hand on his.

"She wouldn't say much more about it, other than repeating that she couldn't stay here."

"But I won't be here. There's no reason why she can't stay. This is where she lived before, why would she not be willing to be here, in the future?"

It was all Patricia Webb could do to bite her tongue and not bring Blanche Hollis into this discussion, but she somehow managed.

"If you're asking me to speculate, I'd say that it's simply because this is your house and not hers.

"But to be honest," his mother continued, having spent a great deal of time thinking about it, "I'd say the real reason is because she doesn't want to put you in a position to later have to ask her to leave."

Again, Patricia took great care not to mention Blanche Hollis but added, "I'm sure Iris knows that if you eventually become engaged to someone and wind up getting married that your wife will certainly insist that you tell the beautiful, single woman living in your house that she has to go. Iris is not going to wait around for that to happen, Barrett, and she's not going to put you in the position to have to tell her."

He was bewildered. "Why is Iris thinking way down the road about something that's not even on the horizon?"

"She may have reason to believe that it's not as far away as you seem to think."

"What does that even mean, Mother?" He continued to stare at her in wonder, and his father also looked at his wife, as if suspecting that she was avoiding saying something. He knew her well.

"Maybe you should ask Iris," she sighed, pushing back from the table and heading upstairs to check on their Aunt Sadie.

Chapter Nine

Blanche Hollis had seen Barrett Webb coming out of the feed store and quickly hopped out of her car to intercept him before he could leave.

"Imagine running into you here," she sang out, as he flung the heavy bag of sweet feed into the bed of his truck.

Barrett suppressed a look of irritation and simply nodded at her. "Hello, Blanche."

She had intentionally come around to stand in front of his truck door and now smiled up at him, all the while ignoring his reluctance to talk to her.

"I'd begun to think you'd moved, Barrett. No one seems to have seen you around here for a while."

"I've not been around," he confirmed, wondering if he was going to have to ask her to move.

"Tobey said you'd bought another farm," she breezed on, intent on keeping him from leaving. "He said it was out near Fairfield."

"Yes." Barrett pulled out his phone and checked the time pointedly.

"Are you still going to live here, though? I mean, I know you spend some time on the different properties you acquire, but you seem to always come back here, sooner or later."

"I expect I will," he answered shortly.

He reached a hand around her to grip the handle of his truck's door, in an effort to make it plain that he wished to leave.

"Did you get my message?"

"I haven't checked my messages in a while," he admitted.

"No, I mean..." Blanche checked herself. It was clear to her that he was unaware that she'd driven out to his new farm.

"It wasn't important," she hurried to assure him. "Just a silly dance. I'm sure you're too busy for that sort of thing."

Barrett raised a brow in surprise. Blanche Hollis never thought her parties and dances were silly.

"How's your family, Barrett?"

She managed to surprise him again. His opinion of her was that she was too wrapped up in herself to even acknowledge his family, let alone inquire about their wellbeing.

"They're fine. We're just dealing with family member's hospice care, which takes a toll."

Blanche didn't have to fake her surprise. When Patricia Webb had mentioned a family member's illness, she had no idea it was actually that serious.

"Hospice," she repeated, hoping that she sounded sympathetic and caring. That was certainly what she was going for. "I'm sorry, Barrett, for trying to reach you about such foolishness as a dance, when you're going through something this serious."

"You didn't know," he replied, kindly but impatiently. "I need to get this feed delivered, Blanche."

"Oh, sure!" She moved to one side, and he climbed into his truck. "Barrett, I'm really sorry for what your family's going through. Let me know if I can do anything."

He offered a brief acknowledgement and drove away, still puzzled by Blanche's attempt to express concern. It was completely unexpected and made her seem much less annoying.

Blanche watched Barrett Webb drive away with a look of determination in her eyes. It was clear that her display of compassion was something that the man seemed to respond to, rather than her flirtatious cajoling for him to escort her to various activities. This was the first time she could remember Barrett Webb actually looking at her when he spoke.

She smiled slowly to herself as a new campaign began to unfold for claiming Barrett Webb for herself.

She hopped into her car to keep her appointment to have her nails done. When she arrived and her manicurist let her know she was available, she held up her hand to stop her from reaching for her usual shade of bright red.

Blanche stood thinking, remembering the simple allure of the stranger who was living in Barrett Webb's newly acquired farmhouse. She began to realize that the woman was probably a caregiver, but that didn't mean that Barrett Webb was blind to her natural beauty.

"I think I'm ready for a change, today. I think I'd like to try being really subtle and soft." Her words caused the nail technician to widen her eyes in surprise.

She gestured toward a display of colors and stood waiting for Blanche to choose her shade, completely shocked when she pulled an almost nude tint of pale pink from the shelf and handed it to her.

"Subtle and soft," she repeated to herself smugly. "That ought to do it."

Iris sat next to Aunt Sadie's bed, resting her head on the mattress close to her lifeless form, still clinging to her fingers as she freely allowed tears of farewell to fall and waited for the Webbs to arrive.

Aunt Sadie had lingered in a coma for the past couple of days before slipping away just moments ago, to find her Malcomb.

Once Iris had been able to detect her slowing respiration and faint vitals, she called Patricia Webb and advised her that Aunt Sadie was passing. Patricia assured her that they were on their way and that she would find Barrett, who had left the farm early that morning and had not returned.

The hospice nurse had advised Iris that she was en route to officially pronounce death and prepare Aunt Sadie for transport.

Iris lifted her head and reached a finger to touch the silver picture frame that Aunt Sadie had been clinging to when she'd lapsed into her coma, and was still resting her hand on.

Whenever anyone tended to her, the photo of her beloved Malcomb was carefully placed back into her hands as a fond gesture, knowing that the woman who was still in love, after all these years, would be grateful.

The hospice nurse entered the room quietly and came around to rest a compassionate hand on the back of Iris's head. "I'm so sorry," she whispered, smiling down at Aunt Sadie's tranquil, lovely face that was relaxed and free of pain.

She stood quietly, not wanting to rush her duties at the expense of a grieving loved one, and allowed Iris to lean over to lay a kiss on Aunt Sadie's head before standing up and offering her a sad smile.

"Are the family on their way?" the nurse asked softly.

Iris nodded. "They should be here any moment."

The nurse looked at her with a smile of apology. "I need to perform some checks, sweetheart, before I can legally pronounce death. You're welcome to stay if you'd like, but also feel free to step out if it might bother you."

"I'm okay," Iris answered in a small voice. "I've been through this part before."

The nurse began to check for respiration while looking at her watch. She placed a stethoscope on Aunt Sadie's chest, then continued with testing for vitals, fixed pupils, and any response to deep tissue touching. When she had satisfied the procedures required, she crossed over to the other side of the room and made a quiet call to advise Dr. Reese that Miss Webb had passed and took a seat at the small desk to document the official time and cause of death, before arranging for transport.

"She opened her eyes before she passed," Iris said, almost too softly to be heard.

The nurse turned and looked at her with a smile. "That's certainly been known to happen. Do you feel that she saw you somehow, despite her blindness?"

"Maybe," Iris answered, wiping her cheek. "Her eyes looked different, like they were clear. Really, I think she saw her Malcomb. She smiled."

The nurse looked over at Aunt Sadie's sweet face with a tender expression. "That's a nice thought," she said, before standing up and moving toward the door.

"I have to arrange for transport, Iris," she advised quietly. "I'll step out to do that and give you some time."

She slipped out and Iris watched her go before laying her head back down and closing her eyes, wondering if Aunt Sadie really did see her Malcomb, or who it was that she saw, who made her smile.

She felt a hand rest lightly on her back and sat up to see Barrett looking down at Aunt Sadie with unshed tears brimming in his eyes.

Iris sat up straight to give him room but he stayed where he was and stared down at his aunt, his face a storm of strong emotions that he had difficulty controlling, although he made a great effort.

Iris stood up and began to move but Barrett slipped his hand around her waist and wordlessly compelled her to wait.

"Thank you, Iris," he finally whispered, looking at her with a few tears escaping, despite his best attempt to contain them.

He appeared to be hoping for some kind of response and Iris ached to put her arms around him and comfort him, but she realized that this was for some other woman to do.

She simply told him that she was glad if she'd been any help to him and tried again to move away but Barrett tightened his hold on her and seemed to be silently pleading with her. Iris allowed him to pull her close for a hug.

He wrapped his arms around her and just stood with her for a long moment, not realizing that he was breaking her heart.

She finally pulled away and gave him a brief smile, just as Stuart and Patricia Webb came into the room.

Iris only lingered in the room a few moments more before slipping away and going outside to sit in the sun and be alone with her thoughts.

She walked through the pasture and stopped at the corral to reach for Howie, who had seen her coming and had whinnied a greeting. She stroked his head and grabbed a handful of feed from the bucket for a treat, then made her way over to sit on the large rock by the stream.

Iris knew it wasn't a good time to make plans, so she tried to simply be in the moment, but plans had to be made. She had already met with John Mabry again and he told her that his friend, a local minister, had a little rental house just outside of town that she'd easily be able to afford, if she felt she needed more time before making the commitment to buy a home.

Iris was to meet with him this evening and decided that she'd go ahead and keep that appointment, since nothing more could be done for Aunt Sadie and the funeral wouldn't happen for a few more days.

She looked up as she heard a vehicle approaching and saw that the funeral home was arriving to transport Aunt Sadie's body. She didn't want to be around for that.

She had stayed when Glenn's body had been transported and although it was done with respect and dignity, she simply didn't want to go through it again. Besides, this was a moment for family and regardless of how often Patricia Webb tried to convince her otherwise, Iris knew that she had been nothing more than a caregiver to their aunt and there was nothing else she could do for Aunt Sadie. The family didn't need her now.

She looked down at the flowing stream and tossed a pebble into it while she began to mentally prepare herself to go ahead and pull back from her involvement with the Webb family, and begin to find a way to fend for herself.

Nip had spotted his owner and came to her with a great deal of enthusiasm. It was a rare thing for him to find her outdoors lately and he was eager for her to pet him.

Iris welcomed him by putting her arms around him. After a few moments, she finally burst into quiet sobs and the faithful cattle dog looked at her with soulful eyes and tried to gently nudge her.

She made the effort to reel in her grief and tried to convince Nip that she was better, then looked over at the house and watched from a distance as the Webb family came out onto the porch and waited for Aunt Sadie to be carried out and placed into the waiting hearse.

She watched them embrace each other and stand looking after the departing vehicle before Patricia and Stuart Webb went back inside the house. Only Barrett remained on the porch, leaning against a post and looking down at the ground.

She wished she knew what he was thinking. There was a time when the two of them had begun to be able to discern such things about each other, but that was gone now.

Barrett saw that Iris's truck was still there and knew that she was somewhere on the property. He looked out toward the stream and saw her sitting with Nip.

They stared at each other for a long moment, neither attempting to approach the other.

Even from a distance, Iris couldn't fail to see the intense longing in him as he stood gazing at her, but she told herself that grief was making him feel vulnerable and that if his girlfriend were here, he would be turning to her for comfort.

The thought made her look away and Barrett drew in a deep breath before getting into his truck and driving away.

Iris smiled at the kind, white-haired minister and his wife, as they greeted her in front of the little cottage that John Mabry had told her about.

The couple introduced themselves as Pastor and Mrs. Welch, although they had certainly seen Iris around town over the past few years and felt as if they knew her. She remembered seeing them, as well. They had just never formally met.

She returned their greeting quietly and was surprised when the pastor's wife gathered her up in a hug.

"You'll have to watch out for Miss Katie," Pastor Welch warned her, with a grin. "She's a hugger."

"I am!" she agreed, proud of it. "If you don't want me hugging you, you'd better turn and run the other way."

Iris laughed softly at that and instantly liked the old couple. It had been a long while since Iris had been able to find humor in anything and she was relieved to discover that she could still laugh.

The pastor unhooked a very heavily loaded key ring from his belt loop and stood fingering through it.

He glanced over at Iris with another grin. "They say that you can tell how powerful a man is by how many keys he has on his key ring."

"Well, I don't know about that," his wife declared, getting another little laugh out of Iris.

The pastor finally located the key he was looking for and opened the door to the little cottage.

He let his wife and Iris go in ahead of him and Iris stopped to let her eyes roam around, taking in its sweet charm.

"Now, it's empty as it sits," Pastor Welch pointed out, "because John Mabry told us that you had furniture already that you'd probably want to use, but if that's not the case, young lady, then we have plenty of things in storage to make it nice for you."

Mrs. Katie Welch eyed the beautiful young woman with a question. "What do you like to be called, honey? Do you want us to call you Mrs. Anderson, or Iris? Or, I can just make up a nickname for you."

"You don't want that!" her husband laughed.

She smiled at them. "Iris is fine. Not Mrs. Anderson."

"Well, I'm Pastor Ben or just plain Ben, and everyone knows my wife as Miss Katie, although she's not technically a 'Miss' anymore and hasn't been for over fifty years."

"Fifty-two," his wife added happily. "This front room is what I guess you'd call the living room." She indicated it with a wave of her hand. Iris's eyes were drawn to the stone fireplace and Miss Katie noticed with pride.

"Ben laid every one of those stones," she informed her, bragging on her husband a little. "Most of them came from down river."

"It's beautiful," Iris told her sincerely.

They led her on into the little dining room and Iris told herself that she had a table that would be just about right for it.

The kitchen was larger than Iris had expected, and Pastor Ben had apparently continued his masonry skills here, as well. Iris was impressed by the section of backsplash behind the sink area that had been made with much smaller river rocks and black mortar.

She stood studying it closely, complimenting Pastor Welch and wondering why she had never tried anything like that.

The rest of the cottage consisted of two bedrooms and a fairly large bathroom.

The tour continued out through the back door and Iris was glad to see the tall pines and oaks and breathe in the woodsy smell. The cottage was secluded enough to feel private and the river that Miss Katie had talked about could be heard just beyond the trees.

"It's very close," she told Iris, after she asked. "If you like fishing, you'll enjoy being able to just walk out a little way and catch your supper."

Iris brightened considerably at thought of being able to do that and was beginning to feel a sense that this was where she needed to be.

When they went back inside, they discussed the rent and told her what was included and Iris wrote them a check on the spot to secure it, hoping to be able to begin to move her things a little at a time, whenever she could do it without being stopped and questioned.

She reluctantly returned to the farmhouse, suspecting that the Webbs were probably still there, or at least Barrett. When she drove around the circle and parked, his truck was where he normally left it, but after she entered the house and began to move around in it, she could tell that he wasn't there.

Iris thought it unlikely that he would be out in the fields today just after losing Aunt Sadie, especially when he paid other men to do that sort of thing. She decided that he must have ridden back with his parents to help them deal with selecting Aunt Sadie's casket and providing the clothes for her burial.

Iris didn't envy them the chore that these sorts of things could become and hoped that it could all be done quickly so that the family could begin to get back to normal.

She knew that she couldn't avoid Aunt Sadie's funeral, regardless of how much she wished she could. She felt that it would be selfish and an insult to Stuart and Patricia Webb, after all the time she had spent with Aunt Sadie. There was nothing for it but to attend and then focus on moving out of the farmhouse and looking for a job.

Iris climbed the stairs and opened the door to what had been Aunt Sadie's room and stood looking around, realizing that the bed had been stripped and remade to look as it had, before Aunt Sadie had arrived.

All of Aunt Sadie's personal effects were gone and the window next to the bed had been left cracked open to allow the fresh air in.

She could see that someone had taken the time to wipe down all the surfaces and mop the floor and the equipment that had been rented from the medical supply company when Aunt Sadie first arrived had obviously been picked up.

She stood leaning against the doorframe and let out a quiet sigh, realizing that all evidence that Aunt Sadie had ever been here was all gone. All she had left of her was the memory.

Chapter Ten

Iris had arrived at the church without much time to spare before the service was to begin. She had gotten rid of all the black clothes she owned after her late husband's funeral and hadn't even considered what she might have to wear until the last minute, which caused her some delay.

She'd finally found a sleeveless teal green silky dress that featured an intricate sheer teal overlay with embroidered darker lace botanical imagery over the bodice that spilled down below the fitted waist onto her slender hips, then repeated upward from the hemline of the overlay.

The dress had sheer bishop sleeves that gathered at her elbows and it suited her willowy form to perfection, although that was hardly what she had been fretting over. She'd simply wondered if it might be too frivolous for such a somber occasion, but there was nothing else.

She'd finally located some heels and took a quick look at herself in the hall mirror to make sure there was no grease she'd missed when she bathed then dashed out to her truck, in order to not be late.

Iris hadn't bothered to notice that the dress was a perfect complement to her lovely, long, coppery curls, or to remember that no one in the Webb family had ever seen her in anything but jeans and summer tops, with or without shoes.

She had slipped in quietly to take a seat in the back but when Stuart Webb glanced up from speaking with another man, he saw her and came to get her, insisting that she accompany him to the front to sit with the Webbs.

Iris realized that it would create more of a scene if she were to continue to protest than it would to simply agree, and allowed him to take her arm and bring her to be with his family.

Iris had never seen Barrett in a suit and drew in her breath at how naturally and perfectly he wore it, effortlessly changing from a farmer and cattleman to someone who would very much be in command at the head of any boardroom meeting.

He looked up at her, unable to hide the startled look in his eyes that witnessed her standing before him, as beautiful as any woman could possibly be. He stood to quietly greet her then moved down to let her sit between him and his mother. Patricia leaned over to whisper to her that she was absolutely stunning, and to give her a maternal pat on her arm.

Iris was as aware of Barrett's nearness as he was of hers, but she didn't allow herself to look at him again, glancing instead toward the beautiful casket where Aunt Sadie rested in repose, with the photograph of her beloved Malcomb beneath her slender fingers.

She wasn't surprised that seeing the photograph caused tears to immediately well up in her eyes but she felt a tissue being tucked into her hand and realized that Barrett had noticed. She offered him a weak smile and looked down at her hands, waiting for the service to begin.

All of this was observed by a livid, seething Blanche Hollis who'd heard her parents talking about Stuart Webb's aunt passing away and had hurried to find the obituary on the funeral home's web site. She had every intention to attend and offer her condolences and give comfort to Barrett, when the opportunity presented itself.

Now, she glowered at the woman who had been living in his house and had now been ushered up to the front for all eyes to see, as if she were a member of the Webb family. She had seen no mention of the caregiver in the obituary but she wouldn't have known the name, if she had. She sat staring daggers into the beautiful, nameless woman who was sitting so close to Barrett that they were touching.

It took everything Blanche had to refrain from taking advantage of the service not yet having begun, and going up to the front to greet the family, and settling down on the other side of Barrett as if it were the most natural thing in the world, but the minister's approach to the microphone foiled that plan and she was forced to sit and stare.

The reading of the obituary had begun and when First Sergeant Malcomb Howard's name was read, Iris needed her tissue again. Suddenly, she heard her own name and stared up at the minister in disbelief, not daring to believe that the Webb family had listed her as one of Aunt Sadie's survivors.

Tears insisted on running furiously down her cheeks. Barrett saw her distress and reached to take her hand in his, giving her fingers a light squeeze.

She allowed her hand to remain in his, admitting that she was grieving as well and accepting that his gesture was simply an attempt to recognize that and to offer some small comfort.

The minister invited Stuart Webb forward to eulogize his great aunt and he managed to do so with incredible self-control, although as he dwelt on her final days with the family, he had to stop and gather himself. He mentioned the invaluable help Iris had been to them and she lowered her head and gazed down at the floor, surprised and deeply touched by his kind words.

When the minister returned to the podium, he began to speak about eternity and the need to be prepared for it. Iris tried to listen but Barrett had unconsciously laced his fingers into hers and she couldn't stop herself from thinking about how her hand felt in his.

She didn't mean to, but she glanced up at him and he smiled softly at her and rubbed her hand gently with his thumb.

When the service ended, everyone except the family was asked to stand. They were directed by the funeral home staff to exit forward and out the side door beginning with the last row, in order to pass by where Aunt Sadie's body rested and ultimately leave the family alone with their loved one, before following the procession to the cemetery.

Barrett hadn't been looking up and missed the fact that Blanche Hollis had attended the funeral, but Patricia Webb and Iris saw her.

Patricia muttered something unexpected under her breath and surprised Iris, who looked over at her with wide eyes, causing Barrett's mother to grin and shake her head.

At last, the family stood and Barrett retained Iris's hand in his as they approached Aunt Sadie's lifeless form. The Webb family were all Christians, which enabled them to view this as a temporary parting but Iris knew nothing of eternal life and felt a pang of sadness that caused her to close her eyes tightly and press her lips together, as she felt the pain of it.

Barrett put his arm around her and whispered comforting words to her until she was able to draw in a deep breath and nod to him that she was okay.

He escorted her to the limousine and allowed her to enter, then slid in beside her to sit while they waited for his parents to receive some last minute instructions from the funeral director before the procession began.

"Are you okay?" Barrett asked quietly.

"Yes." Her response was faint. "Are you?"

"I've had better days," he admitted with a grin, causing her to smile sadly and nod.

"When this is over, can we talk, Iris?"

She sat still, not sure how to respond. It depended on what he wanted to talk about.

She finally looked at him and shook her head. "Not if you want to try to convince me to stay at the farm. We can't talk about that, Barrett."

He tightened the muscles in his jaw and drew in a breath.

"I won't try to convince you to do anything you don't want to do," he said, taking her hand again and coaxing her to look at him. "But please don't abandon me to have to work through endless unanswered questions about why you felt you had to leave me."

She studied him closely, completely thrown by his words. How could he not understand that he had a commitment to another woman that he needed to honor? Why was he speaking to her as if the other woman didn't exist? Another question presented itself to Iris, and she gave voice to it.

"Why wasn't Blanche Hollis sitting with the family, today?"

Barrett looked at her in complete bewilderment, as his mother and father were invited into the vehicle by the funeral home staff to join them, putting an end to discovery and leaving them both confused.

As the car followed the hearse into the cemetery, Iris began to feel a sense of dread, knowing that Blanche Hollis would certainly make an appearance there as well.

Patricia Webb seemed to somehow realize that Iris was worried and looked over at her with a meaningful expression.

"You belong with us, honey," she whispered, having not missed the color that had rushed to Iris's cheeks when she saw Blanche Hollis walk up to the front of the church and then turn to deliberately look straight at her before following the others outside. "Don't let that silly old Blanche get under your skin!"

This further served to confuse Iris, as she reasoned that if Blanche Hollis were really in a relationship with Barrett, surely his mother wouldn't be having such a negative reaction to her presence, or calling her that 'silly old Blanche'. It was all very strange to her.

When they stepped out of the limousine, Iris felt a tug on her fingers. Barrett had claimed her hand again and led her to sit beside him in the seats lined up alongside the closed casket.

She refused to look anywhere but at the minister, grateful that the interment service was brief and relieved to once again have Barrett as a shield, as they walked back to the limousine to depart the cemetery.

"Are we going back to the church?" she asked him, suddenly remembering that she had driven to the church in her truck and would need to somehow get back to it, in order to return to the farmhouse.

"I'm sure we are," he said. "Most of us arrived at the church in our own vehicles. From there, we're going to Mom and Dad's house."

"Would you please excuse me if I don't, Barrett?"

He looked at Iris with his disappointment clearly visible.

"Iris, you really won't come?"

She blinked rapidly and looked out the window. "I don't belong there," she said under her breath, but he heard and immediately looked at her in consternation.

"Why would you say such a thing?" he asked, trying to keep his voice low and quiet, but wanting to yell at her. "Do we make you feel like you don't belong?"

"No," she answered quickly, hoping to appease him enough to keep his parents from overhearing and realizing that he was upset.

Barrett stared out the window past her, a stern frown resting around his mouth, silently resolving that whatever it was they needed to clear up, it was long overdue.

He was determined that if he had to follow her truck out to the farm and not attend the gathering at his parents' home he would, but one way or another, he was going to make her tell him what it was that made things change between them.

Stuart Webb exited the vehicle first, then offered his hand to his wife. Barrett wanted to tell them to close the door so that he could have it out with Iris right here but he knew that the funeral home staff would have a problem with that. He slid across the seat to stand and reach for Iris's hand.

She was tempted to open her own door and walk around, but she didn't want to upset Barrett any more than he already seemed to be. She allowed him to help her out of the car, then turned to hug his parents and say a hasty goodbye.

Patricia stopped her and began to ask Iris the obvious question, intent on reasoning with her while Barrett stood silently, regarding Iris with a blend of confusion and anger.

Stuart took it all in, then laid a hand on his son's shoulder.

"Don't do any damage that you can't undo, Son," he advised quietly. "You don't want to take your frustration out on that young woman. Iris has gone from one traumatic experience to another, in rapid succession. She's walking a tightrope right now and you don't want to make her lose her balance."

He nodded, but made no reply and continued to watch his mother pleading with Iris to come be part of the family.

Iris was looking down at the ground listening, but Barrett knew her well enough to know that she was going back to the farm and regardless of his father's advice, he was going to get in his truck and follow her.

Just as he'd known she would, she gave Patricia Webb another tearful hug, then started the Apache and drove away.

Patricia returned to her husband and son with sad eyes.

"I'll be back later," Barrett muttered, heading to his own truck and driving in the direction of the farm.

Stuart looked after him with a sober expression, then put an arm around his wife and led her to their own vehicle.

After they drove away, Blanche Hollis decided that she knew where both the caregiver and Barrett were headed. There was no need to stay right behind them. She was very well acquainted with where the farm was.

Iris had been sure that she wouldn't be able to stop Barrett from following her to the house, but it couldn't be helped. She had already decided that she was going to locate an old cot she had in the utility room and spend the night at her cottage.

Barrett was too determined to force her to talk to him and she couldn't trust him not to leave and then show up again in the middle of the night, if he was still angry. If that happened, then she just wouldn't be there. Besides, it was his house. She was the one who needed to leave.

She knew that it wasn't the fact that she didn't want to go to his parents' home after the service that had upset him. She realized that she had been giving him mixed signals. She didn't blame him for being frustrated, but all that was about to stop.

It was the way Iris had changed toward him, that Barrett couldn't seem to get past. But why did he expect things to stay the same, especially since Blanche Hollis had made it clear that she was in a relationship with him? Iris might not like the woman, but she wasn't the type to willfully accept affection from a man who wasn't free to give it.

She wasn't surprised to look up in the mirror and see his truck enter the farmhouse road behind her. She blew out a breath she had been holding and tried to talk herself into staying calm. She felt that if she tried to be reasonable and give him answers to his questions, he might accept them and then leave her alone.

When she pulled her truck around the drive and parked it, he pulled in next to it, and hopped out to confront her, having worked himself into a state of irritation during the drive out to the farm.

She stood next to her truck, unsure of how he would approach her, but she knew he would definitely approach her.

Barrett stood looking intently at her, his brown eyes sparkling with anger, and forced himself to take in a steady breath and let it out slowly.

"Tell me why, Iris, and please don't waste our time by saying that you don't know what I mean."

"I do know what you mean," she admitted quietly.

He rested troubled eyes on hers and seemed more emotional now, than angry. "Did I get it all wrong? Everything about us? How big of a fool am I, Iris?"

She drew in a breath, as she saw the hurt in his eyes.

"No, Barrett, don't... "

He had moved closer and was searching her eyes with an intensity that took her breath. Once again, there was a longing in him that seemed to be pleading with her.

"I don't want to fight," he said, in a whisper.

He drew her close and rested his forehead on hers, closing his eyes and trying to dial himself down. She stood quietly leaning into him, with her own eyes closed. Both their hearts were pounding.

Iris slowly began to realize that she heard another vehicle and was dismayed to look behind Barrett and see Blanche Hollis's red car pulling around the driveway.

Barrett moved to turn and look and a streak of white-hot anger rushed across his face. He muttered something and glared at Blanche as she began to walk toward them, abandoning her original plan to pretend that she had only come to offer Barrett her condolences and becoming belligerent as soon as she reached them.

"So, you're not just a caregiver to the elderly, I see."

"Get out of here," Barrett gritted through clenched teeth.

"Of course, Barrett is not as helpless as his aunt was, so I can't help but wonder how you managed to convince him that he needs you to care for him, as well."

"Get out of here, Blanche!" he thundered.

Iris turned to head into the house, but Barrett caught her by the arm and pulled her roughly against him, capturing her mouth with his and kissing her angrily at first, and then hungrily, leaving Blanche Hollis speechless, as she turned and fled to her car, speeding away from Barrett Webb as fast as she could drive.

Iris resisted him at first, then yielded so completely to him, that it took a long moment for her to begin tell herself what his kiss really meant.

She drew back from him, staring with wide eyes, before looking down the road in the direction Blanche Hollis had just taken. She covered her mouth with her hands and backed away from him.

"You kissed me because you were mad at your girlfriend? You did it to make her leave?"

She wanted to hit him but instead, she turned and ran into the house, leaving him completely stunned.

Chapter Eleven

Barrett was perfectly still as he looked out the large wall of windows that afforded his parents an amazing view of the lake behind their impressive home. He wasn't sure why he'd returned here last night, instead of going to his own home, but it wouldn't surprise Stuart and Patricia Webb to come into the large den and find Barrett here.

That was his mother's discovery, as she padded softly into the room and stood looking at her son while he remained motionless, staring at nothing with his arms crossed and his jaw clenched with stress.

"Have you been here all night?" she asked him quietly, noting that other than removing his suit jacket and flinging it over the back of a chair, he was still in the clothes he'd had on when he left to follow Iris back to the farm.

"I have," he admitted in a dull voice, not turning around.

Patricia sighed and came across the room to slip an arm around his waist and look up at him with tender eyes. "Come have coffee with me," she suggested.

Barrett pulled his eyes away from whatever it was he'd been looking at and rested them on his mother. "I'm okay, Mother, I'm just... I have a lot to think about, I guess. I should be doing it at my own home. I don't know why I came here."

"You came here to talk about it, sweetheart," she pointed out, correctly. "Come sit and have coffee with me. Dad's still upstairs on his phone. Come."

She nudged him gently in a way that reminded Barrett of Nip, and he gave her a reluctant smile, and let her convince him to join her.

Patricia had already been in the kitchen making coffee, and had wandered into the den, as she did every morning, to stand and look at the lake while she waited for it to brew. It was ready now, and she filled their cups and brought them over to the kitchen table.

Barrett pulled out a chair for his mother, before settling heavily into his own and taking his coffee gratefully.

"I should have listened to Dad," he confessed after a long moment of just sitting, not sure how to begin.

Patricia smiled faintly. "If I had a nickel..."

Her son grinned and nodded. "I'm sure you'd rule the world, if you could cash in the number of times Dad was right."

She pursed her lips into a grin and nodded.

After another long moment of quiet, she reached over and touched his hand.

"So, you followed Iris to the farm and..."

"And who do you think showed up?"

A stormy expression returned to Barrett's face and his mother drew in a sharp breath.

"Oh, that foolish girl!" she exclaimed, seeming to be as annoyed as her son. "What, in the world, is she trying to pull?"

"Whatever it is, Lester Hollis better reel her in, if he ever expects to do business with me again," he stated grimly. "There are plenty of other auction houses. I don't need him, if his lunatic daughter is part of the deal."

"I'd be willing to bet that Lester has no clue that Blanche is behaving this way toward you," Patricia said. "But I think he should be made aware."

"She's just a silly kid, Mother, and I've never given her any encouragement at all but for whatever reason, she has latched onto me to the point of stalking. You're right, her father needs to know that she could very well cause me to find somewhere else to do business."

He gripped his coffee cup between his hands and sat still, but he was quietly seething inside.

"I haven't said anything about this," his mother began slowly, as her son looked up at her expectantly.

"Blanche has been out to the farm before," she said flatly.

Barrett just stared at her.

"Not long after hospice began working with Aunt Sadie, I heard someone at the front door and it was Blanche. I didn't even ask her what she wanted, I just told her that you weren't there and that we were dealing with a family illness.

"I told her to call next time, before she drove all the way out and of course, she began gushing with concern and asking me to let her know if she could do anything. All that crap."

Barrett couldn't resist smiling at his mother, as she said a word that she fussed at him for saying.

"Anyway, Iris just happened to walk out of the kitchen with a pan and took it upstairs to the hospice nurse, and Blanche looked at her as if she wanted to stab her. The odd thing is that I could somehow tell that she'd already known she'd find Iris there, and was actually looking for her."

Barrett couldn't hide his surprise but waited to comment.

"Later, I encouraged Iris to go outside whenever I was there or hospice, just so she could breathe in some fresh air and get a change of scenery, and she went out to the stream.

"I decided to go check on her and I asked her if Blanche had been there before, and she had." Patricia's displeasure began to mirror her son's.

"Iris admitted that she had been told by Blanche to give you a message but that she'd forgotten and I'm sure that's true, with everything that poor woman was having to deal with. Blanche told her that she was checking to see if you were still going to a dance with her and she wanted Iris to remind you. She implied to Iris that the two of you are a couple."

Barrett's steady gaze faltered and he looked down at the table in disbelief.

"That's why Iris asked me why Blanche didn't sit with the family at the service. And that's why she began avoiding me."

"I'm sure you're right," his mother agreed with a fed up scowl. "Barrett, somebody has got to stop Blanche, before she antagonizes every cattleman her father tries to work with."

A flush of regret swept across Barrett Webb's handsome but sad face as he remembered how Iris had backed away from him yesterday evening and accused him of kissing her to make his girlfriend mad. He couldn't grasp what she could possibly be talking about but it was becoming painfully clear.

"I did something stupid," he admitted softly to his mother.

"Did you do what your dad told you not to do?" she asked, with a smile of sympathy.

"I did." He sat thinking about how hurt Iris had been and how she had turned and run from him.

"I just wanted her to tell me what I'd done, Mother. I had to know. I didn't plan to follow her to the farm but I did ask her if we could talk. She said that I couldn't try to talk her out of moving out of the farmhouse but she seemed willing to talk.

"But after she upset me in the limo, when she wouldn't come here, saying that she didn't belong here, I didn't try to hide the fact that I was angry. She knew by then that I fully intended to follow her to the farm and have it out."

Patricia studied him with a sober expression, suspecting that Blanche had probably arrived on the scene just in time to interfere with that. "You said you did something stupid. What did you do, Barrett?"

He leaned back in his chair and returned her gaze with troubled eyes. "We both pulled our trucks in and got out and I demanded that she tell me what I'd done. But at the same time, I didn't want to fight with her.

"She didn't want that either and we both dialed it back and got quiet, just being close, alone together, only to have Blanche drive up and immediately begin saying ugly things to Iris, implying that she was much more than a caretaker, as far as I was concerned."

Patricia Webb was full on angry now and if Blanche Hollis had been anywhere nearby, she probably would have slapped her heavily made up face, until her head spun around. She silently admitted to God that she needed to repent.

"I yelled at her to leave, but she just doubled down on what she'd already said. Then Iris began walking away and..."

Barrett stopped, realizing how he'd treated her, although unintentionally, and feeling ashamed of himself.

"I grabbed Iris and kissed her," he confessed.

On the surface, it didn't sound so bad but of course Patricia was a woman, and completely understood why Barrett had just told her that he'd done something stupid.

"In front of Blanche?" She gasped softly when he nodded. "Oh, Son! She thought you did it *because* of Blanche!"

He nodded, confused as to why his mother could see that so clearly and he hadn't had a clue.

"Blanche tore out of there of course, and I hope that's the last I'll see of her but Iris just stood there, backing away from me and accusing me of kissing her to make my girlfriend mad." He looked at his mother with a silent appeal.

"I couldn't understand why Iris was calling Blanche my girlfriend, Mother. Believe me, the last thing I was thinking about was Blanche. I just didn't want Iris to leave me again. It was desperation on my part; I admit it. But I love her."

Patricia nodded, having already figured that part out.

⁂

Iris stood watching, as the movers cleared her old farmhouse of the last of her possessions. This final load had to go to a storage facility since she'd already furnished the little cottage with what it needed, without it becoming cluttered.

She stood looking around at the empty old house not even trying to figure out what she was feeling. She couldn't handle feelings right now.

She'd already walked out to the cattle sheds early that morning to advise Barrett's foreman that she was leaving Nip to work the cattle and that Barrett would decide what to do with the horse, goats and chickens. She asked him to remind Barrett about that, allowing the foreman to assume that he knew.

She put her house keys on a nail by the door, knowing that there would be enough of Barrett's crew around the property to discourage anyone from breaking in. Even if someone did, there was nothing to steal, other than Barrett's clothes in the bedroom he'd been using downstairs. She'd locked that door, for now.

Iris got into her truck and followed the moving van to the storage facility and once everything had been loaded into it, signed the work order and paid the man who was overseeing everything. She made sure it was locked, then drove over to her little cottage, which had begun to feel more and more like a haven to her.

There was no past, here. Everything was new and she felt she could breathe again and stop constantly feeling regret about everything, except for Barrett. She couldn't think of him without a stab of pain but Iris believed, or at least hoped, that time would help her with that.

She stopped in the kitchen to brew a quick cup of coffee, then took it out to the little backyard patio to sit and stare into the trees and try to think a clear thought.

Barrett hadn't been back to the farmhouse since following her there after Aunt Sadie's funeral. Iris had been relieved that he hadn't returned to try to convince her not to move but it hurt to realize that he had become her past, along with the farm. She wondered how long it would take her to stop caring.

She figured that he must have worked things out with Blanche, since she'd also not returned to further antagonize her.

Iris breathed in the steam of her coffee and tried to push back the tears that always seemed to threaten whenever she let herself think of Barrett.

She knew she needed to focus. She had been considering the hospice nurse's suggestion that she might consider working as a hospice aide.

The nurse had learned that Iris had already passed her certified nursing assistant exam when her husband was first diagnosed with cirrhosis, and had also been certified in CPR. She knew that Iris would pass her health and background checks. She just needed to pursue her hospice certification, and she had no doubt that Iris would sail through that.

She'd advised Iris that it was not a high-paying job but Iris only needed to be able to pay her rent without having to dip into the money in her account that she had already had to touch to get her things moved and get into the cottage.

She let the sunlight that filtered through the trees warm her face and sat with her eyes closed, wishing there was someone who could advise her.

She had tried to tell herself that she should be able to make basic decisions without having to run everything past someone. Mr. John Mabry had been invaluable to Iris as she dealt with the aftermath of Glenn Anderson's reckless squandering of everything they'd owned.

She thought of the good Pastor Welch and Miss Katie and wondered if she might someday be able to talk to them about her situation. She'd always supposed that ministers were used to that sort of thing so maybe they'd be willing to at least listen to her and even pray for her, since that wasn't something she knew how to do, herself.

She wondered if she would have to attend their church, in order to receive counsel from them. She doubted if they would force her but she also didn't think she'd mind as long as they didn't do anything odd in church. She honestly didn't know about churches although she knew that the Webb family could be considered as church people and she respected them.

A sour expression washed across her face, as she correctly imagined that the Hollis family were also probably church people, so apparently that didn't stand for a lot.

Iris lifted herself up from the glider she'd been slowly rocking back and forth on and headed back indoors to finish unpacking her things, in an attempt to create a home for herself.

※※※

Barrett stood looking around the empty farmhouse with a tightness in his throat that was making it difficult for him to breathe. She was gone.

He'd had no idea that she would move so swiftly to find a place but she obviously had already accomplished that, in order to be able to so quickly and completely rid the house of any evidence that she had ever been here.

He fought to hold back the tears that seemed to have finally found him at thirty-eight years of age, despite the fact that he'd spent a lifetime with the reputation of being completely in control of his emotions.

She didn't love him. He understood that, now.

It didn't matter what Iris convinced herself of, regarding Blanche Hollis. He didn't believe she could just leave him, if she really loved him but she was gone. That was that, then.

Barrett stepped out onto the porch and put his hat on, then wandered over to the side pasture to check on Howie. He had no plan regarding what to do with him, yet. As far as that went, Barrett didn't have a plan for his next breath.

He stood patting the Morgan absentmindedly, deciding to just trailer him and take him and the goats back to his primary residence where there was always someone around to feed and look after the livestock. That wasn't the case yet, on this farm.

He headed off to advise his foreman of his intention and also asked him to find out if any of his men wanted to have the chickens. Iris had seemed to sort the issue of them not laying, and the eggs needed to be taken to their homes, as well. The foreman said he'd look after it.

He went back to his truck and drove into the town, to pick up what he needed in order to be able to brew himself coffee in the farmhouse from time to time. He finished that errand, then headed to the square to see if he could locate a map of what he'd purchased, other than the one Iris had given him when he'd first seen the property. She'd only had an aerial map and another one showing property lines. He needed to know more about the actual topography.

Nothing like that had been provided at closing, but since it was a cash deal, he'd simply told John Mabry that he'd get it later. He was able to find what he needed, and decided to make a few changes to the farm.

He expected that he would probably end up selling it in the future and wanted to make sure he made his investment turn a profit. There was no reason to take Iris's feelings into account, now. He didn't have to consider her, he told himself.

Barrett turned around as he heard his name, and saw John Mabry walking away from his own vehicle and using his fob to lock it.

He waited for him to catch up, then nodded a greeting.

"I see you finally found that information," the banker acknowledged. "I'm sorry that wasn't available before, Barrett."

"No, it's fine, I haven't needed it until now."

John looked at him steadily. "I heard about your aunt, Barrett, and I sure am sorry. It doesn't matter that we know age will take our elderly. It's still a disappointment."

He nodded and looked away, wondering if John Mabry had called out to him to simply make small talk. He liked the man, but they weren't the sort of friends who had the need to get caught up.

"I guess you've discovered by now that Iris has moved."

Barrett lifted a hand to stop him. "I don't need to know where she is."

John looked at him silently, not believing him but not pursuing it, since his demeanor warned him not to.

"If there ever is a reason to, Barrett, I can get a message to her," the banker offered quietly. "For what it's worth."

"I can't see that being the case, but if it ever is, I'll call you," he said in his crisp way that most of his workers were used to hearing.

"Good day to you, Barrett," John Mabry offered, deciding not to detain him further. Maybe Barrett Webb was right to not continue to concern himself with Iris Anderson's wellbeing. A man had to look out for himself.

Barrett nodded to him and got into his truck, as John Mabry watched him drive away with a sigh of disappointment.

Chapter Twelve

Barrett stopped in his tracks and closed his eyes, taking in a deep breath and knowing full well that he was about to lose the battle for self-control as the shrill, hated voice of Blanche Hollis pursued him with a greeting.

He couldn't believe she had the nerve to ever try speaking to him again, let alone smile and wave, as if she had done nothing to upset him.

He waited, since she could be counted on to scurry over and begin prattling on to him about some stupid party. When she did just that, he lifted a hand and fixed a look on her that made her forget what it was she was saying.

When Barrett finally spoke, his words were calculated, measured, and ice cold.

"If you ever approach me again for any reason, I will slap a restraining order on you so quickly that it will make your head spin. You get back into that silly toy car of yours and go home and tell your daddy that I will never do business with him again, and that it's your fault. The Webb and the Hollis families are done. I will soon contact your father myself, to determine if you delivered my message."

He turned and continued on his way, leaving her staring after him, as the fear of how her father was going to respond began to cause Blanche Hollis to panic.

Barrett got into his truck and slammed the door with unnecessary force, and sat scowling at the dashboard, waiting for his blood pressure to return to normal.

He started to return to his house to give Howie an injection for his joints, but remembered that he needed to run by his parents' home and drop off something for his father.

When he arrived, he was still angry about being stopped by Blanche Hollis, and entered the house without remembering to check his temper at the door.

Stuart and Patricia Webb looked up at him and then at each other, as it became obvious that their son was irritated.

Barrett set a package on the counter, then indicated it with his hand before turning to leave.

"That's the lime-sulfur dip you wanted, Dad. Abner said to tell you not to give it any more often than every twelve days if it's still needed, and to not let the horse lick where you treat him, but I don't know how you're going to avoid that, if that's where the mange is."

His father nodded and continued to eye him, waiting to see if he had to ask.

His mother was not so patient. "What's going on?"

Stuart glanced over at her with a little grin, then looked back to see if their son was going to tell them.

"You may as well know," he muttered. "I shouldn't have spoken for you, Dad, but when that pain-in-the-neck Blanche Hollis tried to talk to me today like she hasn't been stalking me and doing everything she could to interfere in my personal life, I told her that if she ever comes near me again, I'm taking out a restraining order against her. I also told her to tell Lester that I wasn't doing anymore business with him and that she could tell him it was because of her."

"How did you speak for me, Son?" Stuart asked quietly.

"I told her that the Webb and the Hollis families were done. I apologize for that, Dad, because my issue shouldn't become your issue. I don't expect you to fall in behind my decision. I'll let Lester know that I'm only speaking for myself, but I did tell Blanche that I will be contacting him to find out if she delivered my message."

Stuart liked Lester Hollis well enough, but he was not the only show in town. He looked at his son with a mild expression and gave him a smile.

"I don't mind that, Barrett. The Webbs stick together. Patty told me what Blanche did and I sure am sorry to hear it. I have to admit, I do think it's a shame that no one is stepping up to tell Iris the truth but that's your business, so I'm not going to wade off into it."

"If she had really cared about me, Dad, it wouldn't have mattered what Blanche said," Barrett replied, crossing his arms and looking off toward a window. "It didn't take much for her to hightail it out of the farmhouse, as if she'd never even been there. She didn't leave so much as a bottle cap. John Mabry seemed to want to tell me where she was, but I told him I didn't need to know."

Patricia looked down at her nails, as if one suddenly needed attention and just shook her head, then blinked back tears. She loved Iris and she knew that Iris loved her son. Of all the times for Barrett to show his stubborn streak!

She looked up at her husband and he gave her a soft look. He knew what she was feeling.

"Well, Son, if Lester asks me if you're speaking for me too, I don't mind telling him that we're more than a little put out over what his daughter did, and the way she's been dogging you. I do find it hard to believe that no one has ever complained to him about Blanche's behavior, so I expect he'll just be hearing something he's heard before.

"It's a mighty shoddy way to run a business though, to let your spoiled daughter run off your best customers."

Barrett laid a hand on his father's shoulder and gripped it with affection. "I appreciate it, Dad."

He leaned down and gave his mother a peck on the cheek. "I guess I'd better get home and give that old Morgan an injection. He's a little stiff."

He stopped at the door and put his hat back on, then nodded to the both of them before leaving.

Stuart and Patricia watched him go with disappointment. Whenever their son got this dug in about something, not much would move him. Not even the woman he was in love with.

Patricia let out a heavy sigh. "I do wish Iris hadn't been in such a hurry to go. I wish they both could have just slept on it and tried to talk again. It's a shame Iris made her decision based on a lie."

She lifted her sad brown eyes to her husband. "But Barrett won't tell her the truth. He's too angry at her for believing Blanche."

"Well, that's the reason he's come up with to allow himself to be angry instead of hurt, and keep his pride intact. But you're right. Barrett never told her anything different, Patty," Stuart agreed. "Why shouldn't she believe Blanche? Sure, he got offended at Iris for believing her, but he never just up and said it was a lie.

"What was the girl supposed to do? He didn't give her the one thing she needed from him. But I can tell you this. I watched the two of them at Aunt Sadie's service and there's no way anyone will convince me that those two aren't in love. That's pretty clear, regardless of who's living where."

Pastor Ben and Miss Katie sat out on the back patio with Iris and sipped the coffee she'd made for them, with smiles of contentment.

"We haven't sat out here in a long time, have we, Ben?" Miss Katie challenged.

"It's been a while," he agreed. "This area has always had a peaceful feel, Iris. I hope you find it peaceful for yourself."

"I love it out here," she assured him.

"Have you been fishing, yet?" Miss Katie wondered.

"Not yet, but I did walk out and take a look at the river," she admitted. "It's a pretty open trail between here and the river. Did you clear it?"

"We had a son," Pastor Ben replied, the memory of the young man resting in his eyes. "Matthew. He was our only child, and he was always helping us with whatever he could do. He came out here, I expect about ten years ago, and took out the underbrush and cut some saplings back for us."

"He made it real nice," Matthew's mother added, with a wistful little smile.

Iris looked at them, wanting to ask but not wanting to create any awkwardness for them. They seemed to see her questions on her face.

"He was a musician," Pastor Ben told her. "And there was just something about him that was special. I guess he never was long for this world. He played the guitar and wrote some of the prettiest songs. But, of course, he only wrote them for the Lord and himself. He never aspired to share them with anyone else, except our little church."

"We have some movies of him, though," Miss Katie said in a soft voice. "We'll always have those."

"You don't have Matthew, anymore," Iris said hesitantly.

"No, Iris, he's with the Lord, now. I guess he's just about sung every song he ever wrote to Him, by now. He'll have to come up with some new material. Eternity is a long time."

The old Pastor's eyes crinkled up with a smile, as he made his whimsical remark. "He ended up wrecking, probably seven years ago, now. I expect he was about your age. He had just turned twenty-six. Some poor woman had been drinking and was coming right at him, and when he swerved to miss her, his car went down a steep embankment and rolled several times.

"They brought him by helicopter to the hospital and we stayed there with him for about a week. He was hooked up to all kinds of life support but it got to where there was no brain activity and we finally had to let him go."

Iris immediately felt tears forming, just hearing the way this sweet old couple talked so peacefully about the loss of their only child without any bitterness.

There was a lengthy silence as they were all lost in their thoughts before Miss Katie quietly said, "He was beautiful."

"Yes, he was," her husband agreed. "Hair the color of flax, all curly and down his neck. His mother was always after him to get a haircut, but he'd just laugh and tell her he'd think about it."

"Have you ever seen flax, Iris?" Miss Katie asked her.

"I have, it's a beautiful color," Iris answered quietly.

She sat deep in thought, bothered by some of this and wondering if it would be wrong to ask her question.

Finally, she looked at them both and wondered, "How could you be willing to worship a God who took your only child? I don't understand why you aren't angry at Him for that."

"Do you believe In God, Iris?" the kind old pastor asked in a gentle tone.

"I think I do. I did when I was a little girl, but I never went to church. I was raised in different foster homes, but none of those families went to church, if I remember correctly. But I used to pray to God, when I went to bed."

"Who taught you to do that, if you don't mind my asking?"

"Maybe my grandmother. I don't remember her much, but when my mother went to prison, she kept me until she died. After that, I went into the foster care system."

"Can I ask where your father was, honey?" Miss Katie's question was a timid one.

"I just don't know. Everyone has to have a father, I guess, but I don't know who mine was."

She hadn't pondered all of this in many years, probably because she always ended up with more questions than answers.

"I seemed to always think there was a God. I just didn't understand why He didn't like me."

The pastor and his wife exchanged stricken looks.

"Why did you believe that, Iris?" Pastor Ben asked, in his kind way.

"I guess little kids think that way, when they pray for things and they don't get them," she finally offered. "I'm not really sure, except that I heard other people talk about praying and they made it sound like God would talk to them. But He never would say anything to me. So, I finally just quit talking to Him. I guess I just decided He wasn't listening."

He nodded and thought about her words. "Well, if I'm being honest, Katie and I have felt like God wasn't listening at times but as we began to know Him better, we learned that His silences are just as important as His voice. All of Him means something."

Miss Katie smiled over at him. "We sure did beg God to heal our Matthew, didn't we, Ben? But He took him home, and we just had to trust that it was the best thing for him.

"We just have no way of knowing how his life would have turned out, if he'd continued on after his accident. He might have ended up with the kind of life he wouldn't want."

"But I mean, if God could have given your only child back to you and He chose not to, how is that love?" Iris wasn't trying to be argumentative; she was just longing to know.

"Well, honey, who knows more about losing His only Son, than God? Only His Son wasn't killed in a car crash or even murdered. God sent Him to die for all of us, knowing that not everyone would accept the salvation that He brought, but He chose to send Him, anyway.

"At any time, Jesus could have chosen not to go through with it, but he set His face like a flint, and while we were all still sinners, He died for us." The good pastor smiled, as he reflected on his own words.

"But, Pastor Ben, what was the point of Him dying?" Iris was truly confused. "What good did that do?"

"God's anger against sin could only be satisfied by a perfect sacrifice. There was no sacrifice to be found perfect enough, except His Son Jesus, the Lamb of God," the old minister told her. "And so He was willing to come to earth, live as a man and lay down His life, so that His Father's wrath against sin would be appeased, once and for all."

He stopped and looked at Iris, as if he was studying her. "I have something in my car that I want to give you."

He stood and made his way around the cottage and Miss Katie smiled, knowing what he was after.

"Are you liking the little cottage?" she asked, hoping it would be a good home for the beautiful young lady.

"I really do. I was living in an old farmhouse on a lot of land and I was really just rattling around in it by myself, after my husband died. I did have a family there for a while because their great aunt needed hospice care and I watched over her."

Miss Katie was intrigued by that. "Is that what you do, honey, work with hospice?"

"I did for my late husband and then for that family's relative. I'm beginning to think I should continue to do that. I actually wanted to ask you and Pastor Ben what you might think about that."

They both looked up, as he came back around the cottage with an old Bible in his hands and held it out to Iris.

"Iris, this is God's word to us. Everything in it is good, but when someone like you has questions, I always think it's good to start in the New Testament and read the four gospels, Matthew, Mark, Luke and John. I'd like to give you this Bible, in the hopes that you would consider reading a little of it from day to day. I believe that if you'll do that, God will cause you to understand what you read, and your questions will be answered."

She looked down at it and took it into her hands almost reverently, as she once again felt the onset of tears. No one had ever given her a Bible before, or spent this kind of time talking with her about God. She looked up at him with a grateful look in her blue eyes and quietly thanked him.

"I'll read it," she promised.

He smiled and gave her a thumbs up, looking very happy.

"Ben, Iris has worked with hospice, before," Miss Katie informed him. "She might do it again."

"Is that right, Iris?" He seemed interested. "What would you be doing?"

"I'd work as a nurse's aide and tend to the patient, as far as bathing, helping them dress, taking their vitals, cleaning their room, running errands. Just whatever I can do to make their remaining days as nice as I can."

"I think that's a noble thing to do," he commended her.

Iris hesitated, as she looked down at the Bible in her hands. "Is your church far?"

"Not at all," Miss Katie replied. "We're just right back in town, as you head there, from here. Would you like me to write it down for you somewhere?"

"If you don't mind," Iris said. "You never know, you may look up someday and see me walking in."

"That would be wonderful, honey!" the minister's wife declared, looking as happy as her husband did.

They both agreed that they needed to get back home, and Iris stood up and walked with them back into the house.

She found a sheet of paper and a pen and Miss Katie wrote down the address of the church, along with the service schedule and added their phone number.

"Honey, if you get lonely over here now, you just give us a call and let us know what you need," she instructed her, adding one of her famous hugs to her words.

Pastor Ben gave her a little pat on the elbow and then reached down to touch the Bible she was still holding.

"Make this your friend, Iris, and you'll never be alone."

They gave her a wave and she watched them climb into their car, before closing the door and looking down at the Bible, feeling more free to allow a few tears to fall, now that she was alone. And she really was alone, she told herself.

She had once found a wonderful family who loved her and now they were all gone. She doubted she'd ever see Barrett again. The thought made her ache, and the pain was real.

She brought the Bible over to a chair in the corner and hoped that Pastor Ben was right. She needed a friend.

Chapter Thirteen

Barrett stood watching the excavator working outward from the center of what was about to become the lake. He had come to realize that it needed to be exactly where Iris had always envisioned it.

There was a time when he had planned to build the lake for no other reason than to please her. Now, his motivation was to simply increase the value of his investment and generate a quick sale. He just wanted to be rid of it.

His contractor, Grant Foley, approached him with a smile and stood looking with him out toward the rapidly changing parcel of land.

"If ever there was a place that was begging for a lake, this is it," he declared, with satisfaction. "Did you already know about the underground stream, or did we just get lucky?"

"I had some idea that it was there, pretty much for the same reasons that you noticed," he answered quietly.

Barrett observed their progress as he rested his left arm across his waist to support his elbow, and absently stroked his stubble beard with his right hand.

"You can see water already pooling where Leon's moved away," Grant pointed out, as the excavator driver continued forward in a straight line and the spotter stepped in to check the depth. "This is going to turn out to be beautiful."

Barrett nodded, looking neither pleased nor hopeful. His face was unreadable. Since he had been denied the joy of doing this for Iris, it was just another chore that needed to be done and the sooner it was finished, the sooner he could list the property.

Grant clapped a hand on his shoulder and headed off to see why the dump truck driver was waving an arm at him.

Barrett continued to let his eyes travel over the developing lake and remembered Iris telling him that she liked to go fishing. That was something he liked doing as well, although he had less and less time for anything like that. He made a silent decision to stock the lake with fish, stubbornly trying to convince himself that it would only be in order to add value to the farm.

He watched for a few moments more, then looked down as Nip showed up to find out what all the noise was about.

He reached out his hand, and the cattle dog enjoyed a gentle scratch behind his ears. Despite his wanting to rid himself of everything that connected him to Iris, Barrett had a soft spot for Nip and reasoned that animals were exempt from the conflicts of their humans, which influenced his decision to move Howie and his goats to his personal property.

He looked up again at the beginnings of the lake and satisfied himself that his contractor was on top of things, before he slapped his thigh to signal Nip to come with him to check on the milo he was testing in this soil.

Nip matched him step for step, looking up at him as if he were speaking and trying to anticipate the need to herd something. Barrett smiled to himself, as he appreciated the intelligence of the Australian breed, then made his way toward the orchard to determine if it would add to, or detract from the property's overall value in its current state.

His eyes traveled over to where he'd parked his truck, the day that Iris rode with him around the farm, pointing out various aspects of it, as the two sat together on the tailgate, and she agreed to stay in the farmhouse and care for Aunt Sadie. He thought about her misunderstanding him, and wondering if he was asking her to stay for himself and grinned, in spite of himself, as he remembered her dismay and wide-eyed reaction.

This only served to create a sense of loss and longing in him, and he hurried to push it away and tell himself again that she had never loved him as he had loved her, and that he just needed to let it go and do what he could to flip this farm and then move on to buying the next one.

He removed his hat and wiped his brow with his sleeve, then headed back to the house to find something cold to drink. Nip only walked with him as far as the fence, since he'd have nothing to do but lie on the porch, once Barrett went inside.

Barrett swung his leg over the fence and crossed the yard to step up onto the porch of the farmhouse.

He stopped to glance over to where Iris was known to sit on the big rock by the stream and muttered to himself impatiently, heading into the house to throw some water on his face and get a drink.

After he'd cooled down, he pulled out a chair that was part of the small dinette set he'd picked up in town and could drop off at a charity when he was ready to sell the farm, then sat down to think about the rest of his day.

The table and chairs were the only furniture in the house now, except for the bed that Iris left in the bedroom he'd been using. When he dropped the dinette set off at a charity, he'd give them the bed, as well. She probably would never contact him about it, and if it did turn out that she wanted it back, he'd just have another one shipped to her.

He pulled a small pad out of his pocket and made a note to pick up some antibiotics for a couple of Herefords, then sat mulling over the best use of the rest of his day.

He sighed, as he remembered that his mother had asked him to join her and his father to order a headstone for Aunt Sadie. Of course, he did want her to have a beautiful stone, and he appreciated his parents wanting him to be a part of the decision, but heading back into that county was the last thing he wanted to do today.

He could never guarantee that he wouldn't run into Blanche Hollis, although Lester had called him and apologized profusely for her behavior and assured him that there would be no further incidents.

Barrett allowed a dour expression to rest on his face. He expected that Lester would say whatever he had to, in order to keep him and his father as customers.

He did remark to the girl's father that one more attempt by Blanche to pursue him in any manner, and Lester might as well not bother calling again, because he had no intention of putting up with her foolishness and he'd be quick to make good on his promise.

Barrett pushed up from the table to go grab some clean clothes from his bedroom before getting a quick shower. His showers had all become quick ones, because he didn't like to stand in silence too long and think. His thoughts all brought him back to the same place, and he didn't want to linger there, anymore.

When he was dressed, he found his hat then headed to his truck in order to not disappoint his parents. He'd given his word and it needed to be done. Barrett was not a man to avoid his duty, just because he didn't feel like performing it.

Iris slipped her shoes off and rested the soles of her bare feet on the cool stones of the backyard patio. She reached her arms high in a stretch and smiled to think that she had passed her hospice certification exam and was officially employed as a nurse's aide.

Her first assignment had been to temporarily replace an aide who had to be away from her job. Iris's supervising nurse thought this would be a good way for her to begin, since she would only work with that patient for a couple of days and wouldn't form any sort of bond. Iris was glad of that. After Aunt Sadie's death caused her to grieve in a way that she hadn't expected, she was hoping that the longer she worked at her job, the more professional and less personally effected she'd become.

She looked off vacantly into the peaceful pines that stood tall between the river and her cottage. The sun was beginning to hint at going down, and it cast an orangish-golden light through the tops of the pines. Iris noticed that the air was beginning to feel cooler, and was surprised to see a slight bit of color in some of the hardwoods in the distance. Autumn seemed to be trying to sneak in, not fully arrived, but making the promise to come soon. Iris breathed in the evening air and felt a sense that her life might be moving in the right direction.

After reading the scriptures that Pastor Ben had told her about and attending their little church, she understood enough to be able to recognize her need for salvation and had prayed with the couple, after the service. She knew she had a lot to learn, but she did grasp the concept of grace and embraced it gratefully.

Now she sat reflecting over the way God seemed to be leading her and she knew what Pastor Ben meant by telling her that God's silences were as important as His voice. He and Miss Katie advised her to pursue peace, and she took hold of that counsel and found that it was how God seemed to direct her.

Iris recognized the peace of God that very day, after her shift was done. She had to drive through downtown Fairfield on her way home.

When she stopped for a light, she saw Barrett coming out of one of the county offices on the square. If he had glanced up, he would have recognized the old Apache truck, but he was looking down at the papers in his hands intently, and she drove on when the light changed, without his ever being aware of her.

Her heart immediately filled up with her love for him, and she keenly felt his absence in her life. She missed him more than she could express, but at the same time, some sort of steady, calm sensation blanketed her in such a way that she knew God had His hand on her.

Rather than focus on her pain, she used the time during her drive home to talk to God out loud about Barrett. By the time she stopped her truck in front of the cottage, she sensed that He had listened to every word she'd said.

Part of her had wanted to tap her horn, to get Barrett to look up at her, but as far as she knew, he could very well have worked things out with Blanche, now that she had moved out of his house and wasn't around to confuse him. She told herself that if God ever intended for them to reunite, He would speak to Barrett about it. She was surprised to have reached that conclusion, but it felt right to her.

She lifted her hands to clasp her forearms in a comforting hug, and felt the same rush of tears that always threatened her, whenever she thought of Barrett Webb, but she would just have to trust God to heal her heart and, knowing that Barrett was a Christian, she prayed that if she had ever hurt him, he would forgive her and that God would heal his heart, as well.

She knew that was a dangerous prayer, because if his heart was healed, it might mean that he would move on and have a life with Blanche Hollis or some other woman, and wouldn't even look back at the time they'd shared. All this did was create more tears and Iris drew in a deep breath and told herself to think of something else, anything else, besides Barrett Webb.

She started a new assignment in the morning. All she'd been told about the patient was that he was an elderly gentleman farmer who had been treated for coronary artery disease for several years and was now in the end stages of advanced congestive heart failure.

His name was Oren Frazier and he had served many years as a member of the local area's cattlemen's association. Iris was told that his wife, Lillian, wanted his hospice care to take place in their home, so that their grandchildren could be able to see their grandfather.

Iris wasn't sure how she felt about children being present when a loved one passed, but she hadn't been told how old the grandchildren were, so perhaps they were old enough to be able to process everything.

She would have to drive a bit further out to get to the Frazier home, which would make it necessary for her to start her day earlier than normal, so she decided to get up from the glider and head inside to throw some sort of meal together and turn in early. She hoped to be able to study some from her Bible before she became too sleepy to read it properly.

As she came into the kitchen and locked the door, she thought about Nip and chided herself for constantly thinking about people and animals she loved, but were no longer part of her life. She became so emotional that she finally fussed at herself out loud and laughed.

She could just imagine Nip having the time of his life, running around doing a lot of important barking and nudging, with nothing but fields, pastures and cows and all day long to enjoy it all. The thought made her smile and she decided she was happy for her cattle dog, and maybe just a little bit jealous.

She still hadn't thought of anything she felt she wanted to eat, so she just turned off the kitchen light and headed off to get a shower, then turn in to say her prayers and ask God to not let her dream about Barrett Webb tonight.

⬥

Patricia Webb moved slowly through the aisles of the local Christian bookstore, browsing out of boredom, rather than need. She was supposed to meet a friend for lunch, but she'd called to tell her that she was running about a half hour late. Patricia had wandered across the street from the restaurant's parking lot to look around the shop and pass the time, rather than just sitting and waiting.

She had pulled a book from the shelf to read the blurb on the back, when she suddenly looked up with a wrinkled brow and a confused expression. She listened carefully, as she heard a woman asking a salesperson about audio Bibles. That, in itself wasn't unusual, but the soft, low, husky voice asking the questions certainly was.

Patricia drew in her breath and hurriedly put the book back, then stepped around to the other side of the aisle. She stopped with surprised delight to see Iris resting her beautiful blue eyes on the salesperson, who was advising her of the version of audio Bibles most people found easiest to listen to.

Iris thanked her and began to move toward Patricia, while she continued to study the back of the packaged set. When she realized that she was about to walk into someone, she glanced up to apologize and just stared at Patricia with the same tears rushing to her eyes that seemed to be filling Patricia Webb's.

The two women stood smiling sadly at each other before Patricia reached to gather Iris into her arms and just hold her for a long moment.

"I have missed you so much, sweetheart," she whispered to the only woman that her son had ever loved and the one that he was still grieving over, even if he wouldn't admit it.

"I've missed you too," Iris replied brokenly.

She pulled back to look at her and had to smile when Patricia instantly found the tissues that they both needed. She had always been quick to provide them.

"Honey, what, in the world, are you doing here, of all places?" Barrett's mother demanded. "You're in an entirely different county!"

Iris laughed quietly. "I'm working in this area for a while. I'm a nurse's aide for a hospice service and I've been sent out to work for a local family. His wife mentioned that they are Christians and that it was hard to find anyone to read the Bible to her husband. She can't see well enough to do it, so I offered to come and see if I could find one he could listen to."

"That's a lovely idea," Patricia breathed. She tilted her head and looked closely at Iris's beautiful face. "You look different, Iris. Not in a bad way," she added hastily, when Iris gave her a comical roll of her pretty eyes. "Definitely not in a bad way. What's changed, sweetheart?"

"I guess I have," she admitted, suddenly feeling a little shy. "I'm a Christian now, and I guess I'm slowly becoming a little less sad and a little more at peace."

"That's what it is!" Patricia felt like crying all over again. "My goodness, Iris, you don't know how many prayers I have prayed for you. I kept telling God that you were just too wonderful and too special to our family for you not to be with us in eternity."

Iris looked down with a self-conscious blush. "Well, at least special to some of your family." She immediately felt regret for her words, and looked back at Patricia with remorse. "I'm sorry, I shouldn't have said that."

"The only reason you shouldn't have said it is because it's not true," the kind woman assured her. "You're wrong, if you think you're not special to my son, Iris."

She reached and took her hand to make her look at her. "And you're wrong about something else, too."

Iris shook her head and looked down.

"Yes. You are, Iris. Blanche Hollis just flat out lied to you. She and Barrett were never a couple and they never will be. She made that whole thing up."

Iris began to feel more tears make their way down her cheeks. "I guess it doesn't matter, now. He's probably pretty angry with me for believing her."

"He wants to pretend he is, but his father and I know better," Patricia replied flatly. "That man is so in love with you that he's becoming harder and harder for us to be around, without picking something up and whacking him with it!"

Iris smiled at Patricia Webb's expression.

Patricia's face softened, as she began to sense Iris's need to return to her job. "Won't you let us know where you are, honey? Or me, at least?"

She longed to. She had missed Patricia Webb so much. She was just what Iris imagined, when she dreamed of what it could have been like to have a mother.

She hesitated. "I just need to pray about it, if that's okay."

"It is, honey. I won't press you about it. But you have my number. Please call me, whenever you want to visit, and I'll hop in my car and run right over."

Iris pressed her lips together and nodded, before reaching for Barrett's mother and giving her a tight hug.

"I love you," she whispered in Patricia's ear.

"I love you, too, sweet girl."

She gave her another hug, then headed out, so that Iris could complete her purchase and return to her job. She stopped at the door and gave her one last wave and smile before she left, and Iris drew in a deep breath and thanked God for letting them have this moment.

Chapter Fourteen

Lillian Frazier seemed to be much younger than her husband, and Iris noticed it every time she saw her. She had been informed that Oren Frazier was seventy-four, but his wife looked no more than sixty, if she was even that.

Perhaps it was because the tall, gracious man was so ill, she told herself. He had beautiful, wavy white hair and long, tapered fingers that made him seem more likely to play the piano, than to work cattle.

Mr. Frazier possessed a very cultured, intelligent way of speaking. Even though he seemed to be talking less and less because of the toll that the effort took on him, when he did speak, it was with a gentle, thoughtful manner, as if much thought had gone into everything he said.

His wife stayed devotedly by his side, with a small, elegant hand always touching him in some fashion, if only to finger the sleeve of his pajamas. She would look at him with every intention of keeping tears out of her eyes, and if she knew she was failing, she'd glance out of the window by the bed, and draw in a deep breath to steady herself.

It was Lillian Frazier who made Iris's heart hurt the most. Her husband appeared to have an incredible amount of peace, and his quiet smiles seemed genuine, rather than forced.

His wife tried to display peace as well, but it was obvious that her heart was breaking. Her husband knew and would sometimes simply lift a hand to indicate that she should come closer, and she would lay her head down on the mattress while he ran his fingers through her hair and soothed her with hushed words of endearment.

Iris would often have to step out of the room and regain control of her emotions, because the love between this couple was so overwhelming.

The Frazier's daughter, Katherine, spent a great deal of time there, along with her husband, Michael Bishop, and their two children, Jack and Daisy. Little two-year-old Daisy was taken with Iris and constantly followed her in and out of the room, crinkling her eyes and returning all of Iris's gentle smiles.

Lillian had been quick to reassure Katherine that their grandchildren weren't bothering Papa and that he loved seeing them. They weren't loud children and Iris could see for herself the way Mr. Oren would study their mannerisms and listen to their conversations with amusement.

Iris smiled at the family as she came in to place the oximeter on Mr. Frazier's finger and wait for his oxygen levels to display. She removed it and quietly fitted him with the nasal cannula he'd told her that he would prefer over a mask, and set the amount of flow.

"Mr. Frazier, let me know if you need some gel, if you feel this is drying you out," she said quietly. He gave her a nod, then closed his eyes for a few moments, trying to decide if this was helping him feel better.

Iris stood waiting and he finally opened his eyes and gave her a brief smile and another nod.

She moved away from his bedside and began gathering items that needed to be taken downstairs to the laundry.

Ordinarily, Lillian Frazier would protest her taking on doing the laundry as well as her other duties, and would implore Iris to let their housekeeper know what needed to be washed, but Iris was able to convince her that this was a regular part of her duties and that she was happy to do it.

Iris couldn't very well admit to Lillian Frazier that it was difficult to witness the devotion between her and her husband without her heart breaking for them, and that the busier she was, the less likely she was to give in to embarrassing and unprofessional tears. She sent up a silent prayer and made herself focus on taking care of her patient.

She carried the laundry to sort it and begin a wash load, and while she was separating it, she glanced up to see that young Jack Bishop had followed her.

She smiled at the stoic seven-year-old. "How are you, today, Jack?" she asked, watching him fidget with his fingers, as if he had something on his mind.

"Is Papa going to die?" he asked, with everything in his troubled green eyes begging her to say no.

Part of her training had touched on having these sorts of conversations with the family members of a terminally ill patient, but Iris hadn't expected to have to deal with it so soon. She left off what she was doing and leaned against the washer to give him her full attention.

"What did your mom and dad tell you, when you asked them, Jack?" she questioned gently.

He twisted his mouth to one side and looked away. She suspected he was struggling with tears.

"They said that everybody dies, but I already knew that."

Iris looked down at her feet for a moment, wordlessly asking God to help her with this sad little boy. After a moment, she rested her kind eyes on his face and offered him a faint smile, unaware that Jack's mother had come into the kitchen looking for him, and could hear their conversation.

"Well, Jack, your parents told you the truth about that," Iris began hesitantly. "And the reason that it's hard for you to accept that, is because we weren't created to die."

He looked up at her and seemed to be thinking about what she said. "Then, why do we?"

"Do you know what sin is?" she asked him, watching him nod his head.

"Sin first existed in Satan but it hadn't yet entered the world. It was a perfect world. But when God's creation, Adam and Eve, let Satan talk to them when they shouldn't have been listening to him, he made them doubt God. They made a decision to do something that they both knew God had told them not to do, and they disobeyed. It was done on purpose, and there had to be consequences."

She stopped and rested a hand on his shoulder. "Have you learned in school what consequences are?"

"What happens because of something you did," he answered, and she could see that he did know.

"That's right. God couldn't just ignore what they'd done. The world had just changed. Their disobedience brought evil into the world and now, there would be consequences.

"Ever since that time, Jack, we all live in what is called a fallen world. That means a world that it is no longer perfect. Now, we struggle every day with not just sin, but tornadoes, earthquakes, poverty, sickness and death, and a lot of other things that we were never meant to deal with. Are you understanding what I'm saying to you?"

Katherine leaned against the wall just outside the laundry room and wiped her cheeks as she heard the gentle and loving way that Iris was giving her Jack all the time and attention he needed. He loved his Papa dearly, and he was hurting.

Jack nodded up at Iris, his eyes misting over, but calmly considering everything she was telling him.

"The sadness that we feel, Jack, when we know that someone we love is dying is about a lot more than just the fact that we'll miss them. Something deep inside us begins to resist accepting death, because our spirits know that it's wrong, and that it was never meant to come to us. But it does come.

"And sadly, it will come to your Papa and to all of us, someday. But God made a way to beat death."

Jack thought he knew what God's way was. "Jesus?"

"Yes, Jesus." Iris answered, giving his shoulder a little caress. "The world is no longer perfect, but Jesus is. He was all God could look at after that, because God is so holy, that He can't be around sin and evil. He won't look at it, but He can look at His Son." Iris paused a moment.

"You probably learned this at church, right?"

"Some of it," the little boy admitted. "I didn't know that God could only look at Jesus after that, though."

"Jesus became a man, because it was man who caused sin to come into the world. He became a human in every way. The only thing that made Him different was that He was perfect, with no sin at all in him. God could look at man now, because He was looking through Jesus. You know the rest, don't you?"

Jack nodded. "He died and that's how we get saved."

Iris gave him a little pat of confirmation. "Absolutely. Because He died, then rose and is alive now, we will also die, and rise again and be alive, if we belong to Jesus, because Jesus beat death. So, what do you think will happen to Papa when he dies?"

Jack took a moment to think about it. "He'll go to Heaven to be with Jesus."

"Yes. Only Papa's body will die, but he won't need that anymore. Our bodies just carry our souls and spirits around while we're alive, like a lantern carries a flame. When we believe in Jesus and we die, we just let our old bodies go, kind of like when a butterfly comes out of cocoon. It doesn't need the cocoon anymore, because it's free.

"Your Papa will be free. He won't be sick anymore. He'll become young and healthy, and he'll actually get to see Jesus, and talk to him. He wouldn't want to miss that, for anything in the world."

Iris knelt down to get level with the child, and looked at him tenderly. "It's alright to feel sad, Jack, when someone we love leaves us for a while. That's normal. But since Jesus beat death, we'll see that person that we love again."

She smiled. "Do you want to ask any more questions?"

"Can I hug you?" he asked bashfully.

Iris scooped him into a squeeze then ruffled his blonde hair with a grin.

"Thanks for keeping me company, Jack. I like talking to you."

His face brightened and he headed off to see his Papa with a little light in his eyes.

Patricia Webb stood looking out toward the lake with her arms folded and a look of disappointment in her brown eyes. She had hoped that Iris would have reached out to her by now and let her know where she was staying.

She longed to see her again and just make sure that she was doing well. She allowed herself a little smile though, as she remembered Iris telling her that she had become a Christian.

She knew she was okay then, but she just missed her and she knew her handsome, scowling, stubborn son missed her too, regardless of how much he pretended that he didn't.

She was annoyed to learn that he'd had a dinner date last evening with Callie Jeffries, not that there was anything wrong with Callie. She was a nice enough girl. She just wasn't Iris.

Patricia knew that wasn't fair, but that was how she felt.

Normally, she'd be tempted to think that Barrett was hoping to make Iris jealous but she had no idea that Barrett had a date, or who Callie Jeffries was. There was simply no way she'd ever find out, so she discarded that notion.

She knew that he was just trying to distract himself and not spend silent evenings alone with his dark thoughts. She also knew that Barrett would not allow Callie or any other woman to think that he cared for her in any special way, if he didn't. That was one thing about her son that she could be confident about.

She looked off to one side, as she saw Barrett's truck come down their long drive. She knew he'd come in the kitchen door and normally, she'd head into the kitchen right away to give him a hug and offer to make coffee but she just didn't feel like doing that today. He could come find her, she decided.

She turned back to look across the lake with a pang of sadness because she could see no reason for Barrett and Iris to remain apart. Iris knew now that there had been nothing between her son and Blanche Hollis.

She twisted her mouth into a scowl. It was Barrett she was upset with. He told John Mabry that he didn't need to know where Iris was but he could just as easily tell him that he changed his mind. But he wouldn't change his mind.

His mother heard the door open and she could sense that Barrett was looking around to determine where she was. He saw her in the den and came over to the window.

"What are you doing, Mother?" he asked.

She didn't answer him or turn around. She just kept her eyes fixed straight ahead, suddenly feeling like crying.

Patricia Webb didn't just cry when she was sad. She also cried when she was angry and right now, she was angry with Barrett. All of this was just wrong!

"Mother?" He came around and looked closely at her.

"Don't talk to me right now, Barrett. I can't deal with you." She turned and walked back into the kitchen and sat down at the table, staring hard at nothing.

He blew out a deep breath of frustration. He knew what this was about. After a moment, he followed her and took a seat next to her at the table.

"Just say it, Mother," he suggested quietly.

She shook her head. "You don't want that."

"You're upset because I had dinner with Callie Jeffries," he said flatly. He leaned back in the chair and crossed his arms in a defensive attitude.

Patricia Webb sat perfectly still and continued to stare down at the table, silently asking God to keep her from reaching over and slapping her son.

"Are you seriously not even going to talk to me?" He was having trouble believing that his usually kindhearted and loving mother was freezing him out.

"What's the point?" she said loudly, actually hitting the table. "Oh, wait, there *is* no point! Good, then we're done!"

She pushed back her chair and marched down the long hallway to her room, leaving her son staring after her in disbelief.

Barrett had come by to drop off a bag of feed for his father and realized as he had driven up to the house, that Stuart Webb wasn't home but he'd simply assumed he could come in and say hello to his mother.

His mother always had a kind word for him and a hug. He'd never seen her like this and it was hard for him to believe that one dinner with a woman that Patricia had known since his high school days would cause her to be this angry with him. This had to be about something else.

He started to just leave and come back later when she'd gotten over herself but he stopped at the door. Something was going on with his mother and he felt he should at least try again to get her to talk to him.

He made himself walk down the hallway to her door and tapped lightly. "Mother?"

When there was no answer, he tapped again and then opened the door. Patricia was sitting on the side of her bed, holding a tissue up to her eyes and crying softly.

Barrett quickly came around and sat next to her. He put his arm around her, completely bewildered.

"Mother, please talk to me," he asked hesitantly. "Please tell me what's wrong."

She simply shook her head. "Don't, Son. I can't talk to you right now. It wouldn't end well."

"Why wouldn't it end well?"

He waited for a long moment, before he tried again.

"If you need for me to know something, I'll listen."

Patricia rested her head against his shoulder and he gave her a little squeeze.

"Why are you crying?"

"Because I'm mad at you," she admitted honestly.

"It *is* because of Callie Jeffries, then? Mother, you've known Callie since we went to high school together. What's wrong with Callie?"

Patricia burst in tears. "She's not Iris! And she never will be! And if you allow Callie Jeffries, or any other woman to think you care anything about them when you're in love with Iris, and you always will be, then that's not fair to them, and you're just being a jerk!"

Barrett tightened the muscles around his mouth and drew in a calming breath. He was disappointed to feel old hurts immediately return with just the mention of her name.

"What difference does it make if I love her?" he asked, after a long silence. "She certainly doesn't love me."

Patricia pulled back to narrow her eyes and stare at him. "Why would you try to make me, of all people, believe that?"

"Because it's true. If she loved me, she wouldn't have rushed to move out of the house the way she did, without even bothering to talk to me."

"Have you ever stopped to think that she left the way she did because she *does* love you, Barrett?"

"That makes no sense," he muttered.

"It makes perfect sense! You never told her the one thing she needed to hear from you. You never said that what Blanche claimed was a lie. You never denied it! You just yelled at Blanche to leave and for all Iris knew, you and Blanche had some unfinished business and you were still in the middle of some kind of lover's spat."

Barrett stared darkly down at the floor, remembering the last time he saw her all too well.

"Mother, we kissed. I told you that. I also told you that we had a sweet moment between us, just before Blanche Hollis drove up. That was real. I knew it and she knew it. But the minute I left, she couldn't pack and get out fast enough. How is that loving me?"

"She loved you enough to give you up, when she thought you belonged to someone else," Patricia said softly, letting out a little jagged breath that was left over from crying.

"I don't even know what that means," he replied in a dull, tired voice.

A long moment passed before Patricia spoke again.

"I talked to her."

Barrett drew his brows and looked at her in surprise.

"When did you do that?"

"Two days ago. I saw her in the bookstore across from Fiddler's."

"Here? Why was she here, and not in Fairfield?" He thought about it. "That's a Christian bookstore."

"Then she was in the right place."

He lifted his brown eyes to study her quietly. "Why do you say that?"

"Iris told me that she has become a Christian," his mother told him, reaching for another tissue since she had just shredded her used one.

"The reason she was here is because she's working now as a nurse's aide for a hospice service. One of her patients lives in this area, and she was there buying an audio Bible so that he could listen to it."

Barrett didn't want to ask, but he did, in spite of himself.

"How did she look?"

Patricia's smile was sad and bittersweet.

"Tall. Graceful. Beautiful. Sweet."

Barrett let out a sigh of regret.

"She's all those things," he admitted, almost too softly for her to hear him.

"I asked her to call me and let me know where she lives now," Patricia admitted, becoming emotional again. "She asked me if she could pray about it."

She began to weep softly and buried her face against her son's chest. "I'm afraid we'll never see her again."

Barrett dropped an instinctive kiss on his mother's head and quietly tried to soothe her.

He wished that he could tell her she was wrong, but he didn't think she was.

Chapter Fifteen

Iris settled back on her couch and fished around for the remote to the TV and DVD player. She told herself that she probably shouldn't do this since she was already sad, but when Pastor Ben and Miss Katie came by to make sure the faucet on the side of the cottage had really been fixed this time, Miss Katie pulled a DVD out of her bag and showed it to Iris.

"If you get to wanting something to look at, I brought this for you," she said, holding it out and giving her a watery smile. "Do you remember me telling you that we had movies of Matthew?"

Iris had nodded and looked down at it as if unsure if she should take it, but Miss Katie insisted that she trusted her with it and placed it in her hands.

It had been a disturbing day at work. Mr. Oren had a rough time and had to be suctioned until enough secretions could be removed to give him some ease. She hated having to put him through it but he seemed to want her to, so she quietly advised that someone take Jack and Daisy out of the room, knowing of course that Lillian would remain by his side.

After that, she had elevated his head a little and gave him oxygen. When she left, he was able to speak and seemed to be at ease but she drove off in tears, wondering if there was any chance at all that she could ever grow to become professional enough to not be emotional when a patient was in distress.

Now she pushed her hair back out of her eyes and decided that she was apparently not depressed enough, so she might as well watch recordings of the dead son that was forever gone to Pastor Ben and Miss Katie, and really cap off her day.

She set the DVD to play and took in her breath at once, as she saw a laughing, clowning young man, with golden curls and slight dimples acting out for whoever was recording him.

The clips were of changing scenes and he was so in the moment and charmingly joyful, that she found herself smiling and even laughed out loud when he picked up a kitten and kissed it, then hurried to wipe his mouth and spit out cat hair.

She watched him sit down on a tree stump with his guitar and begin playing and singing one of the most beautiful songs she'd ever heard. He reminded Iris of a young John Denver, simply because he was proficient with the guitar and he had a beautiful voice and an easy, conversational delivery that was rare.

Iris didn't know much about the music industry, but she felt that if Matthew were still alive, he'd certainly be well known, although his parents told her that he only sang for the Lord and himself, and maybe at church.

She shook her head, not understanding why someone so full of life was taken in such a shocking and unexpected way, then sat back and thought it through, reflecting on the way that Aunt Sadie had passed, and how Oren Frazier was leaving this world. She wondered if Matthew's startling death might have been mercy, after all.

Pastor Ben had told her that Matthew had never seemed to be long for this world and as she watched him now, digging both his hands right into the middle of his birthday cake and getting it all over his face, then trying to chase his mother to wipe it on her while she ran away from him laughing, she thought she could see that special "something" in their golden boy that let them know that they only had him for a season.

Iris reflected on her conversation with Jack and thought about how everything changed in an instant, the minute God's man and woman listened to a lie and decided that God was trying to keep something good from them.

She was probably not the first person in the history of the world that had a strong desire to sucker punch Adam and Eve, she told herself dryly.

Their decision to disobey God started an age-long chain of events that led to this wonderful, golden young troubadour being snatched away from his parents with no warning. It led to poor Mr. Oren gasping now for most of his breaths, while his devoted wife watched him struggle, with her soft eyes filled with both love and pain.

It was no surprise to Iris that when she finished watching the DVD, she had to sit for a while and mop up her tears. She knew that Miss Katie hadn't been trying to upset her. She was proud of her son and just wanted Iris to see how special he was.

She was glad to know that when she returned the DVD to his mother, she could tell her very genuinely how much she enjoyed getting to see their son, and how handsome and gifted he was.

Iris turned the DVD off and leaned back into the couch, closing her eyes and trying to decide if she was hungry enough to go to the trouble of finding something to eat, or if she just wanted to go to bed.

The evening before, when she left the Fraziers house, she stopped at a restaurant, preparing to order curb service to bring dinner home with her. While she was glancing at her phone to look at their pickup menu, she quickly looked back up again and saw Barrett escorting a woman into the restaurant.

She had never seen the woman before and the two of them certainly did seem to know each other. It didn't look like a blind date.

She laid her hand on her heart and felt a tightening in her throat that warned her that a good cry was coming. Her breathing became shallow and she put her phone away and prayed desperately for God to help her.

She drove home mechanically, not even remembering the trip. She was on some sort of strange autopilot but the minute she opened her door and was safe inside the cottage, she dropped everything and knelt down on the floor, sobbing as if her heart had just been destroyed. She had waited too late.

She felt that she had cried all night, but when she woke this morning, there was an odd calm in her spirit, as she decided that Barrett had moved on. She felt that she didn't have to pray about letting Patricia know where she lived, then.

She didn't think she should continue to have a relationship with her, if her son had found someone else to care for. After all, the woman might very well become Patricia and Stuart Webb's daughter-in-law. It was time for Iris to close that door.

As she thought about all of it now, she couldn't honestly say that she felt peace. She just didn't feel anything.

It was eerily similar to the way she felt following the death of her late husband. There was a strange relief, just knowing that she was done.

∞∞∞

Lillian Frazier looked up at Iris, as she leaned down to put her arm around her and give her a hug.

"I can't even tell you how sorry I am, Lillian," she said in her soft way. "I've watched how very much you and Mr. Oren loved each other and I wish I had something to share that would help, but I guess the sad truth is that the greater the love, the deeper the pain."

She knelt down and Lillian put her arms around Iris's neck and wept softly, as Iris cried with her. She held her for a long while, just stroking her hair and giving her soft caresses on her back and praying for her.

Katherine came into the room and rested a hand on Iris's shoulder, before leaning down and whispering that the RN had just arrived.

Iris nodded and got up to go meet her, as Katherine took her place to try and comfort her mother.

Iris was only gone briefly then came in to let the family know that the RN would need to complete the procedures for pronouncing death and notifying Mr. Frazier's physician.

She told them they were welcome to stay but that they should also feel that it was okay to step out, if they thought it might be too hard.

Although Lillian had stayed by her husband's side day and night, she stood now and allowed her daughter to take her out of the room to go sit with her son-in-law and grandchildren.

The RN competently completed her checks and phoned the doctor, then filled out the necessary paperwork. She came over to the bed to stand next to Iris and look down at Mr. Oren Frazier's still form.

"He was a very distinguished, handsome man, wasn't he?" she mused quietly.

Iris nodded. "He was very eloquent and kind."

The RN shook her head and rested a hand on Iris's shoulder. "I'll call and arrange for transport. I'll stop and tell the family what I'm doing. I expect his wife may come back in, but I hope the children remain where they are."

"When Lillian comes in, I'll step out and offer to sit with them, in case their daughter and son-in-law want to be with her," Iris said and the nurse nodded in approval.

"I'll let them know that."

Iris waited alone with Mr. Oren, looking down at the gentleman with sad, tear-filled eyes, knowing that he was with the Lord but hurting for his wife, whose heart was broken.

She looked back as the door opened and Lillian came in, standing back for a moment, clasping her hands and staring at her husband with wide eyes, now seeming to be in shock.

Iris came to her and put an arm around her and didn't try to urge her to approach him, if she wasn't ready. Katherine and her husband opened the door slowly and Iris smiled at them and motioned them into the room.

"I'll just be with Jack and Daisy," she whispered, and they smiled gratefully at her.

<hr />

She hadn't stopped to consider what sort of people she could expect to see at Oren Frazier's funeral. She stood beside his widow and rested a hand on her back as Lillian steadfastly remained by the casket, staring down at the face of the man she had loved for so many years.

Iris slowly began to remember that Oren Frazier had been a long-standing member of the cattlemen's association and told herself that it should have been no surprise when she glanced around the funeral home's large chapel and saw Stuart Webb speaking quietly to another gentleman near the entrance.

She immediately willed herself not to look for Patricia or Barrett. She didn't need to know if they were with Stuart.

She applied herself to attending to Lillian's needs, even though her duties as a hospice aide were completed. Lillian and Katherine had asked her to come to the service and she simply agreed, not anticipating that there would be any reason for her to regret doing so.

She glanced down as young Jack reached to claim her hand and smiled sweetly at him before kneeling and pulling him close for a hug.

"How are you doing with all this, Jack?" she whispered.

He seemed to treat her question as a serious one and gave it some thought. "I just feel kind of quiet inside."

Iris nodded. She knew that feeling.

"You're allowed to feel whatever you feel and if it's just quiet, then that's okay. Remember, Jack, that Papa has left his old body behind with all the pain and sickness that was in it. He doesn't need it anymore, now that he's with Jesus."

He nodded solemnly and laid one arm around Iris's neck, as he often did when she positioned herself low enough to be on an equal level with him.

"Does it bother you to see Papa's old body, Jack?"

Again, he thought about it then shook his head. "No. But it bothers Nana, I think."

Iris looked up at Lillian wiping tears.

"Well, Jack, that's because Nana and Papa shared a long life with a special kind of love that's different from the kind the rest of you shared with him. They were sweethearts, so Nana's going to grieve in a different way and it will be more painful for her. It may take a while before she's quiet inside."

Iris felt annoyed at the tears that were running down her own cheeks as she said this, but she should have known they would come. "Nana knows that Papa is free now and no longer sick. She's glad for him, but she'll just need some time."

He gave her a sad little smile and nodded.

Iris lifted herself to stand and laid an arm around Jack's shoulder, unaware that Barrett Webb had witnessed all this from the back of the chapel with a blend of strong emotions that he couldn't possibly unravel.

He couldn't help but watch the beautiful woman, as she quietly found little ways to comfort Oren Frazier's family.

She was wearing a simple, sleeveless black chiffon dress that fell around her slender form in beautiful lines, with a midi-length hem. Her arms were toned and tan from the amount of time she'd spent in the sun on the patio and her hair seemed to have grown longer and even richer in color.

She hadn't looked in Barrett's direction and it didn't seemed as if she would, but he found himself hoping that she would rest her fascinating blue eyes on him.

Little two-year-old Daisy had claimed Iris now, so she lifted the petite little girl up and rested her on one hip, smiling at her while the child combed her fingers through Iris's long hair.

Patricia Webb had seen Iris but didn't think she should make an attempt to greet her this close to the service starting, since she'd have to go up to the front in order to do it. She just stepped over to stand next to her son and the two of them looked at Iris in silence.

Both of them wondered who the man was who approached her and said something quietly to her. They didn't know Michael Bishop, and his casual manner with Iris sparked similar reactions in the two of them.

Iris listened intently to what he was telling her then reached over to touch Katherine and bring her into their consultation.

Barrett's relief, when Katherine put her arm around the man was so great that he felt weak for a moment. He heard his mother let out a sigh and they exchanged faint smiles, without comment.

The service was a touching one that seemed fitting to the dignity and reputation of Oren Frazier. Several community leaders took the opportunity to come forward and share their words of regret at his passing, along with their appreciation for the life he'd lived.

One of those was Stuart Webb, and he seemed to be particularly touched as he said goodbye to his long-time friend and associate. He directed a few words of comfort to Lillian and her family, before returning to take his seat.

When the service concluded, Iris sat with Daisy in her arms as the people began to file forward and out, stopping to offer a silent acknowledgment beside the casket.

Iris was studying Daisy's perfect little face, since she had fallen asleep and never looked up to see the Webb family as they moved past the front and walked outside to join the procession.

She rode with the Frazier family to the cemetery but stood back in the distance when they gathered alongside the casket under the tent for the graveside interment service.

This was the same cemetery where Aunt Sadie had been laid to rest and Iris knew that she would have to leave when the Frazier family did in order to have a ride back to the funeral home and get her truck.

She took the opportunity now to wander off in the direction where she remembered Aunt Sadie being buried and eventually stood looking down at her beautiful headstone with a rush of emotion.

Along with the Frazier family, she had been given a single rose to lay on Mr. Oren's casket but she knelt now and laid it on Aunt Sadie's grave, then stood looking down at it with unshed tears crowding her eyes.

"Do you like her stone?"

Barrett's low voice rumbled through her slight frame and she closed her eyes and took a deep breath, without allowing herself to look at him.

"It's beautiful."

He came closer and stood beside her, glancing down at Aunt Sadie's grave before allowing his eyes to wander aimlessly about, unsure if he should say anything else. He couldn't read Iris's deceptively calm demeanor.

"How are you, Iris?" he finally asked quietly.

"I'm doing well," she replied in her soft way. "Are you here alone?" she asked, before she could stop herself.

"Mother and Dad are here," he told her and she nodded.

"Yes, I saw them."

Barrett furrowed his brow, confused. If she saw them, then why did she ask if he was alone? He wondered if she was expecting to see Blanche Hollis here.

"You saw them? Then the answer to your question is yes. I'm here alone," he said, crossing his arms and letting out a sigh. After a long moment, he looked over at her.

"Mother said that you work with hospice now. Was Oren a patient, then?"

"He was. I normally don't come over into this county to work but it just turned out that way, this time."

"Oren was a good man," Barrett observed, glancing back in his family's direction. "Lillian will have an especially hard time with this. They were together since Lillian was in high school."

Iris made no reply but nodded in agreement.

"Have you been out to the farm since you moved?" he asked, not missing her surprised reaction to his question.

"You'd be welcome, of course," he added. "I was just wondering if you had stopped by to visit Nip or see some of the changes."

"No." She continued to quietly stare down at Aunt Sadie's headstone. "I imagine that Nip's forgotten me by now, although Howie might know me. Horses remember."

"Nip wouldn't forget you, Iris," he chided, grinning at that. "You're his person."

She smiled and he allowed another moment to go by before speaking again.

"Howie and his goat friends live at my place, now. He needs regular care, and I can accomplish that easier with him close by."

"Thank you for doing that," Iris murmured. She made no further remark, but turned to look back at the service being held behind them. "I suppose I'd better go back. The Fraziers are my ride back to the chapel."

She made a move to go and Barrett reached a hand to touch her arm. "Iris?"

She wouldn't look at him. That's all he wanted, but she wouldn't raise her lovely eyes and just look at him.

After a silent moment, as her struggle to remain in control became visible, she did finally did lift her gaze to his, and it took his breath away.

"I'd better go back," she repeated softly.

She turned to do that, then looked back at him. "It was good to see you again, Barrett."

He stepped away from the grave and came to stand close to her and wait for her to look up at him.

"Iris, when I kissed you... it wasn't what you thought," he told her, watching closely to see if she understood what he meant. "That wasn't true. It was never true."

She looked down, as a faint blush came with the memory, then glanced back up at him. "I'm sorry, Barrett," she offered.

"I've missed you," he whispered, in spite of all his intentions to never admit that to her.

She wiped her cheek and smiled sadly, more beautiful in this moment than he had ever seen.

"I've missed you, too."

She caught his fingertips and lightly squeezed them, then quietly took herself away, to return to the service.

Barrett watched her go, as the overwhelming sense of longing that she used to effortlessly stir in him returned.

Chapter Sixteen

Patricia Webb had been so sure that after talking to Barrett at the cemetery, Iris would let them know how to reach her but there had been no word.

She sat in her car and idly watched people milling around the square and wondered if she would do more harm than good if she went through with her intention. She knew she was taking a risk and that her son might even be angry and accuse her of meddling or trying to manipulate him but she had to know, if only for herself.

She got out of the car and walked resolutely through the double glass doors of the bank and after leaving her name with the young man who greeted her, was soon shown into the office of John Mabry.

He knew Stuart and Patricia Webb, if only by reputation and of course, he knew Barrett. He welcomed her warmly and invited her to sit before taking a seat himself and asking what he could do for her.

She pursed her lips and looked at him with her direct brown eyes. "I'm just going to say it, Mr. Mabry. I need to know how I can reach Iris Anderson."

He wasn't surprised, but he'd hoped that Barrett would be the one to finally ask him. He hesitated and picked up a pen on his desk, turning it absently in one hand, as he sat in thought.

"I tried to broach the subject of Iris moving to her new place to Barrett one day when I saw him out on the square, and he was quick to inform me that he didn't care to know where she was," he said quietly, wondering now if that might have been for the best.

John Mabry had always felt protective of Iris and if anyone posed a threat to her on even the smallest scale, he wanted no part of it.

"My son is a stubborn man, Mr. Mabry," Patricia pointed out reasonably.

He laughed softly. "I've seen him in action, so I can't argue with you there."

The banker looked at Barrett Webb's mother with curiosity. "I have to assume that Barrett has no idea that you're asking me this."

"You assume correctly. I'm not asking for him. I'm asking for myself." She gave him a meaningful look. "I have to talk to her."

John Mabry drew in a breath and tried to picture Iris's reaction when she learned that he had given her address to Patricia Webb. She might not be pleased if it were Barrett, but he'd been led to believe that Stuart and Patricia Webb had grown especially fond of Iris when she cared for their Aunt Sadie and he knew that Patricia certainly meant no harm.

He silently reasoned to himself that she had never actually asked him not to tell anyone where she lived and he had never told her that he'd keep it a secret.

He reached for a stack of sticky notes and quickly jotted down the address of the little cabin before he could change his mind, then tore if off and handed it to her.

"Pastor Ben Welch and his wife Katie own this little cottage. It's tucked into some trees on a dirt road, so if your GPS tells you to turn on one, it's not wrong. I'm not sure if you'll find her home though, Mrs. Webb. Iris pulls some long hours and extra days, just to be able to have Sundays off."

She took the address gratefully. "Thank you, Mr. Mabry. I appreciate it so much. Iris is one of those people that you just can't bear the thought of losing touch with."

He nodded. "I agree. I've had to walk with Iris through some very hard things the past few years, and a lesser woman would have let it make her hard and bitter, but Iris simply took each piece of bad news in stride and kept moving forward.

"That's one of the things I admire most about her. I've always been quick to guard her. God knows, that character she was married to turned out to be just another person she needed to be shielded from."

He said this with a grim expression and Patricia hesitated before bringing herself to ask.

"Where are her people, Mr. Mabry?"

He shook his head. "All gone. Iris was raised in the foster care system from the time she was a toddler until she graduated high school."

His face was bleak. "As soon as she graduated, that little football playing jock who was after her all through school talked her into running off with him to get married and when his grandmother died, she left him the farm. She'd have done better to just sell it before she died, and treat everyone she knew to a cruise," he said sarcastically.

"Of course, he barely knew how to spell farm, let alone run one. All he cared about was running around with his old high school buddies and staying drunk. Iris was the one who applied herself to learning as much about farming as she could, and she had the potential to really make something of it.

"She could have, too, if Glenn Anderson hadn't drinked up every dime they had until his liver failed, and then it was Iris who stayed with him day and night, nursing him and doing what she could." John Mabry looked down at his hands with an impatient scowl.

"He couldn't even die right. He had to eat an entire bottle of opioids and chase it down with a bottle of whiskey and then leave Iris to once again clean up another one of his messes."

He saw Patricia Webb's shocked expression and relented.

"You'll have to forgive me, Mrs. Webb. I suppose I was too close to the situation and I've formed some pretty hard opinions. I did everything I could to keep Iris from ending up in foreclosure.

"That's why I have a warm spot for your son. If he hadn't stepped in, the developers were already circling, trying to practically steal the farm and turn it into cheap housing. I'm indebted to Barrett for keeping them away from her."

Patricia nodded and gave him a little smile, almost as an afterthought. She wondered if Barrett had ever known all this about Iris.

"I know what you mean about admiring her," she said softly to the banker. "I've never known anyone like her and if I could have had a daughter, I would have wanted it to be Iris."

John Mabry grinned. "Well, if you'll forgive me for being blunt, I'd been hoping that your son would make that happen."

"Don't give up hoping," she replied, standing to leave and reaching for his hand. "It's not over, yet."

⁂

Iris couldn't believe she had been able to find the nerve to drive out to the farm. Of course, Barrett had told her that she was welcome to but she never thought she would do it.

He had asked her if she had been by to see the changes and her curiosity got the best of her as she wondered what sort of changes he meant.

She was glad to see that there were no vehicles parked near the house. She purposely waited until the evening, since that was normally when Barrett's crew quit for the day and he usually left when they did. That seemed to be the case, as she stood by her truck and listened carefully for the sound of any equipment or vehicles.

Nip came running to her with so much excitement that he could hardly contain himself. He stopped just before he reached her then approached her slowly, his entire body shaking with gladness. Iris knelt down and held her arms out and he nudged his way in and looked up at her as if he were laughing.

"I love you, Nip," Iris crooned, giving him little caresses and pats and fussing over him. "I've missed you so much."

He had obviously missed her too, and when she stepped back to open her truck door, he jumped right in. Wherever she was going, he was going with her.

She grinned at him and pulled her truck around the farmhouse, then opened the gate, closing it after she'd driven through.

"Show me what all you boys have been up to, Nip," she said, feeling a rush of adrenaline and hoping that no one would discover her presence, as she began driving around in the fields.

After a few minutes, she stopped and let her eyes travel across the landscape, happy to see all the cattle roaming around in the pastures. Everything was fenced so nicely, and she could see some calves with their mothers, in a separate area.

Barrett had placed them so that they could have access to the far end of the stream and there were plenty of trees for them to gather under when the sun was hot, although the air was much crisper and cooler now.

A big smile of pleasure rested on her pretty face as Iris began to see this farm becoming what it was always intended to be. Nip sat up straight and alert when he saw the cattle, but noted nothing that needed his immediate intervention and was content to stay in the truck with his person.

Iris finally continued around past the orchard, which had been nicely cleaned up and pruned. She couldn't remember it ever looking like this.

When she pulled the truck around the bend and saw what was waiting for her up ahead, she stopped and got out, almost without realizing it.

She lifted a hand to her throat and held her breath. Tears ran freely down her cheeks when she saw the lake.

"Thank you, God," she whispered. "I realize that it's not for me, but thank You for letting me see it. It's so beautiful."

Nip had hopped out with her and now sat beside her, looking up at her then looking at the lake. He seemed to be asking her if she liked it.

Iris gave him a tearful smile and reached down to scratch his ears before walking toward the lake bank and continuing to take it all in. There were already ducks or geese down at the far end. She couldn't decide which they were from that distance, but she loved seeing them swimming around in a little group.

She realized that the sun was beginning to set and it was quickly becoming too cool for her to continue to be outdoors in her sleeveless top. She folded her arms to hug herself and could feel that her skin was almost cold.

She very reluctantly opened her truck door and allowed Nip to jump in, then finished driving around to the place where she could see where Howie and his goat pals used to live and the big rock by the stream where she'd spend the past few years deep in thought.

Iris brought the truck around to where she'd started and managed the gate, finally closing it and locking it carefully after driving through, then stopped the old Apache under a tree and got out to signal to Nip that their ride was over.

She suddenly felt that she needed to hurry and gave Nip a tight hug, then pulled away from the farmhouse, looking back at it in the mirror and wishing that she hadn't left it so bare since Barrett could have used some of the furniture.

She breathed out a sigh, feeling a sense of loss, and pulled out onto the highway on her way to the cottage. She was so engrossed in her thoughts that she never saw Barrett's truck pass her, or caught the look of shocked recognition on his face.

His first instinct had been to whip his truck around and follow her, but he managed to restrain himself and continue on to the farmhouse.

As he pulled in, he noticed that Nip was on the porch, instead of out in the fields where he'd normally be. He got out of his truck and looked over at the tree where Iris used to always park and his heart sped up a bit when he saw fresh tire tracks.

"Was she here, Nip?" he wondered out loud. He walked past the house to the back gate, then saw the way the chain was double-wrapped and smiled to himself.

Iris had come to see the farm. He was glad that he'd told her that she'd be welcome to. He was sorry that he'd missed her, but he realized that the only reason she took the opportunity to see it was because she felt she would be alone.

Barrett leaned on the gate and looked around, his brown eyes reflecting the thoughts that were racing around in his mind. He wondered if her beautiful face lit up when she saw the lake. He was sure it had, and felt a sting of sadness that he had missed getting to see that.

He could envision her driving her truck around the pastures, discovering the new calves and seeing how the entire farm had been properly fenced.

The handsome cattleman ached inside, not to have been able to share all this with her. He'd wanted so much to make a life with her here. Even though he had his own large, impressive ranch, he would have let it all go in a heartbeat, just to remain here with Iris for the rest of his days.

Barrett thought of Oren and Lillian Frazier. Although there was a marked difference in their ages, their entire marriage was lived out together, sharing the same vision and having the same goals.

Barrett had hurt for Lillian, as he saw how devastated she was to have lost her husband. Stuart had told him how Lillian's parents were firmly against her marrying Oren, and had tried in vain to keep them apart, but Oren quietly waited until she was older and no longer needed their permission and the two eloped and never looked back.

Anyone who had ever spent any amount of time with the two of them could see that they were deeply in love. Lillian looked so lost without him at the service that it was almost too much to witness.

Barrett ran a hand through his dark curls and clenched his jaw, willing himself to move away from his sad thoughts.

He prayed last night and asked God to please help him to either win Iris's love or no longer desire it, but to please not leave him with a longing that would never be filled.

Right now, his longing for her was overpowering, so he knew that he needed to keep praying. He wondered if she had ever prayed about the two of them, as well. Part of him hoped so and part of him was afraid for her to do that.

Iris was the kind of principled woman who would do what she felt was the right thing, even if it hurt. If she felt that God hadn't intended for the two of them to be together, no amount of handholding or long conversations, or even passionate kisses would cause her to give in. He knew that about her, and he both respected her for it and resented her for it.

From the first moment he had driven up to the farm and found her brandishing the water hose in the chicken pen, then looking up at him and back down at her dirty clothes in dismay, he suspected that she just might be the one woman who would ever manage to capture him.

When he came back a couple of days later and saw her legs sticking out from under the hood of her old truck as she tried to convince it to yield to her efforts, he was sure of it.

He had loved her ever since, more deeply than he had ever been aware that he had the capacity for. He loved her now, and it kept him awake until the wee hours and reminded him every morning that it was still there.

"Help us, God," he whispered, the presence of lonely tears clouding his vision.

Barrett glanced down at his phone and saw that his mother had just sent him a text.

He wiped his eyes on his sleeve and looked more closely at it, frowning with confusion.

Why was she sending him an address?

Chapter Seventeen

Stuart and Patricia Webb both looked up when they heard their back door open and Patricia wasted no time donning a frown of disapproval.

"What are you doing here?" she demanded.

"Heck of a way to greet your son, Mother," Barrett returned, pulling out a chair and settling down, then reaching a hand over to give Stuart Webb an affectionate clasp on his arm.

"Didn't you get my text?" She continued to regard him with an air of exasperation.

"I did, but I had no idea what you were on about, so I stopped by on my way home to find out. I don't text if it's not an emergency. You should know that."

"Well, it was an emergency! I don't text either, and you should know *that*."

Barrett laid his hat on the empty chair next to him, and ran a hand through his hair, favoring his father with a look of exasperation and causing him to chuckle.

"How can an address be an emergency, Mother? Was it on fire? I'm not the one you contact for something like that."

She reached over and popped his arm. "That's where she lives! Sometimes, Barrett Webb, I just wanna smack you upside your handsome head!"

He looked at her for a long moment, then pulled his phone out and read the text again. "How was I supposed to know that? It doesn't say Fairfield."

"No, but Fairfield is not the only town in that county. You know perfectly well where Dover is!"

"How do I know perfectly well where Dover is?"

"The locals don't call it that," Barrett's father told him. "They insist on calling it Hyatt's Creek."

Barrett looked back down at his phone and realized that he would have had to go right by there, on his way home. His disappointment was evident and his mother decided to stop being mad at him.

"Well, it's not like she's suddenly going to move out before you can get over there," she offered. She intended for that to make him feel better, but he shot her a dark look.

His father belted out a laugh. "Too soon?"

Patricia put her hand over her mouth to keep Barrett from catching her grinning, but it had gotten into her eyes.

"I'm sorry, honey. I didn't mean it like that."

He begrudgingly allowed a slight smile and continued to study his phone, wondering how in the world Iris ended up at Hyatt's Creek.

"Well, I wouldn't just show up there anyway, Mother."

"Both you and Iris seem to have forgotten how to use these." She reached over and yanked his phone out of his hand, then shoved it back at his face.

"What makes you think she'd answer, if she saw a call come in with my name on it?" he retorted.

"Because I saw the two of you at the cemetery. You were able to talk then, apparently."

"Not really," Barrett sighed. "I just asked her if she liked Aunt Sadie's stone and there was some small talk. She felt the need to get back to Lillian's family before they left, because her truck was at the funeral home."

"Why didn't you just offer to take her to her truck?"

Barrett looked at his dad with wide eyes. "Make her stop."

He grinned and gave his wife a pat on her shoulder. "We weren't over there with them, Patty, so we don't know how all that was playing out. She had come with Lillian, so of course she would have refused to leave with someone else."

Patricia knew he was right, but she didn't like it. She handed Barrett's phone to him, and leaned back to cross her arms in her mildly combative way.

"Well, you know where she is, now. If you don't jump on that, then you can't blame me if someone else decides to take an interest in her. What single man in his right mind wouldn't?"

Barrett narrowed his eyes and tried to determine what made her say that.

"You and I had the same fear when we saw Katherine's husband talking to Iris, and you know it, Barrett. We didn't know who he was, and it upset the both of us when we thought she was there with a man. This is not the time for you to play tough guy, so you might as well admit it!"

She gave him a pointed look. "One of these days, when we see something like that, we'll be right and it'll be too late to change it."

Barrett's jaw tightened with the evidence of stress, as he remembered the enormous relief that had washed over him, when he realized that the man speaking to Iris was Katherine's husband and hadn't come there with her.

"I'll think about it."

"I wouldn't think too long, Son," his father advised in a soft tone.

"Did you tell her that she was wrong about Blanche?" Patricia demanded, watching his face carefully.

"I told her that it wasn't what she thought."

She processed this silently. She had also told Iris that she was wrong and that Blanche had lied. So she knew the truth and was still being evasive. Why was that?

"What did she say, Barrett, when you told her that?"

He reached for his hat, indicating his intention to leave. "She just said she was sorry."

Patricia drew her brows and frowned and he tried to interpret what that meant.

"When I saw her at the bookstore, I told her that Blanche had made the whole thing up and that none of it was true."

Barrett settled back into his chair and examined her. "And what did she say?"

"She said it didn't matter anymore because you were probably angry with her for believing Blanche."

He raised a brow and thought about that.

"Our interaction at the cemetery should have proven to her that I wasn't."

"So then, go see her, Barrett," his mother pleaded.

He drew in a deep breath. "She came out to the farm."

His parents shared a look of surprise.

"When did that happen, Son?" his father wondered.

"Yesterday evening. I passed her truck as I was driving back out there to leave some barbed wire up against the fence for the men to pick up in the morning. She had apparently just turned out onto the highway.

"When I pulled in, I could see where she had parked and when I walked back to check the main gate she had secured it like Fort Knox, the way she always did."

"Reckon why she came out there, Barrett?" Stuart felt that it must have been an impulse.

"I told her at the cemetery that she'd be welcome to. I guess she was curious about the place and wanted to see the changes. She made sure to come at a time when no one would be around, though."

"Well, I expect she was nervous, coming back after everything ended up as it did. She might have thought you were just being nice by saying that to her."

Barrett got back up and put his hat back on. "Well, it's already dark, and I need to give Howie his shot. These brisk nights aren't exactly helping him."

"Are you gonna blanket him?" his dad asked, standing up to walk out with his son.

Patricia watched the two men head out, discussing the needs of Iris's beloved old horse and sat replaying the past few moments over in her head.

She had gotten to know Iris pretty well over the past several months and if Iris believed what she and Barrett had told her about Blanche lying but she was still keeping to herself, there had to be a reason for it.

She knew that Iris loved her son, and it was certainly an established fact that he loved her, so why was she continuing to stay away when she knew that Barrett's family adored her and wanted her to come be a part of them?

She got up to go wash out a few things in the sink and quietly continued to mull it all over.

Finally, she put a dishtowel over the drying rack and reached to turn out the light over the window with a look of grim determination.

Patricia could tell that Iris was bothered by something and that it was enough to cause her to keep her distance. Barrett didn't seem inclined to find out what it was. If she wanted to know she'd just have to ask Iris, herself.

༺༻

Iris came around Mrs. Estelle Tarver's chair and knelt to see where the glasses her patient dropped had landed. She finally located them under the chair's upholstered skirt and fished them out.

"They're not broken, so that's a good thing," she informed the elderly woman with a smile. "They look as if they need a little cleaning, though."

Mrs. Tarver, who normally had a sour remark for Iris and anyone else who dared trying to speak to her in a cheerful tone while she was obviously waiting to die, sat in silence and simply held her hand out expectantly.

Iris checked the lenses after wiping them and handed the glasses back to her.

She looked over at the door as Estelle Tarver's grandson came into the room and flashed a smile of greeting at the beautiful nurse's aide before giving his grandmother a dutiful kiss on her forehead.

The old lady seemed to endure, rather than enjoy his light expression of affection although it bothered her slightly less than if a complete stranger had kissed her.

Her grandson grinned at her. "Don't you act like you don't love me, Gram, or I'll kiss you again."

Harris Clark reached a finger to tap his grandmother on the chin and she gave him a reluctant smirk, rather than her usual belligerent scowl of displeasure.

He glanced over at Iris who had busied herself with changing the linens on the cancer patient's bed, now that she was in her chair.

"Let me help with that," he offered.

She knew he'd eventually talk her into it since he always did, so she simply allowed it.

"Fitted sheets are the bane of my existence," he informed Iris with an exaggerated sigh. "Have you ever been able to fold one of these things?"

"I normally lay them flat on a bed then tuck the corners together and fold them lengthwise before I finish. I think that helps," she replied.

He seemed to think about that.

"So, my method of holding them up in the air and trying to bring the corners together then rolling it all into a ball, muttering something that only Gram is allowed to say, then stuffing them into the linen closet is incorrect?" he asked facetiously.

Harris's grandmother cackled dryly at that and Iris looked over at her with an amused smile.

"There are probably better ways," she replied.

"I'll never master it," the blonde, good-looking man said ruefully.

"And that's just another reason why you're not married!" his grandmother snapped, waving a bony finger at him in admonition. "You never would let me teach you anything. All you know how to do is that computer stuff!"

"Gram thinks investment banking is computer stuff," he explained to Iris, who glanced back at her again, glad to see her interacting with her grandson rather than retreating into her normal dark moods. Iris sometimes wondered if she typically woke up angry simply because she did wake up.

The elderly patient knew fully well what lay ahead of her and seemed to want to confront it with anger.

"I *have* learned how to make your biscuits, Gram, so I guess I did let you teach me something, after all."

She sat thinking about that for a moment, almost pleased until she'd managed to think about it for too long.

"What good is it? You make a whole pan of biscuits and then just eat two and throw the rest out. That's wasteful!"

He laughed at her and she waved him off with a dismissive hand and made a sound of impatience.

"She right, you know," Harris confided to Iris as they both pulled the cases onto the pillows and placed them on the bed. "I actually do that."

"You should freeze them," she said with a quiet smile.

He stopped and widened his blue eyes, darker than hers but equally expressive. "You can do that?"

Iris lowered her brows and shook her head. "You've never seen frozen biscuits in the grocery store freezers?"

He paused before laying the folded blanket across the foot of the bed and thought about it.

"You can't tell him anything," his crotchety grandmother announced to Iris with a grimace. "He knows it all, except how to fold sheets!"

"That's actually correct," Harris grinned, viewing his blanket-folding skills critically then stepping back to allow Iris to pick up a soiled towel he had apparently been standing on.

"Only, now that you've enlightened me as to how to conquer the fitted sheet, I now know everything. But I won't let it go to my head," he quipped, laughing heartily when his grouchy grandmother let him know that his head was where it was supposed to go.

Iris watched their combat with an indulgent smile and finished gathering the towels and linens from the floor and packing them into the laundry basket.

"I'm just going to get this load into the washer, Mrs. Tarver, while you and Harris visit," she informed her.

Iris breezed through the door before he could offer to take the laundry downstairs for her and smiled again as she heard her patient demand to know why her grandson suddenly had time to visit her, when he never had before.

Iris had already made her way down the stairs and out of hearing range, when Mrs. Tarver accused Harris of only coming to see her because of the pretty nurses' aide, something he

163

laughingly pleaded guilty to, only making his grandmother grumble and wave another hand of dismissal in his direction.

<hr />

Patricia was relieved to see Iris's truck, indicating that she was home from work. She sat for a moment in her car, looking at the sweet little cottage and thinking that it suited Iris somehow even though she had been disappointed when she first learned that Iris had moved out of the farmhouse.

As long as she had continued to live there, Patricia knew there would be frequent exchanges between Barrett and the beautiful woman that he had lost his heart to. Now she was removed from their family and seemed to be finding her way without them.

Patricia couldn't resent that. She just greatly missed her and she could only imagine what her son was feeling.

She got out of her car after another moment and gave the front door a timid knock. Iris was sitting on the back patio and didn't hear her, even when she knocked again, a bit louder.

Patricia almost returned to her car, then decided that since she had driven all the way here she might as well take the little stone path that swept around the side of the cottage and see if she might be home, after all.

Iris looked up with startled eyes, as she saw Barrett's mother come around the corner and stop to give her a little wave and smile.

"Is it alright?" she asked hesitantly when Iris didn't greet her immediately.

Iris shook herself out of her suspended state and stood up to welcome her.

"I'm so sorry, I was just surprised. Of course it's alright!"

Patricia came to her and gave her an affectionate embrace.

"How did you find me?" Iris asked, still unable to believe that she was here.

"I might as well admit that right off the bat and get it off my chest," Patricia laughed.

She sat down in the chair Iris indicated next to hers and rested her soft brown eyes on the young woman's lovely face.

"I'm afraid I asked John Mabry to please tell me how I could find you," she confessed.

Iris nodded quietly, then raised her eyes with a question in them. "Is anything wrong?"

"No, dear, we're all well. But to be honest Iris, I have missed you to distraction and I just wanted to see your face and visit with you."

Iris smiled gently at her. "I've missed all of you, as well."

Patricia reached a hand and patted her arm.

"You'll be pleased to know that Howie and his goats are doing well. Howie gets a blanket put on him every evening to keep him warm and frequent injections to keep his joints from hurting him so much. He's enjoying the fall weather."

Iris's smile grew much brighter. "I really appreciate that. I don't think I could have been much help to him and I felt so badly about that."

Patricia smiled. "Did you ever name the goats, Iris?"

She drew her brows and thought about it. "I don't guess I ever did, which is odd. Even the chickens had names but I guess the poor goats were just Goat One and Goat Two."

Patricia laughed at that. "Stuart went over there to see how your horse was doing and when he came back, he informed me that he'd just named the goats Stonewall and Beauregard."

Iris laughed with her. "I see he kept to the Civil War theme. That's pretty funny."

Patricia glanced out into the piney woods and drew in a breath. "This is lovely!"

Iris followed her gaze with her own. "I think so. It's a much different view than I had on the farm but I love it."

She pointed toward the trees.

"Right through there is the river. Can you hear it?"

Patricia listened with a little smile of pleasure.

"I can! It sounds very close."

"It is," Iris confirmed. "If it wasn't for about the first twenty yards of trees, you'd be able to see it. I think that when the leaves finally fall, it can be seen. That's what Pastor Ben says."

"Is Pastor Ben your landlord, honey?" she asked.

Iris nodded. "He and Miss Katie, his wife. He pastors a little church not far from here."

"Oh, I'm so glad you met them," Patricia said sincerely. "They sound so nice."

"They are," Iris agreed.

The two women sat together in a silence that was comfortable at first but became a little awkward.

Finally Patricia asked her question.

"Iris... what changed?"

She shook her head silently.

"Maybe I'm not sure what you mean, I guess."

"With you and Barrett. I mean, I explained to you about Blanche Hollis lying to you and Barrett finally told me that he spoke to you at the cemetery and told you that things weren't the way you thought. But you still stay away. Is it us? Do you wish that we'd leave you alone?"

Patricia's eyes began to gather tears and Iris had to wipe at her own eyes.

"It's not that."

"Then what, sweetheart?"

Iris knew that Barrett's mother wasn't going to leave without some answers and although she'd be tempted to accuse any other woman of meddling, she knew Patricia Webb was sincerely trying to determine what they could have done to hurt her in any way.

"When I saw that Barrett has moved on, I just had to let it go," she finally said, looking down at her hands.

Patricia wrinkled her brow. "Honey, what made you think that Barrett has moved on?"

"I saw him with his date," she finally admitted, again reaching a finger to wipe a tear away before it could escape.

Patricia's eyes were wide with surprise.

"Oh, honey! No, that was just Callie!"

Iris looked at her vacantly and Patricia hurried to explain.

"That was just Callie Jeffries. She and Barrett have known each other since they were kids in school. Going to dinner with Callie would be like going to dinner with any one of Barrett's old school buddies. There was never anything between them and there's nothing between them now."

She touched Iris's arm again. "I admit it Iris, even though I've known Callie since she was a kid, I was so mad at Barrett for taking her to dinner that we had a huge fight, not because I was worried that he had feelings for her but because I was afraid of what you might think, if you found out.

"He only had dinner with her that one time and he hasn't seen her since. They ran into each other in town and Barrett simply hates eating alone."

Iris sat taking all this in without comment and Patricia watched her carefully, unable to read her expression.

Finally, she looked up at Barrett's mother and gave her a look of regret.

"I need to be honest with you, Patricia. I'm actually seeing someone, myself."

Patricia looked as if Iris had just slapped her. She raised her hand to her throat and stared at her in dismay.

"I guess I shouldn't be surprised," she finally managed to say, faltering a little. "I mean, what man wouldn't want to spend time with you? But..."

She looked at Iris with such sorrowful eyes, that it stung her heart.

"Do you not care at all for Barrett then, Iris? Even after knowing that he was never in a relationship with Blanche and that he hasn't moved on?"

Iris hung her head and stared at the ground.

After a long moment, Patricia stood and paused next to her, laying a gentle hand on her head.

"I'd better go. Take care of yourself, sweetheart."

When Iris finally looked up, she was gone.

Chapter Eighteen

"Honey, I don't think we necessarily need to say anything to Barrett about this," Stuart Webb advised his wife.

She looked at him in surprise. "Don't you think he'd want to know? Barrett doesn't deserve to be made a fool out of."

"I don't think Iris is trying to make a fool out of anybody, Patty," her husband said quietly. "It might just be that the two of them aren't meant to be together and if that's the case, maybe we should both step back and stop encouraging them."

Patricia rested her head in her hands and stared down at the kitchen table with disappointment.

"I wasn't planning on running to Barrett with it, Stu, but I guess I hate the thought of him reaching out to her again only to have her tell him that she's seeing someone else."

She slapped the kitchen table in frustration. "I told him that this could happen but he just ignored me!"

"Honey, you're getting way too upset with all this," Stuart Webb soothed. "They're both adults and they have to find out for themselves if they love each other and if they do, whether or not that's worth fighting for."

"How can they possibly know if they love each other if there's someone else involved, now?" She dabbed at her eyes.

"I was so mad at Barrett for taking that Callie Jeffries to dinner and wouldn't you just know that Iris saw them, the very minute he was escorting her into the restaurant?"

Stuart Webb simply nodded without comment.

"Iris didn't just say she dated someone, she said she was seeing someone. So I guess she must like him, at least."

"She must," her husband agreed softly.

Patricia looked at him impatiently. "Why aren't you more upset by this?"

"It's not that I'm not upset," he answered. "I love our son and I don't want to see him hurt anymore than you do. But he's a grown man, Patty, and this is all just part of life.

"Barrett has been handling all this fairly well as far as I've been able to observe. There was that incident at the farm after Aunt Sadie's service but that wouldn't have become an incident without Blanche Hollis turning it into one, so all in all, even though Barrett hasn't denied how he feels about Iris, he hasn't pushed himself on her. He doesn't want her to have to be talked into loving him."

Patricia looked at him for a long moment. "I haven't been trying to talk her into loving Barrett," she said tightly.

"No, and I didn't accuse you of it either, Patty," her husband returned, getting up from his chair and reaching for his hat before going outside.

She watched him head off to check on their cattle then got up and wandered into the den, settling down on the couch that faced the large windows and staring absently at the lake.

She fully intended to sit and pray until she found God's peace in all this but for the next few minutes, she intended to have a good cry.

◆◆◆

Barrett pulled onto the highway and silently ran through the list of things in his head that he needed to accomplish, before leaving this county to head back to his own residence.

He glanced down at a paper bag on the seat of his truck and realized that he needed to take care of that, as well.

He slowed his truck to a stop as a tractor attempted to cross the highway and glanced over at a coffee shop with a look of astonishment in his eyes. He looked ahead after the tractor had made it across the road, then pulled his truck into the parking lot of the coffee shop, stopping next to Iris's Apache and wondering why there was a for sale sign in the window.

Barrett drew his brows with a look of disappointment. Was she having financial difficulties, in spite of working?

Barrett got out of his vehicle and glanced in the Apache's window to confirm to himself that it was actually her truck and not one that just looked like it. It was hers. He pressed his lips together, noting that she had left her keys in the ignition.

He walked around and opened the door, taking them out and heading into the coffee shop to let her know and to return them to her.

He looked around for a moment, then located her in a booth across the room and his heart reacted to seeing her.

She chose that moment to glance up and stared at him with an expression of dread and dismay that surprised and saddened him then swept her eyes around the room, as if looking for someone else.

Barrett came over to her and held out her keys.

"I saw your Apache and stopped to look at your for sale sign," he said quietly. "You left you keys inside."

She looked down at the keys then slowly reached her hand to take them.

"Thank you," she said softly.

"Why are you selling it?" he asked. "You love that truck."

She drew in a breath and swallowed. "I guess I'm just ready for a change."

Barrett looked steadily at her, as Harris Clark returned to their booth with two coffees.

"Hello," he said pleasantly. "Are you a friend of Iris's?"

Barrett regarded him briefly. "I'm not sure."

He returned his disturbing gaze to Iris, who was looking back at him with tears brimming in her eyes.

"Ready for a change." He looked around the room with a dry, ironic smile. "Got it. Well, if you don't find a buyer for your truck, you might give my dad a call. He likes old Apaches."

Barrett touched the brim of his hat and walked out, getting into his truck and seeing the paper bag on the seat. He was supposed to give that to Iris but he wasn't going back inside.

He sat still a moment, staring hard at the coffee shop and trying to think clearly. Finally, he pulled his truck out onto the highway and drove to her cottage.

He reached into his glove box and pulled out a scrap of paper and penned a hasty note before attaching it to the bag with a paperclip and leaving it on the cottage's front door step.

He took a moment to steady himself, then drove away.

⁂

Iris left the coffee shop as soon as she realized Barrett had gone. She came to work, hoping to be able to focus on her job and stood folding Mrs. Tarver's gowns and linens in silence as the elderly lady observed her curiously.

She noted the young woman's flush of color and the fact that she was obviously close to tears and lifted her hand to indicate a chair next to her bed.

"Come sit over here," she commanded in her rough way.

Iris looked over at her and placed her stack of folded laundry on a chair before coming to sit in the one her patient had indicated.

"Are you alright, Mrs. Tarver?" she asked, looking for any sign of pain.

"I'm fine! But you are *not* fine. You're upset," she said, giving her a pointed look. "Has my grandson been up to his usual foolishness?"

Iris shook her head. "Not at all, Mrs. Tarver. Harris is a very nice man."

"Harris is a fool," his grandmother informed her dryly.

She thought that the old lady was simply being her testy self but something in her manner checked the smile Iris was about to give her and caused her to wait.

"He thinks that I don't know," she continued, "but his old grandmother is not nearly the imbecile he believes me to be. That's why he's in for a surprise when my attorney gives him the bad news."

Iris suddenly felt uncomfortable and lifted her hand. "I don't think I should be hearing about personal family matters, Mrs. Tarver."

"And why not? I'm dying. If I want to unburden myself to a stranger on my way out, are you going to deny me that?"

Iris knew that part of her duties was to keep her patient calm and listen if she wanted to be heard, but she wasn't sure she was up for this.

Estelle Tarver could see her struggle and silently admired her for not wishing to be privy to personal information but she had decided that she liked the girl and didn't want her to be toyed with by her worthless grandson.

"You can't possibly convince me that you actually have feelings for Harris," Mrs. Tarver said blandly. "For one thing, you barely know him and for another, you seem too intelligent for that."

Iris allowed a faint smile, unsure of where she was headed with all this.

"Do you know how many times Harris visited me before I was given this death sentence by my doctor? Never, that's how many times!

"But as soon as he finds out that his rich old grandmother is going to kick the bucket, he suddenly shows up as if he and I are as thick as thieves. How stupid does he think I am?" she demanded with a scowl.

"He's a grifter, that's what Harris is," the irate old lady continued. "But he's going to find himself fresh out of luck, when my attorney lets him know that he's grifted his last dime out of me!"

Iris heard all this with reluctance and wasn't sure if it was simply the rambling of a cantankerous old woman who was struggling to come to grips with her own mortality or if Mrs. Tarver was sincerely trying to warn her.

"What were you thinking about before?" she demanded of Iris, quite out of the blue.

Iris seemed startled by her rapid change of topic and stammered her response.

"I'm not... I don't know what you mean."

Estelle Tarver waved her words away.

"Nonsense! You've been crying, and you know it! Tell me it wasn't over Harris. Don't waste any tears on *that* crook!"

Iris shook her head. "No, it wasn't, Mrs. Tarver."

"Good! He's not worth crying over," she said.

Iris wasn't sure how to respond to that, but the lady didn't seem to need a response.

"Someone has made you cry and since it wasn't Harris, then who was it? Don't worry," she added. "Your secret is safe with me. I promise to carry it to the grave," she declared with an ironic little laugh.

Iris smiled at that but didn't offer an answer.

Mrs. Tarver regarded her shrewdly. "A special man. That's who did it."

Iris didn't want her to stay fixated on this and she didn't want to talk about Barrett so she stood up and began to put her sorted laundry away.

Mrs. Tarver watched her move around the room and could see that she was doing whatever she could to stay busy and not think about who it was who had hurt her.

"Iris," the old lady said, calling her by her name instead of the usual "Hey, girl." She waved her back over. "I want to tell you something."

Iris reluctantly returned to her bedside and waited.

"This man who made you cry... do you love him?"

Iris looked out the window by the head of the bed and Estelle Tarver could see that her beautiful eyes were bright with unshed tears.

"You don't need to tell me," she sighed softly. "I can see that you do. Just don't make the same mistake I made."

Iris lowered herself to sit again when the old lady tugged on her hand.

Mrs. Tarver watched her for a moment and Iris looked down at the floor, waiting for her to say what she obviously felt she needed to.

"My name is Estelle Tarver."

Iris furrowed her brow, and the woman grinned.

"My name is Estelle Tarver, but it wasn't supposed to be. My name was supposed to be Estelle Perry."

The old woman seemed to be looking back into the distant past and whatever she was seeing back there caused her dimmed eyes to brighten with tears.

"Wendell Perry was the most handsome man I'd ever seen in my life," she said softly. "He had dark hair and his eyes seemed to always have a laugh hiding in them."

Iris watched her face soften and was surprised at the transformation. She began to look much more youthful.

"I met Wendell at a dance and when he walked up to me and never even glanced at my girlfriends who were all prettier than me, I thought, but looked right into my eyes and asked me to dance, I held out my hand and he led me away with him. We danced all the rest of the evening, then he walked me home.

"I was smitten, so I don't mind admitting it," she claimed, glancing over at Iris with a sad smile.

"After that, we saw each other as often as we could and went to every dance together. It wasn't too long before we had fallen in love."

A shadow began to pass over her face and her expression became solemn.

"One night, I was supposed to meet Wendell at a dance but I arrived a little late because my boss wouldn't let me leave early. Most of us girls worked at the textile mill and old Mr. Carmichael acted like he hated all of us, especially me.

"He told me that if he caught me leaving early to not bother coming back and of course, back then it was hard times and if you were lucky enough to have a job, you tried to keep it.

"I had to stay but the minute my shift was done, I hurried into the restroom to change into my dress and then flagged down a ride to the dance. When I got there, I looked all over for Wendell and finally saw him with Ruth Bailey. She and the group of girls she ran around with always hated me.

"I was ready to march right over and demand to know what was going on but I somehow made myself wait and kept watching them and when Ruth stepped up on her toes and kissed him, I saw it.

"I didn't wait around. I took off out of there like I was on fire and when I got outside, I saw John Tarver standing around with a few of his friends, smoking and just talking, as men do. He saw me come out and look around and he could tell that I was searching for a way to leave. He said, 'Estelle, can I give you a ride?' and I quickly told him yes."

She laid a hand on her forehead and seemed to be seeing it all play out in front of her.

"Well, John took me home in his very nice car, just as much a gentleman as you could hope for and asked me to call him sometime if I ever wanted to maybe have dinner. He said he'd always wanted to ask me but he thought I was taken by Wendell Perry. I was still mad and I told him I wasn't taken by Wendell or anybody else, so we went ahead and made a dinner date right then.

"One date turned into another and whenever Wendell would call, I'd tell my brother to tell him I wasn't home. I saw what I saw and I didn't want to hear anything he had to say.

"I never felt the same way about John of course, as I had felt about Wendell but I was done with him. Eventually, John and I were engaged and the announcement was in the paper. We had a big wedding planned. Wendell read about it and he showed up at the rehearsal dinner and insisted that I let him explain. I told him it was too late for that.

"He begged me not to marry John until I let him tell me what had really happened that night, but I had too much pride. John and I were married and the years passed. Wendell had ended up marrying Clara Sanders. We had our family and they had theirs.

"When Wendell passed away, his son found a letter in his personal things and managed to get it to me. He had written it and sealed it up. It had never been opened. It was to me and it was written the night before I married."

Estelle Tarver was unaware of the tears that had gathered on her wrinkled cheeks until Iris gently touched a tissue to them and smiled down at her. She returned her smile and took the tissue into her thin hands and waited to compose herself before she continued.

"Wendell said that Ruth Bailey and the girls she was there with had asked him where I was and he told them that I had to work my full shift but that I would be there. He said that it must have been right when I walked into the room that Catherine

Ainsworth started telling Ruth, 'She's looking! Do it now!' and Ruth suddenly kissed him."

Mrs. Tarver shook her head and looked up at the ceiling at nothing. "I would never let him tell me. I had already made up my mind that he was guilty and I wanted to punish him. But I ended up punishing myself, Iris, and my punishment has been having to live out the rest of my life married to one man and in love with another. I've never forgiven myself for that."

Iris felt a surge of compassion for a woman she had mistakenly concluded was simply mean and bitter.

Estelle Tarver looked over at her beautiful young nurse's aide and reached her hand through her bed rails to touch her slender arm.

"Iris, the man who put those tears in your eyes... he's the man you love. I don't know what he did to you or if he deserves your love or not, but if you weren't in love with him, he wouldn't be able to do that to you. Don't settle for a counterfeit or get involved with someone you already know you don't love, just to get even. When it's too late, it's just too late. I wouldn't wish that kind of sad, empty life on anyone.

"Don't let Harris charm you with the same lines he uses on all the women. He's not someone you can trust, and more important than that, you don't love him. You love the man that you cry for."

∼∞∼

When Iris pulled her truck to a stop in front of her cottage, she gathered her things and got out to go inside but stopped when she saw the paper bag with a note attached to it that had been left resting against the door.

She stood staring down at it then looked around, as if wondering if the person who'd put it there might be watching her, before opening the door and stepping over it to put her things down inside.

She turned and picked up the bag carefully then brought it inside to the kitchen table.

When she pulled the folded note out of the paper clip, she put her hand to her heart and immediately gave a soft gasp, as she saw Barrett's unmistakable handwriting and signature.

She reached to turn on the overhead light and smoothed it out to read, mouthing his words silently to herself.

I dismantled the bed you graciously allowed me to use while you continued on at the farm, caring for Aunt Sadie. As I took it apart to either be returned to you or given to charity, I found this fixed to the underside of one of the slats. It was sealed and I did not attempt to open it but I would assume, since the bed is yours, it belongs to you. Thank you for helping us with our aunt. My family is indebted to you. I wish you a happy life and have enjoyed knowing you.

Barrett Webb

Rather than being curious to know what was in the bag, Iris was stung by the polite but impersonal tone of his note. It sounded like a goodbye and she knew that this was what he intended.

The look in Barrett's eyes that he rested on her before he turned and walked out of the coffee shop told her that he was done. Taking the bed apart meant that he was obviously not returning to the farm, probably because he intended to sell it.

Iris sat down at the table and laid her head on her folded arms and cried unashamedly, knowing how much she loved him but accepting that the two of them would never be together.

She thought of the hurt look in Patricia Webb's brown eyes when she admitted to her that she had been seeing someone else. Patricia was very loving as she left, but she had been unable to hide her disappointment.

She didn't really want to date Harris Clark or anyone else, but she knew it would finally close that door that she and Barrett couldn't seem to stop opening between them. Iris told herself that it needed to stay closed.

It was a while before she was able to spend all her tears and then sit quietly, with an occasional gasp or a shiver shaking her slight frame.

Iris heard Estelle Tarver's words in her ears as she'd told her that it was the man who made her cry that she loved. She sat up straight and pushed her long hair back out of her eyes and rested her forehead in her hands, trying to think.

Finally, she allowed herself to look over at the bag and pulled it closer to open it. She frowned in confusion and removed a small packet that was covered in some sort of bubble wrap and then bound with packing tape.

It hardly weighed anything and Iris suspected that most of its weight was the wrapping.

Iris was reluctant to try cutting through the wrapping but she took her time and was finally able to expose what turned out to be a letter.

She saw that it was addressed to her but she had never seen it before, although it had been opened. Her face darkened as she realized that her late husband had opened it and had apparently hidden it from her, as he had hidden everything else.

Iris removed the letter from the envelope and glanced at it before focusing and staring hard at the contents.

Chapter Nineteen

John Mabry had been surprised when he was informed that Iris Anderson was waiting to see him.

He sat across from her now, glad to welcome her but wondering what brought her to his office since all her financial obligations to both the bank and her creditors had been satisfied by the sale of her farm.

When he asked how he could help her, she simply removed a letter from her bag and held it out to him. He took it from her, thinking that it might be a late-arriving bill. As he began to examine it, his expression was not unlike Iris's had been when she read it.

The banker sat studying the letter for a long moment before looking up at Iris, who clearly had no idea what to think.

"How long have you had this, Iris?"

"Barrett Webb left it at my door yesterday. He found it fastened to the underside of the bed he had been using when he was taking it apart to move. I'm sure Glenn hid it."

"Has Barrett seen it?" the banker asked, still trying to determine how to help Iris.

"No, it was wrapped up with a lot of packing tape around it. He just removed it from the bed slat and put it in a bag then left it in front of my door."

Iris blinked rapidly to control the emotion that surged to her eyes as she thought about the note he had also left.

Her friend nodded and then shook his head in wonder, as the same question Iris had asked herself now dawned on him.

"Why, in the world, would Glenn Anderson have hidden this? You would think he'd have been jumping up and down with glee and pushing you to reply to it."

"I can't understand it," she admitted. "If it's real, it could have solved all our problems, or at least some of them."

He breathed out a sigh and looked back down at the document. "Maybe, or it could have just been something else that he would have frittered away. His hiding it may turn out to be a blessing."

"Do you think it's real?" Iris asked him quietly.

"It seems to be. I do know of this attorney," he replied. "According to the return address, he's just a couple of hours upstate. It would be simple enough to verify."

He sat for a moment reading over it again. There was just enough information to elicit a reply but certainly not enough to provide an explanation. He glanced up at Iris.

"I would think you might contact his office and arrange for a meeting with him. It's certainly worth a trip to at least determine the true status of what this letter is suggesting. If you decide to do that, Iris, make sure you bring documentation to prove your identity, especially any legal paper that ties you to your maiden name."

She sat considering all this with a hesitant expression and John Mabry gave her a kind smile.

"Would you like for me to make the call?"

"If they would talk to you, that would be wonderful."

"I expect they will just advise me that the information is only intended for you but I could at least let them know that you are only recently in possession of the letter and wish to schedule an appointment. How much time do you need to be able to have someone take your current patient?"

Iris pursed her lips and thought about it. She had stepped in plenty of times when another aide couldn't come to work so she felt that wouldn't be a problem.

"I think if you could schedule in at the beginning of next week, that would give me time to speak to my RN and have someone assigned. It would only need to be for that day."

John Mabry nodded and reached for his reading glasses before lifting the telephone receiver and calling the number on the letterhead. After advising the receptionist that he needed to speak to someone regarding a letter from the attorney, he was immediately connected and an appointment was set up for Iris to come to his office.

He smiled as he hung the phone up. "Mr. Keating seemed very relieved to know that you had gotten the letter. So, next Tuesday at ten o' clock. Here's where you need to go."

He tapped the address on the letterhead.

Iris mentally calculated the driving time and slowly nodded then reached to take back the letter that the banker was holding out to her.

"He wants you to bring this letter with you, in addition to your documentation regarding your identity."

She nodded again, then raised her eyes to his.

"I can't even speculate about what this means."

"Well, speculation never accomplishes much," he replied with a smile. "There's no way to know for sure until you sit down across from the attorney and let him explain. I do have a suggestion though, Iris."

She waited, knowing that whatever it was, it was in her best interest.

"Don't drive your truck. It's fine for local trips but that's four hours, round trip. Can you manage to rent a car for a couple of days?"

She thought about it and a flash of embarrassment swept across her face.

"Don't those companies require a credit card? I don't have one."

"I can take care of that," he assured her. "If you can swing by here Monday morning, I'll see to it that you have one. Since you would need to get an early start Tuesday, you might think about going ahead and renting it Monday after you leave here.

"You can leave your truck in the side lot here and I'll let security know to keep an eye on it. I'll give you a lift to pick up your rental." He leaned back in his chair and gave her a smile.

"I hope this turns out to be the break that you deserve."

She offered an uncertain smile and stood up to head to her job. "Thank you so much, Mr. John."

"I'm always glad to help."

He paused as he thought of something.

"Iris, Patricia Webb came by recently and asked if I would tell her where you were living. I hope I didn't do anything wrong by letting her know. I knew that you and her family had become close, so I took a chance and gave her the address. I'm sorry if I shouldn't have."

She drew in a deep breath, disappointed to discover that the very name Webb instantly created a sense of loss and the threat of tears. She somehow managed to give her kind friend another smile.

"No, that was fine. We talked."

⁂

Barrett sat across from Hugh Jacobs and rested an ankle on one knee, fingering the brim of the hat he was holding and giving him a direct look.

"No developers," he said quietly but firmly to the real estate broker. "No exceptions."

"We certainly won't entertain those offers deliberately, Barrett," the man assured him.

"Do your due diligence," he warned in his measured, quiet manner. "I don't want anyone claiming to be trying to finally own his dream farm at last and then turn it into cheap housing the minute he closes on it. In fact, you might advise anyone who wants to put a contract on the property that I will not be replying to any offers for three months."

Hugh Jacobs raised his brows in surprise. "Three months? You've flipped plenty of farms and sold them practically overnight, Barrett. Why is this one different?"

Barrett set his jaw and stood to leave. "My reasons are my own. Three months. If you don't want the listing, just say so."

"Three months," the broker agreed hastily. "Done."

Barrett gave him a curt nod before putting his hat back on and leaving.

He stepped outside the realtor's office and stood looking around for a moment, trying to determine the best use of his time before his next appointment.

His face reflected his confusion and surprise as he saw Iris Anderson's Apache truck sitting across the road in the bank's fenced in side lot. He thought about it and wondered if John Mabry might have either purchased the truck or had offered to help her sell it. He hadn't seen anything in the classifieds about an Apache, so perhaps Iris's banker had bought the truck, after all. He would have done it just to help out, if she really was in a financial bind and needed it.

Barrett's estimation of John Mabry was that he displayed a fatherly sort of protection where Iris was concerned and always seemed to be willing to assist her in any way he could.

He wondered to himself what she might be driving now but pushed the question away, telling himself that he didn't care one way or another, although the stipulation he had just made to the realtor regarding the sale of the farm would suggest otherwise.

He pulled out his phone when he heard a text message being delivered and studied the screen with a degree of mild surprise. It was from Jackie Coates, asking him to call her when he had some free time.

Barrett furrowed his brow and wondered what that could be about. He knew the woman, although not well. She owned a small ranch east of his parent's land and he may have returned a casual greeting or stopped to answer a question about drenching, or injections, but they weren't necessarily friends. He couldn't understand why her name seemed to already be in his phone.

He thought about it, and then recalled an auction that he and his father attended. She was there. She asked if she could send her contact information to his number in case he decided he didn't want the pair of calves he'd just purchased.

He had told her that it wasn't likely, but he did allow her to put her number into his phone. She must have gone ahead and set it up as a contact and noted his number as well. He checked the time again and decided that whatever it was, it would have to wait.

Jackie Coates was in her early thirties, blonde and tanned, since she spent the majority of her time out in the sun. Her ranch wasn't considered to be a large one, but she seemed to be able to make it profitable, not taking on more than she could manage so that she could employ a few ranch hands.

She sold more horses than cattle but Barrett remembered that she had told him she was looking to build a herd, so he supposed that might be why she wanted him to call her.

He put his phone away and walked around the corner to finish off his list of errands before driving out to the Anderson farm to look around for anything he might want to keep before the realtor began showing the property.

Iris took the seat that Adam Keating indicated before he came around to settle in behind his desk. He had been more than a little surprised when the person he had written the letter to turned out to be one of the most beautiful women he had ever seen, but he had managed to cover his reaction and maintain his professional detachment.

"I certainly do appreciate your driving all this way, Miss Foster. I'm sorry, I've since learned that it's Mrs. Anderson."

"I'm recently widowed and I've been considering returning to my maiden name," she admitted in her soft way. "So that's fine. I just need to get used to it again, before I make any sort of legal change."

He nodded and flashed her a smile. "Miss Foster, then."

He reached into his desk's file drawer and retrieved a folder to place in front of him. "I'm sure the letter I sent you raised more questions than it answered."

"I wasn't aware that there were questions to be asked or answered," she replied.

"If I may ask, Miss Foster, why did you wait so long to respond to the letter?"

She drew in a breath, reluctant to offer an explanation, but supposing that he deserved one.

"I'm afraid that my late husband had a habit of simply hiding any type of correspondence he didn't want me to know about. The letter was found only days ago."

She could tell by his expression that Adam Keating found that to be strange behavior, but he made no comment about it.

Instead, he rested his arms on the folder and gave her a direct look. "You were in the foster care system from age three to seventeen, then spent a few months of your eighteenth year in a foster extension program, according to my research. Would you agree with that?"

She nodded slowly and he could see that she had no clue where he was going with that. "Yes, and then got married."

"You were placed in the system after your mother was incarcerated and your grandmother later died. Is that your understanding, as well?"

She nodded again. "You seem to have all your facts in order, Mr. Keating."

He opened the folder and looked at it a moment, as if he were trying to decide how to begin. Finally, he raised his eyes to study her.

"Miss Foster, since you were only three when you entered the system, my best guess is that you don't remember much at all about either your mother or your grandmother. That is, unless you've invested the time to learn what you could?"

He saw her shake her head slowly, still fixing her lovely eyes on him and waiting in silence.

"You don't know why your mother went to prison," he said, evenly.

"I don't even know what my mother's name was," Iris admitted. "I was busy enough all those years trying to explain why my name was Foster and I was in foster care," she added with an amused smile. "One kid thought I owned foster care."

He laughed at that, then glanced back at his folder.

"Your mother's first name was Adrienne. She was your grandmother's daughter and unmarried, so her last name was Foster, as well. She went to prison not long after you were born for charges that included embezzlement, grand larceny and forgery.

"She was to serve a minimum of twenty years. However, she passed away in prison several years after your grandmother died." He glanced up to see her reaction.

"Why?"

Her simple question caught him off guard and he paused to locate that information.

"The death certificate simply states natural causes, related to apparent heart disease with evidence of heavy smoking listed as a contributing factor."

She seemed to be thinking about it. "I guess it doesn't matter. Dead is dead."

Adam Keating was surprised by her calm, unaffected demeanor then reminded himself that this woman's mother was a stranger to her. She didn't seem to feel the need to display feelings that simply weren't there.

He turned a page in the folder and glanced down at it, but hardly seemed to need it. He leaned back in his chair and looked at her closely.

"Your grandmother was Grace Foster. Your grandfather was Thomas Foster. Do either of those names sound familiar to you, at all?"

"I'm afraid not. Should they?"

"Not if you're unfamiliar with the publishing industry. Your grandparents once owned one of the largest magazine and book publishing companies in the country which for a time, also included newspapers."

He could see that this information was nothing more than merely interesting to her.

"When your grandmother died and you were placed into the foster system, your grandfather was still living, although not with his wife, apparently. He returned from Canada after her death and was informed about the fact that you were now in foster care. I'm sorry, Miss Foster, but for whatever reason, your grandfather did nothing to change that. I can only speculate as to why that was."

"I'd be interested in your speculation," she informed him, her expression betraying her attempt to not feel resentment.

"I suspect that your grandfather was angry with his daughter, your mother, because the bulk of her crime was committed against her own parents. If that was the case, he may have decided that he was simply done. He never tried to contact her and he never tried to remove you from the system. I'm sorry for that, Miss Foster," he added sincerely.

She sat quietly for a long moment. "No, it's just what it is. I guess I don't blame him. I expect I was just another mess of my mother's that he didn't want to have to clean up."

Adam Keating had arrived at the purpose of their meeting and began to feel a sense of relief that he would now be able to share some positive news with her.

"You are Thomas Foster's heir, Miss Foster."

She narrowed her eyes and looked at him as if he were deliberately trying to confuse her.

"Why? He didn't care anything about me."

"Regardless, there was no one else in line for him to name as beneficiary. He named you."

She didn't react, and Adam Keating decided that if she were aware of the size of the inheritance, it might help her grasp the significance of it.

"Your grandfather did bequeath sizeable sums to various scholarships and foundations, so your inheritance doesn't reflect his total worth. Still, your portion should be enough to place you in a comfortable position."

He simply turned the folder around, slid it toward her, and circled an amount with his pen.

It was several minutes before she raised her beautiful eyes and allowed herself to be stunned.

Chapter Twenty

Estelle Tarver seemed to weaken much more quickly than Iris had expected, following her return to work. Her grandson told Iris that she had become depressed by her aide's absence but Iris knew very well the toll that her cancer would eventually take on her frail body and refused to allow him to make her feel that she had somehow accelerated her patient's decline.

Harris Clark displayed an unusual amount of curiosity about where Iris had gone. She was surprised that Estelle Tarver's warning that he was a grifter was the first thing that came to mind when he began to try to ferret the information out of her.

Of course, there was no way he could possibly know that she had met with an attorney and the reason behind it but Iris did wonder if being a banker gave him means of discovery that she was unaware of.

Mrs. Tarver was communicating less and less and beginning to sleep more. When Iris returned, one of the last things her patient said to her was to remind her to not make the same mistake she had made. Iris knew that she was referring to the man who made her cry and her entreaty caused the usual stab of grief in her heart, but she simply stroked her patient's forehead and gave her a soft smile.

Faint responses to Iris's questions about her pain eventually stopped coming and as she slipped into her coma, Iris remained by her side, staying beyond her schedule and holding the woman's hand.

Harris had seemed to make himself scarce. Iris supposed that death wasn't something he wanted to witness, but she was actually relieved to be alone with Mrs. Tarver, other than the random visits made by her daughter and son-in-law, who were Harris's parents.

Iris had approached the subject of life after death with Estelle Tarver before she left to meet with the attorney and the bristly little woman informed her in her acerbic way, although tempered for Iris's benefit, that she might not be God's best child but she was still His and that He was stuck with her. She advised her caregiver not to fret herself about that.

She had made the comment with a sparkle in her old eyes and laughed with her little raspy cackle, before seeming to spend some time thinking about it and smiling to herself.

As Estelle Tarver slipped away from her diseased body, Iris stood looking down at her for a long, tender moment then placed a call to her RN and to Mrs. Tarver's daughter to inform them of her passing.

Iris had already decided that Estelle Tarver would be her last patient, at least for a while. She didn't need to continue working and felt that she should take some time to assess things and pray about where God was leading her.

She did have one desire that she had been praying over, that never seemed to leave her, but it seemed unlikely so she had put it out of her mind.

She decided to drive into town and talk to her friend, John Mabry, about it.

Iris stopped by her cottage first, to shower and change and was surprised to find Pastor Ben kneeling down by the outdoor faucet with a wrench.

He looked up at her and grinned. "This old faucet just keeps on dripping, no matter how much I tighten it. I might just go ahead and replace it and be done with it."

He stood to his feet and regarded her kindly. "You said you thought your patient might pass today. I guess, since you're here, she did?"

"Yes," Iris said regretfully. "She didn't seem to be in any pain, so that's a mercy."

"Yes, it sure is!" he agreed. "Katie and I prayed her passing would be easy."

"It did seem to be, Pastor Ben," Iris told him.

They both stood looking down at the faucet for a moment before Pastor Ben made his observation.

"You might want to think about taking some time off, Iris, and have a little period of refreshing before you begin working with a new patient."

She was surprised by his advice but nodded. "I think I'll do that. I think I need to just take a step back and see if I can hear from God about what happens next."

"He has no reason not to tell you," the old pastor said with a little laugh. "I think that's a good idea."

He moved slowly off toward his truck and gave her a little wave. "I'll be back tomorrow and swap that old faucet out."

Iris returned his wave and headed inside to clean up before driving into town. The bank would be closing for the day soon, so she'd need to hurry.

She was relieved to find John Mabry in his office and he was glad to see her, welcoming her to come sit and tell him what was on her mind.

When she took a seat, he gave her a bright smile.

"It looks like a happy ending at last, Iris. I can't tell you how pleased I was when I met you to return the car and you told me about your meeting. It's about time you got a break."

He shook his head in disbelief. "I still can't believe that you are the granddaughter of *those* Fosters! I never would have suspected that."

"I never knew that those Fosters existed," she confessed. "I don't know anything about the publishing industry."

He smiled at that. "Well, I'm just glad that Barrett found the letter. Otherwise, you might never have found out."

John Mabry didn't miss her flinch when she heard Barrett's name, and smiled sympathetically at her.

"What can I do for you, Iris?" the banker wondered.

"You're always doing something for me and I'm beginning to feel bad for asking," she said with a little laugh.

"No, never feel like that. If I can help you, I'm always glad to do it," he assured her with a little wave of his hand.

Iris paused and thought about his words and wondered, as she had many times, why Mr. Mabry treated her so kindly. He certainly didn't wait to exhibit that behavior until after he learned that she had come into money and it was always clear to her that he was sincere.

"Mr. John," she began hesitantly, "why have you always been so helpful to me?"

He looked down at his desk with a little smile. "Well Iris, for one thing, I know integrity and good character when I see it. But, besides that... well, you remind me of someone."

He saw that she was trying to restrain herself from asking and leaned back in his chair with a melancholy smile.

"Mrs. Mabry and I used to have a daughter," he shared softly. "Our little Belle. We had her for twelve short years, before losing her to a drowning accident."

He paused and blinked, deciding not to elaborate other than to add that his little girl had red hair and blue eyes and that Iris always made him think about what she might have grown up to be like.

She sat looking at him with sad, watery eyes and he moved his hand through the air as if wiping away the memory.

"I try not to camp out around that, Iris. But the simple fact is that I like to think that Belle would have grown into a beautiful, good-hearted woman like you. So I may be living vicariously.

"How can I help you, Iris?" he continued and Iris understood that he wanted to move away from the subject of his little girl.

She took a moment. "I realize how this is going to sound, Mr. John, and if you think I'm being ridiculous, please tell me because I'm sure I may be motivated by emotion and that's probably no way to do business."

"You're about to embark on a business venture?" he asked, mildly surprised.

She was suddenly reluctant to go any further but she forged ahead. "I'd like to buy back my old farm."

She had expected her banker to be surprised or register some kind of strong emotion, but he simply looked at her thoughtfully.

"Barrett is not going to work that farm?"

"I thought he was, but I rode out there yesterday evening before I went home and there's a for sale sign at the road."

He seemed puzzled by that.

"Is that when you decided you want to buy it, Iris?" he asked, wondering if it might have been an emotional decision, after all.

She shook her head. "No. I thought about it all the way back from meeting with the attorney and if Barrett had been at the farm yesterday, I planned to ask him if he'd consider selling it. That's when I saw the sign but when I drove on up to the house, no one was there."

John Mabry nodded, pressing his fingertips together and mulling it over. He looked down as Iris slid a piece of paper across the desk.

"This is the realtor. I waited to contact him because I wanted to talk to you first and find out what you thought about it." She watched him study the information.

"He's right across the street," he informed her, still thinking about it. "I know Hugh very well. We grab lunch together on the square, from time to time."

He picked up his phone and dialed Hugh Jacob's personal number, leaving a message for him to call back when he didn't answer.

"I expect he's showing property, Iris," he said. "He'll call back when he sees that it's me."

She nodded. "I may ride back out there since no one seems to be around. The cattle are still there but I didn't see any workers. I didn't see a sale price on the sign but maybe I just missed it."

"Well, if I find anything out, I'll give you a call, Iris. As far as what I think, I'd love to see you get your farm back. It's over six hundred acres, though. You won't be overwhelmed by that?"

She understood his question but smiled and shook her head. "No. I won't want to work all of it and since there's a lake there now, I have some ideas for how to use the acreage around it. But, as far as the rest of it, I expect I'll be able to hire some hands to help."

"Well, Iris, be careful with that," her friend advised. "Especially if you move back into the farmhouse and live there alone. If you do end up being able to buy the farm back, I'd appreciate it if you'd run any potential employees by me first, and let me check them out."

She reached over and laid her hand on his arm. "I will, Mr. John. Thank you so much."

He watched her leave with a little wave and smile then looked back down at the paper she'd given him, wondering why Barrett Webb had suddenly decided to sell a farm that he only recently populated with cattle.

⁂

Barrett waited at the light, glancing around vacantly at traffic, lost in his thoughts. He finally began to move his truck slowly forward as he realized the light had changed and drove in the direction of the Anderson farm. He still needed to pick up a couple of T-post drivers and wire cutters that he'd left on the front porch. He didn't want anyone walking off with those.

Barrett's handsome face was grim as he thought about the phone call he'd made in response to the text Jackie Coates had sent him.

He'd assumed that she'd want to talk to him about buying cattle but she surprised him by asking him what he planned to do with the Anderson farm and if he would consider giving her first right of refusal if he put it on the market.

He'd let her know that it was already on the market and told her that he wasn't ready to consider any offers for three months. She'd reacted by trying to convince him that she would give him the best offer but Barrett knew that it would be her father, Jack Coates, who would actually be purchasing the farm.

It wasn't that he minded but he didn't appreciate the attempt that Jackie Coates was making to hide that fact.

He'd finally told her that he'd think about it and call her if he changed his mind but advised her to not get her hopes up that he would consider her offer or anyone else's any earlier than his three month condition.

He breathed out a sigh of frustration, a frown resting on his face as his thoughts wandered back to earlier this morning when he'd seen his mother.

He'd stopped by to ask his father if he needed him to pick up anything while he was out and couldn't help noticing that Patricia Webb was unusually quiet and solemn.

He had watched her from the entrance of the den, as she sat staring out the window with sad eyes. He finally came in and settled down next to her on the couch, reaching over to take her hand in his.

"Are you okay, Mother?" he'd asked, giving her hand a little squeeze.

He wondered if she'd heard him at first then she simply shook her head.

Barrett sat with her for a few moments longer before asking her if he could do anything for her. She looked over at him with eyes that were threatening tears and just shook her head again.

"No, sweetheart. I guess not."

He thought he knew what she was upset about but he wondered how she'd found out. Rather than ask, he'd simply leaned over to kiss her cheek then pulled himself up to head out and run his errands, leaving her to eventually pray about it, as he knew she would.

Barrett slowed his truck to a crawl, drawing his brows and staring at the Apache truck parked under the tree in front of the farmhouse.

He turned the engine off and sat for a moment looking around, but didn't see the vehicle's owner.

Finally, he let out a mild oath and got out of his truck, heading toward the back gate. He doubted that Iris had gone into the house, since she'd left her keys behind.

He found her leaning over the rails of the gate, completely oblivious to his presence.

Nip hadn't barked, since he knew Barrett's truck, and Iris was so obviously engrossed in whatever she was thinking that she hadn't registered the sound of a vehicle arriving.

Barrett's intention had been to ask her to please not continue driving out to the farm, since his realtor would soon be showing it to potential buyers but as soon as he saw her, with her long hair gently moving in the breeze and her slim form seeming to balance on the top rail of the gate, his heart lurched in his chest and he stopped himself from saying anything.

Instead, he waited, wondering why she had driven out to the farm. He was sure that she had to have seen the sign at the end of the road. He told himself that she probably just wanted one more look at the land, once she realized that strangers would soon be living there.

Barrett knew that this would hurt her heart. He hadn't listed the farm to retaliate after seeing her with another man and hearing her say that she felt she was ready for a change, but he had decided that the farm meant nothing to him without her, and that it would only serve to constantly remind him of her.

He continued to silently appraise her and smiled when she straightened up to pull the pushed-up sleeves of her jacket down over her cold arms and almost lost her footing. She grabbed the top rail and let out a muffled "Whoa, Nellie!" before regaining her balance, then decided to attempt sitting on the top rail.

"I wouldn't," Barrett advised in a low, soft voice.

Iris had to grab the rail again to steady herself, as a bit of panic caused her to shake. She hopped down and made herself turn around to face him.

"I guess you're right," she admitted, with a flush of color washing over her cheeks.

He regarded her calmly before making his way over to the gate and looking down at her curiously.

"How are you, Iris?" he finally asked.

She seemed surprised. She'd thought his first question would be to demand to know why she was there.

"I'm okay," she answered, feeling a bit nervous.

He continued to study her in his quiet way. She wasn't sure where to look so she simply turned back around to gaze out beyond the gate.

"Is it okay that I'm here?" she asked, hoping that he wasn't upset by her presence.

"Why wouldn't it be?" he countered, resting his arms on the gate's top rail and joining her in surveying the fields.

"I just thought..."

She stopped, not knowing if she wanted to finish that.

Barrett didn't allow himself to just brush the coffee shop encounter aside, as if it hadn't upset him. Instead, he said nothing, putting her in the position to have to finish.

"It was just coffee," she finally breathed.

"I didn't ask, but okay."

Iris drew in a deep breath.

"I know it doesn't matter, Barrett, but there haven't been any more coffees."

He resisted the impulse to smile at her revelation.

"Why do you think it doesn't matter?" he asked quietly.

"That's not the vibe I'm getting," she returned dryly, instantly regretting her impulsive remark.

He almost laughed. "Did you just use the word 'vibe'? That doesn't sound like an Iris word."

She twisted her mouth and grinned, her eyes still roaming around the pastures in front of them.

"Am I giving you a vibe, then?" he persisted.

"Actually, yes."

This time, he did laugh. "It's not intentional."

He allowed a brief silence to rest between them, before looking over at her.

"You saw the sign."

She nodded. "That's why I'm here."

He narrowed his eyes, looking at her closely. "You're here because you saw the sign? Are you upset that I'm selling?"

She shook her head. "No, I'm actually glad."

"*Are* you?" His question was asked with a touch of sarcasm and Iris didn't miss it.

"Yes, because I wanted to ask you if..."

Suddenly, she felt she couldn't ask. There was something lurking just below the surface that suggested to her that Barrett wasn't feeling as friendly as he had seemed to be, after she said she was glad he was selling the farm.

He watched her backing away from what she'd begun to say and turned to face her, allowing his eyes to rest on hers.

"You wanted to ask me if..." He waited.

"I'm not sure I can," she sighed, beginning to feel that she was only being sentimental about the farm after all and had no business wanting to own it again.

"Now, you see, Iris," Barrett began after a long silence, "this has always been our problem. We never seem to finish a conversation. One of us always leaves the other one hanging."

She thought about that and agreed. "I know."

"Is there any way, on God's green earth, that you might actually keep talking until we both know what you're saying, or am I asking too much?"

Iris looked up at him to find him studying her with a faint look of amusement.

She took a deep breath and decided that it was now or never and just went for it.

"Would you let me buy it back?"

She couldn't have startled him more, if she had suddenly reached back and hit him. He searched her face to determine if she was teasing him, but she returned his gaze steadily.

"I don't wish to pry into your personal affairs, Iris, but how exactly would you be able to do that?" He suddenly lifted his hand to stop her from answering him and a bit of irritation flashed in his eyes.

"When you ask if I'll let you buy it back, you're not by any chance planning on embarking on a joint venture with the guy from the coffee shop, are you? That would be a no."

She wrinkled her brow. "Why would you think that?"

"Why wouldn't I?" Barrett didn't bother to hide the fact that he was still upset about seeing her with someone else.

"It was just coffee!" she snapped loudly, with a flash of temper in her pretty eyes, surprising the both of them.

Barrett had never heard Iris raise her voice above her typical gentle volume and decided that she had shouted at him in frustration, because she couldn't make him believe her.

"Alright," he finally responded slowly. "Let's say that's true. Back to my original question.

"How, exactly would you be able to buy back the farm? Would John Mabry be willing to hold the mortgage, even after you were forced to sell it before?"

Iris hadn't planned on encountering Barrett Webb when she'd driven out to look at the farm and think about asking him if she could buy it, so she had no ready answer prepared. It took her a moment to take in a breath and meet his eyes with hers.

"It would be a cash transaction."

Barrett had smiled at that, then realized that she wasn't smiling with him. He rested one arm on the rail, and slid the thumb of one hand into his jeans pocket.

"A cash transaction," he repeated quietly.

"Yes."

He held her gaze, trying to determine what she could possibly mean by telling him she would pay cash for the farm.

Finally, Barrett ran his hand through his hair and gave her a long, piercing look.

"The irony of the situation is that you could have had the farm. I would have given it to you."

She stared at him, completely bewildered. "What do you mean by that?"

He leaned his back against the gate and crossed his arms, looking down at the ground with a sad smile of regret.

Iris came closer and tried to read him.

"What does that mean?"

"You don't know?"

She shook her head slowly and waited.

Barrett found it impossible to believe that this woman could stand so close to him and look into his eyes and still ask him what he meant by saying he would have given the farm to her. Was she deliberately pretending not to know that he was in love with her?

"Let me think about it, Iris," he finally said softly. "Can you do that?"

"Yes," she answered, realizing that once again, they had left each other hanging.

Barrett seemed to be ready to go back to his truck, but stopped to question her with his eyes.

"You found the bag?"

"I did. Thank you for taking it to the cottage, Barrett."

He nodded. "It's a nice cottage. I would imagine, being somewhat familiar with Hyatt's Creek, that the river runs pretty close to it."

"Now that the leaves are falling, I can just about see it from my back patio," she told him.

He looked down at the ground with a faint smile. "You've fished in it then, I would think?"

"I did when I first moved in, but there wasn't a lot of time because of having to work so many hours. Now that I'm not working, I'll probably get to go more often."

Barrett examined her closely. "Is that by choice?"

She hadn't meant to let him know that she wasn't working, but there was no way to unsay it.

"Yes," she simply admitted, not adding anything further.

Barrett decided not to press her, although he was certainly curious as to why she was telling him that she chose not to work and had just offered to pay cash for the farm.

He drew in a deep breath and rested his hands on his hips, looking around at his picturesque property before gazing back down at Iris Anderson's beautiful face.

"Alright, Iris," he said softly. "I won't keep you waiting long for an answer but I'd like to sleep on it. Maybe you should, as well and then we'll see."

She flashed a hopeful smile. "Thank you, Barrett."

He simply reached a fingertip to sweep a long, copper curl of hair out of her eyes, then turned and strode toward his truck, leaving her to deal with her racing pulse.

Chapter Twenty-One

Iris opened her eyes and looked around her room in confusion before she realized that the sound of a text message was what had awakened her.

She frowned sleepily and searched the nightstand to locate her phone, then swiped the screen to find the message.

She woke up instantly when she saw that Barrett had sent her a message, asking her if he could stop by to discuss the farm or if she had plans, to let him know what would work for her.

She looked down at herself, still in her gown, and wondered how quickly she could pull herself together. Finally, she forced herself to calm down and texted back, asking him if an hour would be soon enough.

When he let her know to expect him, she hopped out of bed and began to rush around to get dressed and pick up her room, then hurried out to get a pot of coffee started.

Iris tried to tell herself that her excitement was simply because she was just eager to hear what Barrett had decided but she knew that wasn't the real reason for her sudden burst of adrenaline.

She checked her face in the mirror then fluffed her hair with her fingers and tried to decide if she needed any makeup before stopping in her tracks.

She forced herself to consider the fact that Barrett could very easily be coming to give her his answer in person rather than over the phone, in order to let her down easily when he declined to sell the farm to her.

She turned away from the mirror and took in a deep breath, recalling the many times that she and Barrett Webb had seemed to be at cross-purposes. She reminded herself that she had interpreted his dismantling the bed and putting the farm on the market as his way of telling her he was done.

Iris felt a twinge of sadness, remembering the coldness in his voice when she told him she was selling the Apache because she felt she was ready for a change. Even now, she could hear his low, quiet words as he glanced pointedly at Harris Clark, then fixed her with his steady gaze. "Ready for a change. Got it."

She let out a sigh and wandered back into the kitchen much more slowly than she'd entered before, feeling a great deal less excited and a bit more nervous.

She sat out some mugs, then took her coffee outside to sit out on the back patio and breathe in the pine scent, and listen to the early morning birds. She silently whispered quiet little prayers, asking God for His peace.

When she thought she heard Barrett's truck door closing, she sat her coffee down and walked back through the cottage to let him in.

He murmured a good morning to her and followed her, taking a quick moment to glance around before letting her lead him into the kitchen.

Iris poured his coffee and handed it to him and when he thanked her, he met her eyes with some sort of emotion in his own that she couldn't identify. She motioned toward the open back door with a little smile.

"I was sitting outside. Would you like to do that, or I can just bring my coffee back in here?"

He simply nodded toward the back door, still not saying much, but he continued to meet her eyes in a deliberate way that was beginning to rattle Iris.

Instead of taking a seat next to her, Barrett walked to the edge of the patio pavers and stood looking through the trees, and listening to the sound of the river. He realized that Iris was right, and he actually could see it ahead, through the trees that had lost the most leaves.

"It's nice," he commented lightly.

"Yes." She watched him, silently approving his stance and build and the way he seemed to be thoughtfully appreciating his surroundings.

After a moment, he turned and came back to sit down next to her, moving the chair so that he could look at her.

They wordlessly searched each other's eyes and Iris unconsciously began biting her bottom lip, indicating a growing apprehension.

"You're going to say no," she finally decided in a quiet voice, unable to hide her discouragement.

"Not entirely," he returned, still studying her with that odd, calculating manner that he'd obviously never had occasion to let her see before. She wondered if this demeanor was similar to what he might display when negotiating some sort of business deal. In any event, he was impossible to read.

Barrett sat his coffee mug on the little patio table and leaned back in his chair, silently insisting that she look at him.

"You're asking me to sell you back your farm and while it shouldn't matter to me who buys the farm as long as I get it sold, it does matter. You might not believe this, but I actually care about how that farm is treated."

She knew that Barrett was aware that she cared about this as well, so she didn't bother reminding him. She simply waited.

"I have no problem with the fact that you want to maintain a certain level of discretion, as far as your personal business is concerned but at the end of the day, I believe I have gone out of my way since the moment we met, to prove to you that I have your best interests at heart. Is that not true?"

"It is." Iris sensed that Barrett was disappointed in her.

"I only bought the farm because I was led to believe that you were going to lose it due to financial difficulty."

She nodded, wondering why he was reminding her.

"Yesterday, you informed me that you not only want me to sell the farm back to you, but that you are prepared to pay cash for it.

"As the seller, I intend to protect my interests. I had an offer on the table for the farm before the realtor even scheduled his first showing."

Iris breathed in and dropped her gaze. She should have realized that he'd already have offers.

"When I bought the farm from you, Iris, was it not true that you were forced to sell it because of your indebtedness? Was I misinformed?"

"No, you weren't. That was true."

He rested his ankle on one knee and crossed his arms, favoring her with a look that let her know that he had come for answers that he intended to get.

"You and I have to stop playing these little guessing games, Iris," he said in his low, deliberate way. "I want you to tell me exactly how it is that you are suddenly able to pay cash for a property that you were forced to sell.

"I don't ask out of idle curiosity. I ask because I need to determine the level of honesty between us. I'm sure that John Mabry knows every intimate detail of your apparent windfall.

"Yet, when you stood in front of me yesterday and suggested that you were prepared to pay cash, you then clammed up, as if I were some nosy stranger."

Iris had been looking down at her hands, but now she raised her pretty eyes and stared at him.

"I didn't mean to make you feel that way, Barrett," she said softly. "But the last time we spoke before that was at the coffee shop and you were angry with me. I felt like you were done with any friendship between us. When Harris Clark asked if you were a friend of mine, you said you weren't sure."

He looked at her with an impatient frown. "Are you telling me that you can't understand how that cozy little scene I walked in on would have created doubts for me about that?"

"You told me you felt you were ready for a change. Yes, I was angry. Why should I deny that? I honestly expressed what I was feeling. Has that caused you to decide that I can't be trusted? Have I suddenly become the enemy, Iris?"

She lifted a hand to her throat and shook her head.

Barrett read the look in her eyes and correctly told himself that she hadn't realized how she made him feel. He relented and allowed himself to soften his countenance.

"If that is true, then I'd like to know please, Iris, what has generated this obvious change in your financial status."

She swallowed and wondered how to even begin to tell him, then finally just began working her way through it.

"Did I ever tell you my maiden name, Barrett?"

He shook his head slightly. "I think I would remember."

"It's Foster."

He saw the irony of that and smiled at her. "That had to be difficult."

"It was," she agreed. "I spent all my school years having to explain it." She was glad he had finally smiled at her and returned it gratefully.

"I never knew anything about my people, but that was my name. I had no idea it meant anything special."

She let a brief silence help her focus. "The reason I'm able to pay cash for the farm is because of that item that you found under the bed, Barrett."

He wondered at that. "It wasn't a large enough package to hold the kind of cash you'd need to buy the farm, Iris."

She smiled again. "No. It was a letter from an attorney. He asked me to meet with him to discuss an inheritance."

Barrett looked slightly startled, then fixed Iris with a keen look of awareness. "Foster."

She was confused. "You know that name?"

"You don't?" he countered.

"I didn't. The attorney told me they were involved with some sort of publishing company."

Barrett grinned at her words and looked away toward nothing in particular. "You might say that."

"Thomas and Grace Foster were my grandparents."

Barrett looked down at the pavers and faint little smile flashed across his face, before he took on a more thoughtful expression.

"Well, of course they are," he mused to himself quietly. After a long moment, he looked up at her.

"And what was the letter doing fastened to the bed slats, Iris?" He saw her struggle with an expression of disgust.

"My late husband hid it from me, the way he hid everything else. He had opened it, then hid it under the bed."

"Why didn't he just burn it?" Barrett asked, raking his fingers absently through his hair and waiting for her to answer.

"Why didn't he burn all the other stuff he hid?" she returned, giving in to what she really felt about Glenn Anderson's bizarre behavior.

"It was like some strange power trip, I guess. As long as he had hidden it away, he had a secret. Typical drunk," she muttered darkly under her breath, causing Barrett to raise his brows in surprise.

He sat silently with his thoughts for a while, and Iris let him process what she'd told him, wondering if it made any difference to his being willing to sell the farm back to her.

He seemed to be able to read her mind.

"When I listed the farm, I gave the realtor notice that I wouldn't entertain any offers for three months." He watched her wrinkle her brow, wondering about that.

"It's more than six hundred acres, Iris. I'm sure I don't have to point that out to you."

She made no reply, and willed herself to wait.

"The three month period was for my own peace of mind. I didn't want to make any decisions based on my personal desire to just be rid of the farm. I wanted time to find out what I could about the potential buyers and decide who could be trusted to maintain the farm as it is now."

He shifted his position in the chair and rested his eyes on hers. "It's not that I don't already know that I could trust you in that regard, Iris, but you would have to hire hands to work the farm and I would expect that you would surely return to live in the house. I don't want you staying out here with just any old guy who answered your ad for employment hanging around."

"John Mabry asked me to give him the names of anyone who wanted to work for me, and let him check them out, first," she told him.

Barrett appreciated that offer. "John Mabry seems like a decent individual. For whatever reason, he always seems to be looking out for you."

"I remind him of his daughter that he lost," she told him, folding her arms and setting her gaze on the trees again. "He just told me that yesterday."

She glanced back at him with a question in her eyes. "Why do you have a personal desire to just be rid of the farm?"

He suppressed a sound of impatience and looked steadily at her. "I'll just add that question to my long list of all the things that you should know very well, but pretend not to."

"So you're blaming me?" she asked, returning his steady gaze and revealing her own irritation.

"Are we going there?" he challenged quietly, giving her the impression that he was up for it.

When she wouldn't answer, he decided to cut to the chase and not keep her waiting to hear his decision.

"I won't accept your offer to buy the farm, Iris, but I *will* present a counter offer, if you're willing to hear it."

She had just gone from disappointment to hope again so rapidly, that she was holding her breath.

"I'll take you on as an equal partner for an interim period, before eventually accepting your offer."

Barrett watched her lift her eyes to his, making no effort to mask her confusion. She had no idea what that meant, and he waited for her to ask.

"What does an equal partnership look like?"

"We'll both weigh in on important decisions. I reserve the right to overrule, as you might expect," he added, unable to resist laughing quietly at the way she rolled her eyes.

"Am I supposed to prove to you that I can manage the farm before I can buy it?" she asked him.

"At some point, yes. I wouldn't sell it to you until I was absolutely convinced of that. To begin with, I'll work alongside you and determine how much you've already learned, and how much you're willing to learn. We would start with the crew that I provide.

"I don't expect you to hit the ground running, but I wouldn't be surprised to learn that you've been able to acquire at least some working knowledge of farming and ranching, even if you weren't in a financial position to implement what you knew would be beneficial."

Iris considered his offer, then glanced up at him when she felt him studying her, anticipating more questions.

"Would you take the farm off the market, while you're deciding if I can run it by myself?"

"I would. I don't want that to be a stress factor for you."

She smiled gratefully. "What would be your time frame for the interim period, Barrett?"

He seemed to be mulling that over. "It's hard to speculate this early in the game, but if we can manage to work together without yet another one of our infamous miscues, I would expect you could take ownership by spring.

"Getting this farm and the cattle through winter should be enough of a test to discover your capabilities. If you can manage winter, that's half the battle."

Iris knew that much about farming, and nodded in silent agreement.

"Back to our infamous miscues," she ventured, smiling at the way he lifted one brow in amusement.

"It kind of sounds like if we even have one, it's a breach of contract. That hardly seems fair."

He seemed to agree. "I suppose it's a foregone conclusion that we will have them; we seem to excel in that area." He rested his eyes on her, seeming to thing about it.

"Refusing to work through an issue, walking off without finishing our conflict, and aborting the conversation by simply assuming what the other one meant, then drawing the wrong conclusion determines a miscue that we willfully failed to navigate. That indicates that we reached an impasse and were unable to make the partnership successful. Skirmishes are permitted, as long as they are resolved. Does that seem unreasonable?"

Iris laughed at him. "Did you ever think that you and I would have to have a contract to force us to get along, Barrett?"

He grinned and pushed himself up from his chair, preparing to get on with the rest of his day.

"See, you say that as if I'm not expecting you to actually sign one."

She raised her brows and widened her eyes to stare at him in disbelief, as she stood to her feet.

"Are you saying that we're really going to have one?"

Barrett stopped to stand close to her and look down at her with an amused sweep of brown eyes.

"Oh, yes ma'am. The next time you see me, you'd better have a pen on you, somewhere."

He gave her chin a light stroke with his finger and headed off to his truck, leaving her to watch him go with too many emotions clamoring for her attention to even know which one to address first.

Chapter Twenty-Two

Patricia Webb sat cradling her cup of coffee and beaming happily at her two men. Her son glanced over at her with a smile resting in his eyes.

"Mother, you may be celebrating a little early. The ink's not even dry, yet."

His father reached over to rest his hand on his wife's shoulder with a little laugh. "Barrett's right, Patty. One thing we should have learned about those two by now is that just when their train seems to be running smoothly, someone's gonna leave a cow out on the tracks."

She laughed at that. "I can't believe you went over there and made that poor girl sign a contract!"

"Yes, you can," her handsome son returned dryly.

"Well, maybe I can as far as you're concerned, but who would ever have thought that someone as sweet and gentle as Iris is would need to have a contract to make her behave?"

Barrett grinned. "It's not so much her misbehaving, as it is her expecting me to interpret all those heavy sighs and imploring looks she gives me and then hopping in her truck and taking off when I can't. If that girl wants her farm back, she's going to have to hang around and speak up, from now on." He sent his father a grin when he laughed heartily at that.

"What'd she say, Son, when you pulled that contract out of your pocket and asked her if she had a pen?"

"She gave me a heavy sigh and an imploring look."

This remark generated another round of laughter from both his parents, as Barrett stood and reached over for his hat.

"I'd better get on over there," he said. "She's planning on moving back into the house, instead of driving back and forth from the cottage every day, so I expect we'll both be loading our trucks up with her things."

He said this as if he were complaining, but the light in his eyes betrayed him as he touched the brim of his hat, and headed out to go check on his new partner.

His parents watched him go, happy for their son and hoping that this day would be the one that would place Barrett and Iris on the same course, at last.

Stuart Webb picked up the coffee pot to warm up their cups and glanced over at Patricia with a knowing look.

"Of course, you know that Jackie Coates is going to be fit to be tied, when she gets wind of this," he reminded her.

His wife grimaced. "It's about time that Jackie Coates finds out that she can't get everything she goes after, just because her daddy whips out his checkbook."

Stuart grinned. "I expect she does alright as far as her little hundred acre operation goes, but the only way she could hope to manage a place as big as the Fairfield property would be for her dad to send a busload of ranch hands over there. Still, I wouldn't be surprised if she refuses to just move on and let it go. She's the type to dig her heels in."

Patricia thought about that. "If she tries targeting Iris over this, she'll not only have Barrett showing her the road but I wouldn't be so quick to count Iris out, as far as standing up for herself. She seems much more passive than she really is, if I've gotten to know her at all. Jackie might just be in for a surprise."

She rested her chin on one hand and flashed a happy look at her husband. "Those two are going to need a lot of prayer, Stuart, but I've been thinking that I'm just about prayed out."

"Well, you might want to catch a second wind and get right back in there, Patty," he advised, trading a smile with her. "Because our son needs that contract as much as Iris does, whether he wants to admit it or not."

"Oh, I know!" she exclaimed, widening her brown eyes in agreement. "He's every bit as guilty as Iris, when it comes to just walking off. The only difference is that Barrett kicks up a lot of dust, the way he does it."

Stuart shook with silent laughter, thinking about his brooding, scowling son whose entire day, regardless of what he wanted them to believe, revolved around whatever his current situation with Iris happened to be.

"Well, I don't want to see him stroll back in here again with a thundercloud hanging over his head like it was a while back, when he ran into Iris and that guy at the coffee shop after he spotted her truck," he declared. "I couldn't get two words out of him for the rest of the day."

"I didn't say anything to Barrett, but I had gone over to the cottage to see Iris and she told me that she was seeing someone," Patricia told him, noting his surprised look.

"I was so brokenhearted, Stu, I just got up and left. But it seems like all she did was just meet up for coffee and that was it, because I know her well enough to know that she wouldn't get involved with Barrett and this partnership, if there was still another man in the picture. Iris isn't that type, and she wouldn't leave Barrett in the dark, like that. She would have told him and then let him decide if he wanted to work with her or not, even if it meant not being able to get her farm back."

Her husband happily agreed with that.

⊂⊃⊂⊃⊃

Barrett lifted the intricately carved chest out of Iris's arms that she had insisted she could carry and let her open the screen door for him. She led the way upstairs to her old room and pointed to a place for him to set it down.

"Thank you," she said, just as she did every time he'd take something else out of her hands and carry it.

He looked down at the chest curiously. "That's very old."

Iris nodded. "I bought it years ago at a junk store and thought it would be good to keep blankets and stuff in, but I guess I never ended up using it. I thought it was pretty."

"It's nice," he agreed.

He straightened up and rubbed the back of his neck, before giving her a questioning look.

"Were your landlords upset to see you move so soon?"

Iris shook her head with a sad little smile. She loved Pastor Ben and Miss Katie and she had enjoyed their little visits whenever they dropped by the cottage to check on her.

"They weren't upset." She looked down at a quilt she'd been folding.

"You're going to miss them," Barrett observed quietly.

She nodded, then glanced up and gave him a smile. "I can visit them at their church, though."

He returned her smile, then surprised her by asking her if she was having second thoughts about moving back to the farm.

She raised her brows and shook her head. "No, not at all! I love this place."

He couldn't hide his relief, as he placed his hands on his hips and stood looking around thoughtfully at her room.

"It looks very much as it did before." He studied it, flexing the muscles around his mouth in a way that Iris had come to recognize as Barrett's indication of being deep in thought. After a moment, he looked over at her.

"Do you want to leave the rest of your things in storage, Iris, or should we bring it all here? The rest of the upstairs is pretty much empty."

She gave him a teasing glance. "Don't you want to see if I end up staying or not? I might turn out to be a dismal failure, and have you hand me my walking papers."

He grinned and reached out a hand to rest it on her shoulder and give it a light caress. "I would never hand you walking papers and you know it."

He glanced down at her and gave her a soft little wink before removing his hand and stepping toward the door.

"I'm going to go see if I can get a little coffee going."

She watched him leave and raised her hand to place it on her shoulder where his had rested and smiled to herself before putting the quilt across the foot of her bed and coming downstairs to join him.

He had dumped the wet grounds out of the basket of the percolator and stood washing it under the faucet. Iris paused at the kitchen door and watched him, deciding that he seemed very comfortable in the kitchen.

Barrett could feel her eyes on him and smiled to himself. "Have a seat, Iris. Make yourself at home."

She laughed at the irony of his invitation and came over to pull out a chair and perch on it, with one foot planted on the seat and her arms wrapped around her knee.

"You've obviously made coffee a lot, in your lifetime," she observed.

"That, I have," he admitted. "I'm a bit more familiar with a campfire percolator, but I seem to manage."

He turned the pot on, and came over to the table to pull out a chair, amused by the haphazard way Iris had chosen to get comfortable.

"I see you've broken free from the constraints of finishing school," he commented lightly, causing her to laugh.

He reached over to toy with the pen they'd left on the table after they'd signed the contract that Barrett had tossed in front of her the day before. She had stared at him with wide blue eyes, in disbelief.

She had been so convinced that Barrett would confess to only kidding her about a contract that she wouldn't take him seriously, but it didn't take long for her to realize that he was all business.

He looked at the pen for a moment before raising his eyes to meet hers. "Now, Mrs. Anderson..."

"Miss Foster," she corrected, causing him to raise a brow and study her.

"Is that official?" he asked, not bothering to hide his surprise.

She nodded. "I even signed the contract that way."

He continued to look at her as if he'd lost his place. "Let me recover," he murmured, smiling faintly as she laughed.

He leaned back in his chair and folded his arms, fixing her with a questioning look. "What is one of the most important factors in getting your cattle through a hard winter?"

She drew in her breath. "Is this a pop quiz?"

"It is." He waited.

"I'd start with windbreaks, I guess."

He drew his fingers across his beard absently as a slow smile rested in his eyes. "Very good, Miss Foster. Windbreaks. That's what we're going to look at today, if you're up for it."

"Don't I *have* to be up for it?" she asked, hopping up to find some cups and pour their coffee.

Barrett watched her with a sense of comfort. "Yes, you do, but I'd like for you to pretend that you *want* to be."

"I can do that," she said, setting their cups down and returning to her perch.

He smiled, resting his gaze on his coffee and causing Iris to wonder what he was thinking, but he wasn't sharing. Finally, he folded his arms on the table and searched her eyes with his.

"We need to establish some ground rules."

She waited for him to finish, thinking to herself that they had already done that, the day before.

"From what I've observed, whenever you and I have one of our breakdowns in communication, there always seems to be a third party involved. Would you agree, Iris?"

She nodded slowly.

"We're not doing that, from now on. No matter how obvious something seems to be, regardless of what we think we know or what someone else has told one of us, you and I are going to get alone and talk it over.

"We're going to each be the other's source of truth." He fixed her with a steady gaze. "Iris, I'm very serious."

She swallowed and felt a little hesitant, but made herself ask the question. "Are we talking about what happened here, after Aunt Sadie's funeral?"

"That's the best example, yes." He waited until she raised her eyes to his. "That was only about you and me. No one else." He laid the pen down and reached a finger to touch one of hers.

"You wouldn't let me tell you that. You turned and ran into the house, giving more value to what Blanche Hollis, a complete stranger, had told you than what I would have said, if you'd only let me talk to you."

She knew that was true and nodded, glancing down at the way his fingers rested now on her hand. She looked up at him.

"Isn't that what you did, when you walked out of the coffee shop, Barrett?"

"It is," he conceded quietly. "I won't defend myself by remarking that you did tell me you were ready for a change, only to look over and see some man bringing you coffee and asking if you and I were friends."

Iris turned her hand over to lace her fingers into his, revealing an expression of regret. "Barrett, I understand how that must have looked to you, especially after I told your mother that I was seeing someone."

She realized by the startled look in his eyes that he hadn't known anything about that and hurried to explain.

"She came to the cottage after Mr. John told her where I was living. She wanted to tell me that Blanche Hollis had lied to me and I could sense that she was urging me to talk to you, but she didn't ask. I finally told her that and she got up and left."

A single tear found its way down her cheek. "I didn't want to hurt her but I thought it would help her to not keep hoping for something that didn't seem possible."

Barrett listened to all this quietly, processing it before raising his eyes to search hers.

"You'd actually been seeing him?"

"No," she assured him. "I had already agreed to meet him for coffee one morning before work, but that hadn't happened until the day you walked in and saw us."

She gave his fingers a slight squeeze. "Barrett, it really was just coffee. I hardly know him. He's a relative of the patient I was caring for."

Barrett sat considering all this, realizing that it explained why he'd recently found his mother so brokenhearted, sitting alone in the den. She'd kept it from him, not wanting him to feel what she was feeling.

"I suspect, Iris, that all of this could have been avoided if we'd just been able to talk about it. I was wrong to walk out of the coffee shop the way I did, and I wish you hadn't walked away from me, the night that Blanche Hollis followed us."

"I wish that, too." Her reply was soft and regretful.

Barrett seemed to be about to say something else then stopped himself when they both heard the sound of someone's vehicle door slamming.

He stood up and peered from the kitchen toward the living room to see out the screen door, then clenched his jaw in irritation as he came back over and reached his hand to Iris.

She took it and got up, not missing his dark scowl, clearly puzzled.

Barrett came nearer and looked down into her eyes. "You're about to be tested, Iris. Are you willing to follow my lead and then sit down with me after, and let me talk to you about it?"

He was close enough to make her tremble and she held her breath and nodded up at him.

He reached to stroke her hair. "I have a sense of how this conversation is about to go, and I may lose my temper. I'm asking you to trust me now, and give me your questions, after."

She nodded again, as the sharp knock on the doorframe seemed to be the only thing that stopped him from kissing her.

Barrett held onto her hand and led her out to the front room, to stand beside him at the screen door.

"Jackie," he greeted briefly, with a slight nod.

"Hello, Barrett." Jackie Coates immediately saw the beautiful woman whose slender waist he now slipped his hand around, pulling her closer to him.

Jackie was thrown by the unexpected presence of another woman, having planned to use her own femininity to coax Barrett Webb into selling her his farm.

"What can we do for you?" he asked, waiting for her to let them know, and not missing the way Iris leaned in to rest against him. He tightened his embrace.

Jackie Coates managed to recover and swept her arm to indicate the fields and pastures of the farm. "You can sell me this land," she replied. "I just found out it's been taken off the market. You were going to give me first refusal, Barrett."

"When did I agree to that?" he asked calmly.

She let out a loud sigh. "Okay, we didn't have a deal, but I would have thought, since we're friends, that you would have contacted me to let me know what your offer was and give me a chance to beat it!"

"I don't know that I'd call us friends, Jackie. I'd never spoken to you until you approached me after an auction to ask if I planned to keep the calves I had just bought and gave me a number to call you if I changed my mind, but I didn't call you. I know your daddy fairly well, but I wouldn't necessarily call Jack a friend, either."

His measured tones were irritating Jackie Coates beyond all patience and endurance.

"Well, who bought it, then? Maybe I can convince him to sell it to me."

"It wasn't taken off the market because it was sold. It was taken off the market because we changed our minds."

"We." She looked over at Iris with blatant hostility. "Is this your wife, then? When did you get married?"

"We're working on it," he said smoothly, looking down at Iris with a secret smile that she returned.

Jackie Coates began to fume. "Well, I think that's pretty unprofessional, Barrett Webb, to put a property like this one on the market just to tease everyone and then take it off."

"Do you?" He forced himself to look away from Iris and regarded Jackie Coates with boredom.

"I'm sorry you drove all the way out here, Jackie, but you'll have to look elsewhere to expand your operation. We're not selling. Although," he added thoughtfully, "Harper Scott is. It's about four hundred acres. You might give him a call."

"Four hundred acres of scrub land!" she declared hotly. "This is the only available property around with enough water and trees to get the cattle through the winter, and you know it!"

"I also know that it's not available," he informed her quietly, giving her a dark look that told her he was done. "So Jack won't be writing me any checks."

Jackie pursed her lips and fixed Iris with a resentful stare, before finally turning on her heels and stomping her boots across the porch, on her way to start her truck and throw a little gravel, as she made her angry exit.

Barrett watched her go with a slow grin finding its way across his lips, before he looked down at Iris, who was still being held firmly against his side.

"We'd better go warm up our coffee," he suggested, giving her a soft smile. "Get your questions ready."

He released her reluctantly as they returned to the kitchen.

Iris let him refill their cups, realizing that she actually didn't seem to have any questions. That whole exchange appeared to be self-explanatory.

Barrett slid into his chair and handed her coffee to her with a surprised look.

"What are you waiting for, Miss Foster? Should I go find a Bible to lay my hand on?"

She laughed at that, and he gave her a relieved grin.

"So, we're good, then?"

"We're good."

Chapter Twenty-Three

Barrett watched while his foreman consulted with Iris, as he had asked him to do, regarding how she wanted to provide bedding for the cattle behind the windbreaks that she and Barrett had established throughout the pastures, using high stacks of rolled hay as well as taking advantage of various structures and tight groves of trees.

He noted the confident way she seemed to be expressing herself and approved of the way his foreman took her suggestions as seriously as if receiving them from his boss.

Snow had already made a light appearance and more was predicted to arrive, but both Barrett and Iris felt they were in good shape, as far as being able to keep the cattle warm enough and get their feed to them.

Iris had surprised him by instinctively beginning early on to feed the cattle behind the windbreaks before the weather had turned cold, and she had quickly established a routine that the cattle seemed to adapt to right away, finding their way over to the nearest windbreak the minute they spotted her.

Barrett crossed his arms and continued to appraise today's progress before straddling his horse to go check on the repairs to the old barn that hadn't been used in years, but that would be needed this season.

He should have seen to this much earlier, he chided himself, but he'd allowed distractions to skew his focus. He was bent on remedying that now.

Iris had seen him ride off in the direction of the barn and mounted her own horse to follow him, once the foreman had let her know that he'd have his men get the cattle bedding down.

Her horse stepped gingerly into the wide opening of the barn before she halted him and hopped off to see what Barrett was looking at so intently.

He glanced her way with a slight grimace and pointed overhead. "We've got a cracked support beam."

She frowned and came over to look up at what Barrett had indicated. "Just something else that I allowed to go to ruin," she said, breathing out a sigh of disappointment.

He rested a hand on her back and shook his head, still examining the overhead rafters. "You couldn't have fixed that, even if you'd spotted it, Iris. You weren't in a position to pay anyone else to repair it either at the time, so let it go."

He gave her back a light pat. "I had plenty of time to address this barn, but I kept putting it off to deal with other things, so I'll take on the blame for it."

He moved toward the uprights and laid a hand on them to determine their stability, then flashed her a little grin.

"If we can get that beam repaired or replaced, we should be good, at least for this season."

Iris glanced back up at the large crack in the supporting beam, then motioned for Barrett to come toward her. He wrinkled his brow, but stepped over to her, surprised when she took his hand tightly and led both him and her horse back outside to where his own horse was tethered.

"Don't go back in there, Barrett," she cautioned him. Her face was pale and she seemed to be shaking.

He recognized a look of quiet panic in her eyes and gently pulled her into his arms, absently looking out behind her at the stream, while stroking her back and feeling her heart pounding.

"Alright, then." He soothed her softly.

Barrett held onto her, waiting for her to gather herself before drawing back enough to look down at her.

"What is this about?"

She stared at him, her beautiful eyes filled with anxiety. "That whole roof could fall down any minute!"

He smiled and gave her chin a stroke. "This old barn has been standing here for years, Iris, and I expect with a cracked beam for many of those years.

"The roof's not going to suddenly cave in, just because I walk inside. It just needs to be repaired, since it's a vertical crack, but it's not an imminent threat."

She didn't find that reassuring, and let him know with a frown and a twist of her lips.

"I'm sorry," he offered, deciding not to tease her when she was obviously upset. "Of course, sooner or later, someone has to go in there but we'll be careful when we do."

"Not you," she insisted stubbornly.

"Oh, so you don't care about my men, as long as I remain out of harm's way," he observed, causing her to allow a hint of anger to light up her eyes.

"However you want to put it," she muttered.

He laughed softly and pulled her back into his arms when she tried to push away from him.

"Stop that," he ordered quietly.

She stood stiffly, returning his steady gaze with her own, letting him know that she wasn't going to be made fun of.

Barrett studied her demeanor, not used to the way she was refusing to yield to him, and insisting on remaining displeased with him.

"Alright, talk to me," he advised, not needing to remind her of their agreement.

She blinked back tears. "Don't do stupid things."

He sighed. "I had to go into the barn, Iris, to even be able to discover that the beam is cracked."

She knew he was right, and began to feel foolish. He watched her relent, looking away from him with embarrassment. When she attempted to reach for her horse's reins, he only held her more snugly.

"Not just yet," he murmured.

Iris let him pull her close and as he ran his fingers through her hair, she felt herself relax against him, breathing slower and causing his look of worry to give way to a gentle smile.

"If I didn't know better, Miss Foster, I'd think you were beginning to care for me."

He gave her chin a little tap and released her, reaching for his horse and waiting for her to do the same.

She didn't reply to his light comment, but a faint blush swept across her cheeks, as she mounted her horse and led him away from the barn.

Barrett followed after her, then caught up to her, reaching over to stop her horse and advise her that they needed to place some watering tubs around the property and pick up some tank heaters since she'd already let him know that the stream had sometimes iced over in winter, even though it was spring fed.

He asked her to ride into town with him to pick them up, and suggested that they clean up and grab lunch while they were out. She seemed to brighten up at this idea, having not been off the farm for a couple of straight weeks.

"We'll need to stop by my place so I can wash up, if you don't mind, and just get what we need out that way, instead of Fairfield," he told her.

Barrett had opted to return to his own home each night, no longer staying at the farm once he understood that Iris was quite used to being at the farmhouse alone and wasn't nervous about it. He didn't want to create any sort of breeding ground for gossip, regarding their sleeping arrangements.

She nodded in agreement and he took care of some light chores close to the house, while she ran upstairs to shower and change, hurrying down with a freshness to her natural beauty that Barrett had no trouble appreciating.

Iris had never been to Barrett's home and when he pulled his truck through the large gate with the Webb Enterprises logo visible and continued down the long drive to what looked more like an estate than a rancher's residence, she drew in her breath and looked over at him in disbelief.

"You live here?" she demanded quietly.

"I'm not sure if you're impressed or disappointed," he replied sincerely.

"It's nice, but..."

"It's a little much," he finished, understanding. He often felt that way, himself. "It is," he insisted, when she tried to back away from her obvious impression. "Especially considering the fact that I'm normally only here to shower and go to bed."

He came around to open her door and led the way into the entrance, calling out the name "Gladys" and smiling when a middle-aged, gray-haired woman stepped into view, pleased to see him. She looked at his beautiful guest in surprise.

"Gladys, this is Iris Foster. She's managing the farm I bought in Fairfield." He glanced over at Iris with a teasing grin. "Gladys manages me and this house."

The housekeeper waved his remark away with a laugh and took Iris's hand in welcome.

Barrett informed her that they had just stopped by so that he could clean up, and asked her to make Iris comfortable.

She led Iris to a sitting room just off the entrance, after Barrett had slipped upstairs and asked if she could bring her any sort of refreshment.

Iris declined, but thanked her sweetly and the woman smiled in approval.

"Please feel free, Miss Iris, to check out this house, if you like. Mr. Barrett is usually quick when he has to change but you're welcome to pass the time by looking around. I was sorting through some laundry, so I'll get back to that but I'll hear you, if you need anything."

She directed another look of admiration at the beautiful young woman before taking her leave. Iris wondered why she had invited her to check out the house, before realizing with a bit of embarrassment that Barrett's housekeeper must be considering her as a potential mistress of the home. She was glad no one was there to see the rush of color that this thought generated.

She stood and began to stroll slowly about the large, beautiful room and idly looked at several large framed photos of prize-winning stock and certificates of various achievements, not hearing Barrett as he returned to the room and stood watching her move around in his home with a pleased smile.

"Am I presentable?" he finally asked quietly, and she turned to look at him and nodded.

"You're dashing," she quipped, causing him to grin and hold out his hand to her.

"Gladys, we're off," he called out.

The housekeeper hurried back to see them leave, after taking Iris's hand in hers and telling her what a pleasure it was to have met her.

Barrett opened the truck door for Iris, then came around to hop in, glancing over at her briefly while moving his vehicle around the large circle drive.

"Gladys likes you," he said lightly.

"She seems nice," Iris returned.

"You don't realize the importance of my observation," he informed her. "Gladys has never liked even one female who has stepped into my home, other than my mother. Not that many have," he added, seeing her expression.

She shook her head and smiled at that, but made no reply.

Barrett wasted no time, once they arrived at the local farmer's co-op, arranging to have several long tubs and tank heaters put aside for them to pick up on their way back from having lunch.

When he stopped his truck outside the restaurant, he turned to give Iris a look of apology.

"I really did forget to tell you this, Iris, but Mother called me while I was getting dressed. When she found out that you and I were in town, she asked if she and Dad could meet us here. I'm sorry, I should have asked you first."

She looked surprised. "Why should you have asked me? You know I love your parents."

He took a moment to give her a steady, tender look. "I do know that," he admitted quietly, before coming around to take her hand and accompany her into the restaurant.

Stuart and Patricia Webb had opted to simply sit near the entrance, rather than being seated and stood to greet Barrett and Iris as they came in. Patricia immediately gathered Iris into a motherly embrace.

"Hello, sweetheart," she breathed, giving her a little squeeze that Iris returned.

The host seated them when their party was complete and they sat making small talk after their drink orders were given, glancing down at their menus, and waiting to engage in more involved conversations after their waiter took their orders.

Finally, Stuart Webb folded his hands, resting them on the table, and provided his son with a teasing look.

"Well, since you and Iris wouldn't sell the farm to Jackie Coates, she had to settle for Randall Cooksey's place."

Iris heard the way Barrett's father seemed to imply that the farm was owned jointly between her and his son, and the ghost of a smile washed over her lips. Barrett noticed and shot a little wink at her.

"Randall Cooksey's place isn't bad," he replied. "Some of it's a little rocky but he's got some good grass."

His father nodded. "It's alright for grazing, but he didn't get any hay planted this year so she'll have to buy that from someone else. Don't be surprised if she tries to get you to sell her some."

Barrett fixed his dad with a look of quiet exasperation. "All these years and we've never had two words with Jackie Coates. Why has she suddenly begun acting as if we're friends and that we owe her deals on everything?"

"She seems to think you're getting married, Barrett," his father informed him, grinning at his son's expression.

"Iris and I may have let her leave thinking that," he admitted with a little laugh. "It sent her packing though, didn't it?" He directed this to Iris who flashed him a shy grin, but made no comment.

Patricia looked over at the lovely young woman with an apologetic smile, as they both sat and listened to the two Webb men continuing to talk business, getting caught up.

"Did you and Iris get enough hay for your cattle, Barrett?" Stuart asked, prepared to offer some, if they needed it.

"We have enough," Barrett assured him, glancing over at Iris for her confirmation. "I had good luck getting milo to grow out there, Dad. I started with an acre to test, and then ended up with five. I kept it fenced off to keep the cows out of it, so we'd have it to feed this winter. We actually have more than we need, if you want to come pick some up."

His dad looked interested in that and told him that he might take him up on his offer, as their food was brought to them and served.

Iris smiled as the Webb family bowed their heads and Stuart gave thanks, before they began to eat. It made her feel warm to be included, especially when Barrett's dad included Iris in the list of things they were thankful for.

Barrett gave her a soft smile when the prayer was over, seeming to read her thoughts, and she returned it.

Stuart was interested in their efforts to ready their cattle for winter and his questions soon led to the fact that there was a barn on the property but that the roof's central support beam had a large crack in it.

"I'm afraid it's a vertical crack and it's nice and deep," Barrett sighed. "I need to figure out how to repair it without upsetting my partner, here," he added, looking over at Iris with a teasing grin. She rolled her eyes, causing him to laugh, as his parents looked on with happy but confused faces.

"She's afraid I'm going to be crushed by a collapsing roof," Barrett informed them.

Patricia opened her eyes wide and rested a hand on her throat. "Barrett Webb, you hire a construction crew to handle the roof, and stay out of that barn!"

Barrett and his dad both laughed at the women's concern.

"I'm glad Mother doesn't know about that time you and I had to use ropes and carabiners to climb up and patch the top of that old silo, Dad," Barrett said, generating another round of feminine gasps and hearty laughter from his father.

"I've always said what your mother doesn't know won't hurt us," Stuart joked, reaching over and touching her cheek. She made a face at him, then grinned over at Iris.

"I'm so glad to have you around to take some of this off me, honey," she declared theatrically. "These two have pretty much worn my prayer knees out!"

Stuart Webb had been resting a teasing expression on Iris for a few minutes, and she could tell that he was just waiting to kid her about something.

"Well," he began, resting his napkin on his lap and giving her a look of amusement, "which one of you two breached the contract first? My money's on Barrett."

Iris laughed at that, and Stuart's son leaned back in his chair to wait for her response.

"Barrett's been very careful to warn me first, when the potential is there for me to mess up," she confessed, drawing a tender smile from her partner.

"That's because I don't want you going anywhere," he admitted lightly, looking down at his plate and toying with his salad fork.

"Isn't that a little like giving Iris the test and the answer sheet, at the same time?" His father persisted in his teasing and Barrett grinned at him.

"That's exactly what it's like," he agreed, as his father chuckled to himself, finding their situation to be very much to his liking.

Patricia leaned forward to get everyone's attention. "Our house for Thanksgiving?" she suggested, looking more at Iris than at her son, in a way that let her realize that she was to be considered a family member.

Iris looked over at Barrett with a question in her eyes and he nodded. "That sounds really nice," she said, smiling over at his mother and resting a hand on her arm.

"Perfect!" Stuart approved.

"Let's not lock in Christmas just yet, though," Barrett cautioned. "If Iris and I get things running as smoothly as we'd like, maybe we could have Christmas at the farmhouse."

Iris rested her sweet eyes on him and her expression was so beautifully childlike that Barrett decided he'd make it happen.

They prepared to leave and stopped at the entrance to say goodbye reluctantly, but grateful for their visit.

Patricia hugged Iris and promised to get in touch with her about the Thanksgiving details, and Stuart kidded them both about trying to resist eloping just to finish Jackie Coates off, which left the sound of laughter in the air, as they parted ways.

Chapter Twenty-Four

Barrett had arrived at the farmhouse early, and used his key to let himself in to start coffee, suspecting that Iris was still in bed, since daylight was only just now beginning to manifest itself. He imagined that she was probably still asleep, which led to his surprise when he stepped into the kitchen to find her seated at the kitchen table, resting her head on her folded arms, not seeming to be aware of his presence.

He frowned and called her name quietly to keep from startling her. When she didn't respond, he quickly made his way to kneel beside her chair and lifted her hair back so that he could see her face.

"Iris, are you okay?"

She did turn her face to look at him, but didn't answer him, and he reached to touch her face, immediately realizing that she was burning up with a fever.

Barrett picked her up and carried her to the sofa to lie down, while he tried to determine how responsive she was. She seemed to want to answer his questions, but had difficulty finishing anything she tried to say.

Barrett was finally able to understand that she had come downstairs sometime during the night after waking up thirsty, but hadn't made it past the table. She had begun to feel disoriented and was too tired to look for water. Once she found a chair to sit down on, she remained there with her head resting on the table, for the rest of the night.

Barrett's mind was racing, while he tried to decide whether to try to break her fever with some aspirin and a cool cloth, or to go ahead and drive her to the emergency room.

He finally called his mother to get her advice and she had him ask Iris enough questions to feel certain that she was dealing with food poisoning.

Patricia told him that she was stopping to pick up some electrolytes and something for the nausea and fever and that she'd be right on over.

Barrett hung up and continued to kneel next to Iris, looking at her with sadness shadowing his face. He leaned over to lay a kiss on her hot forehead and she opened her eyes to try to smile at him.

"I'm taking you up to bed," he whispered, gathering her into his arms and carrying her upstairs to her room, so that she could be more comfortable. He laid her down gently, and pulled a sheet over her, adding a pillow in the hopes that she wouldn't feel as nauseated slightly elevated as she might, lying flat.

"What can I get you, Iris?" Barrett asked her quietly, from his kneeling position at her bedside. "I think you need to try to drink some water, even though it may trigger your nausea. But I suspect you're dehydrated."

He started to stand, but waited when she reached her hand to touch his face. Tears began to find their way down her cheeks, and he felt his own eyes brimming over, due to his sense of frustration at not being able to help her.

"What is it, sweetheart?" he breathed softly, brushing her hair back and letting his troubled eyes travel the contours of her pale, beautiful face.

"I'm sorry," she said faintly.

Barrett drew his brows in confusion. "You don't need to be sorry. You can't help being sick, Iris."

She shook her head, but didn't try to say anything else.

Barrett waited a moment before attempting to stand up again, thinking that he should bring her waste can over to the side of the bed and wondering if he should try to warm up her chilly room or leave it cool. He wondered all sorts of things, and began to feel impatient with himself for not knowing how to help her.

He tried to stand and Iris stopped him again by reaching her hand to his face.

"Don't go, Barrett," she whispered.

"I won't leave you, Iris," he promised. "But I thought I should bring you a glass of water from the kitchen and make a cool compress to lay on your head. Does that sound like it might make you feel better?"

She nodded but clutched at him again, when he tried to get up to bring the water.

Barrett drew in a breath, wondering if her fever was causing her to be so unwilling to let him go. He thought about the fact that she had just spent an entire night by herself, in a chair, in a lonely farmhouse and began to understand that having someone with her might be what she needed, knowing that his mother could always bring some water up once she arrived.

She found his hand and brought it to her cheek, and opened her eyes to see him smiling softly at her. She gave him a shaky smile. "I'm so sorry," she repeated.

"Honey, you don't need to say that," he insisted. "Don't be sorry. You can't help it."

Iris looked steadily at him, her normally clear blue eyes still beautiful, but listless. She was watching him and he wondered why she was so intent.

Barrett let her read him and rested his eyes on hers, taking advantage of this rare moment between them, that allowed them to say things to each other silently with their eyes that they would never put words to.

After a long moment, Iris touched him again and he closed his eyes, as her fingers softly traced the lines of his face. He slowly opened his eyes and lifted his hand to stroke her cheek with a gentleness that seemed to calm her.

"I ruined everything," Iris suddenly whispered, and he looked at her with a pained expression, wondering if the fever was causing a bit of delusion.

"No, Iris," he soothed. "Nothing is ruined. Everything's okay." He glanced away, as he heard the front door open and his mother's quick, light steps coming up the stairs.

"Mother's come to help, Iris," he let her know, and she lifted her eyes to Patricia, as she hurried over to her side, seeming like an angel to Iris in that moment.

"She hasn't let me leave her side," Barrett said softly to his mother. "Now that you're here to stay with her, what do you need me to bring from downstairs?"

"Get a glass of ice, honey, and a small towel we can get wet for a compress."

He nodded, but both he and Patricia were surprised when Iris once again reached for Barrett and begged him not to leave her. He immediately lowered himself back down close to her.

"But Mother's here, now, Iris, so you won't be alone. I'm just going to get you something cold to drink. I'll be right back, I promise."

She began to cry softly and Patricia laid a hand on Barrett's shoulder. "She wants you, Barrett. I'll go get what we need. The poor lamb is burning up, so I imagine she's a little unsettled in her mind, right now. She trusts you."

Patricia reached into the bag she'd carried in and brought out a blood pressure monitor and took a reading, with a grim face, looking up at Barrett when he asked her if it was high.

She shook her head. "Very low, which I expected."

She hurried out to grab some ice and a towel while Barrett let Iris know that he was close, and that he wouldn't leave her. She seemed to rest when she heard him say that, but her face did seem to register a slight grimace.

"Are you hurting?" he asked, and she touched her head and tried to nod. "You have a headache," he realized. "We'll get you something for that, Iris."

She whispered something that he couldn't understand and he came close and asked her to say it again.

"I love you," Iris said, almost too faintly for him to hear.

Barrett wanted to feel good about hearing her say that to him at last, but he told himself that it was her high fever and her fear of him leaving her that made her say it. Still, when he saw a couple of tears gather on her lashes, he brushed her ear with his lips and whispered that he loved her, too.

She smiled faintly and seemed to drift off to sleep.

When Patricia came into the room, she seemed relieved to see Iris resting more quietly and pulled a chair over to be able to put a compress on her forehead. She poured some of the clear electrolyte drink into the glass of ice, and placed a straw in it, glancing up at Barrett as he moved around to the other side of Iris's bed, and stood looking down at her with his jaw clenching. He was making an effort to control his feeling of helplessness.

"She'll be okay, Son," Patricia assured him with a smile. "We'll try to figure out how she got this when she feels better, but once she's better hydrated and the fever breaks, then she'll be okay."

"She has a headache," Barrett volunteered, and she nodded.

"That's because she's dehydrated and worn out."

"She spent the whole night sitting in a kitchen chair with her head on the table."

Barrett's voice sounded rough with emotion, as he said this, and Patricia looked back at Iris with a sad shake of her head and a sigh.

"My poor, sweet lamb," she fretted softly, touching the cool, wet towel to Iris's hot skin and praying silently for her.

Barrett began to relax when he saw how gentle his mother was with Iris. He watched Iris's sweet face carefully and saw her countenance gradually soften, not realizing how drawn with pain her features had been until he saw them begin to ease.

He didn't know whether to stay or try to take care of some chores while his mother was with Iris, so that he could stay by her side when Patricia needed to go home.

She seemed to recognize her son's dilemma. "Just keep your phone close, Barrett. I'll call, if we need you."

"I won't go far," he replied softly, slowly moving away reluctantly and lingering at the door to look back at Iris, before finally giving his mother a nod and forcing himself to go downstairs.

He stopped at the foot of the stairs and knelt to breathe a quiet prayer for her, before standing and swiping the back of his hand across his eyes and heading out to check on the cattle.

He stood at the fence, waiting to make up his mind if he should leave or not, and took in a deep breath, thinking about Iris and the way she whispered that she loved him. He felt a strange sense of disappointment, instead of feeling glad, telling himself that she was delusional and that the fever made her talk out of her head.

Realizing that this was probably true caused Barrett to feel cheated, thinking of how he had longed to hear her say those words and when she finally did, she didn't mean them.

This only made him more impatient with himself. It wasn't her fault. It was foolish for him to resent her saying that she loved him, while she was delirious with a fever.

He blew out a cleansing breath and strode out across the pasture as Nip spotted him and hurried to catch up.

The sun finally peeked through a slim opening in the curtains to strike Barrett in the eyes and cause him to wake up slowly. It took him a moment to remember that he had slept on the couch downstairs at the farmhouse and his mother had stayed with Iris, on the daybed in her room.

He pulled himself up to think clearly and stood to glance up the stairwell, before heading up to check on Iris.

He didn't knock, in case they both were asleep, but gently opened the door and looked in, slowly coming over to stand by her bed and let his eyes rest on her face. There was more color in her cheeks this morning.

Barrett glanced over to note that his mother was still asleep across the room and tried to be quiet, as he knelt down and watched Iris resting.

She seemed to be aware of him, and slowly opened her eyes then smiled sweetly at him. Barrett stroked her forehead, so grateful to discover that her fever had broken, that tears gathered in his eyes.

Iris reached her hand to his face and smiled and Barrett's heart seemed to miss a beat, as he realized that she wasn't running a fever, but still wanted to touch him.

He looked at her in wonder, and she continued to rest her eyes tenderly on him.

"Thank you, Barrett," she whispered.

He shook his head. "It was Mother who helped you," he admitted. "I didn't do anything."

"You stayed with me," she said, still whispering and tracing his cheek with her finger.

Barrett took in a breath and they exchanged a long look between them, before he asked her if she still felt sick at all.

"Just tired," she admitted. "But I'll be okay."

Barrett looked down at the floor and she watched him, wondering what he was thinking.

He finally remembered something and smiled at her. "We have a new calf."

Iris's eyes lit up. "Can I go see it?"

"Not right now, you can't," Patricia Webb said firmly, pushing herself up from the daybed and giving her a big smile. "Good morning, Sunshine," she added, with a little laugh.

"Good morning," Iris answered, sounding so much better that Patricia hopped up to take a closer look at her patient.

"Oh, look at you," she crooned. She looked over at her son, who had yet to take his eyes off Iris. "Isn't she a beauty?"

"She is," he said simply, and Iris smiled at him.

"When can I get up?" she wondered.

"How's your headache?" he countered, and she thought about it.

"It's not like a headache now. But it feels a little sore, I guess from having a headache, if that makes sense."

"That's not uncommon," Patricia told her.

They looked around, when they heard the front door open and boots begin to come up the stairs.

"It's only me," a familiar voice warned them, and Patricia grinned.

"We're in Iris's room," she sang out, then met her husband at the door with a good morning hug.

He gave her a kiss then came in to see how the patient was, noting the tired way his son was keeping his head down, after he had moved over to sit at the foot of her bed.

He came around to rest a hand on Barrett's shoulder and gave Iris a grin. "Don't you have cows to take care of?" he joked and she gave him a little laugh.

"They won't let me get up," she complained, causing Barrett to roll his eyes and make her laugh again.

Stuart Webb had a newspaper under one arm and brought it out now with a little flourish.

"Iris, what's the last thing you remember eating?"

She thought about it. "When I was downtown, I stopped to get a salad from a food truck."

He handed the paper to Barrett, who looked at the section that his father indicated and began to allow a slow anger to burn in his eyes, as he handed it back and looked out of the window next to the foot of Iris's bed with a firm set to his jaw.

Patricia came over and took the paper to see what had just upset her son and her expression wasn't much better. "Didn't that old man already lose his license to run that truck?"

"I thought he had, but he's back at it, apparently."

Iris looked at their faces, unsure of what they meant, then searched Barrett's face.

"Was it a gray truck with a hand printed menu on the side?" he asked and continued to look out the window darkly when she nodded.

"That's old man Beech, who used to be a truck farmer and then began selling lunches from his truck," Patricia explained. "He never washes anything, Iris. You would think vegetables would be safe, but not if they're filthy, and who knows what he sprays them with."

"He would make a salad with vegetables he didn't wash?" she asked, looking slightly shocked.

"That's what he was cited for," Stuart Webb informed her dryly. "I guess others ended up like you, and he was picked up yesterday evening. It's not his first offense, so there's no way of knowing whether his fine will be high enough to make him stop," he added with a shake of his head.

Barrett promised himself that if he ever caught him peddling out of his truck again, he would make him stop, but he resisted making the comment and decided to focus on being grateful that Iris was going to recover.

Stuart and Patricia visited with her a little longer before Patricia decided that it was safe to leave her in Barrett's care.

She told her husband that she'd follow him back to their house, then leaned down to give Iris a kiss on the cheek and had one to spare for her son, as well.

She flashed him a special smile, meant to let him know that she understood what he was feeling, and he gave her a squeeze and thanked her for helping them.

Iris echoed his thanks and Patricia waved at them both and followed Stuart out to their vehicles.

Barrett moved over to stand at the window and look down at his parents as his mother gave his father another big hug and made him laugh at something she said.

He watched them drive away, with a leftover faint smile on his lips. Iris studied him closely.

"Barrett?"

He looked over at her with raised brows, wondering if she needed anything.

She patted the mattress next to her and he came over to rest beside her.

Iris raised her eyes to his, and a blush of shyness washed over her face but she bit her bottom lip and made herself get past it.

"I heard you," she confided, unable to keep tears from rushing to her eyes.

He looked at her curiously, wondering what she meant.

Iris continued to gaze at him, as if she were trying to prod him to remember, but didn't know what else to say.

"I'm gonna need more," he teased softly, his eyes resting on her with a tenderness in them.

She hesitated, wondering if he hadn't meant what he'd said and was deliberately not remembering. She couldn't hide her disappointment and he lifted her hand to his lips and kissed her fingertips.

"According to our contract, we are required to finish this conversation," he reminded her, smiling at her attempt to look put out with him.

"I mean..." Iris paused. "I just started it, so you finish it."

He laughed quietly. "Is that a new rule?"

She nodded and he laughed again.

"You can't just arbitrarily bring in new rules, you know."

She grinned at him. "I've been sick. Humor me."

He gave her a look that caused her pulse to race. "I'm gonna need more," he repeated in a whisper.

She blushed again, becoming self-conscious.

Barrett reached over to pick up a pillow, then slipped a hand behind her shoulder to persuade her to come forward, leaning close, and positioning the pillow behind her to help her sit up straighter. He had to hover very close to do this, and took his time moving back, pausing to let his eyes search hers.

She held his gaze and after a long moment, he gave her a slow smile.

"I may have heard you, as well," he murmured.

Iris drew in her breath and waited to see if he would continue. She seemed to become nervous.

"Are we going there?" Barrett challenged quietly, fully expecting her to lose her nerve and shy away.

She nodded, and smiled at his skeptical expression.

"You have just managed to surprise me, Miss Foster," he said lightly, watching her closely to determine if she really understood what he was asking her.

"Did I ever tell you what I thought of doing with the land around the lake, if I was able to buy back the farm?" she suddenly asked him, causing him to lean back and narrow his eyes to examine her.

He shook his head slowly, and waited.

"I thought about building a home there," she told him, wondering what his reaction would be.

"So did I," he informed her, enjoying her stunned reaction.

She lifted her arms to rest them on his shoulders.

"That was me, giving you more," she said, furnishing him with a little smirk when he laughed.

"I see." Barrett moved closer, and Iris slipped her hands behind his neck. "I suppose that means it's my move."

"It is."

"Of course you realize that we're only a couple of weeks away from our contract expiring," he pointed out, not missing her frown of confusion.

"Does that change things?" she asked, becoming serious.

"It may," he replied. "At the end of our contract, I'm supposed to let you know if you can buy the farm."

She continued to frown. That wasn't what she wanted, anymore, but she didn't tell him, even though the rules of their contract stipulated that she had to.

Barrett seemed to suddenly wander off after his own sober thoughts. "Over the past twenty-four hours, I was afraid you had decided to buy the farm in the metaphorical sense."

His face was lined with stress, and when he raised his eyes to look at her, they were filled with uncertainty.

"I imagined all sorts of illnesses. I was afraid I might lose you, and it would have ended me. I came very close to coming in here in the dead of night and taking you to the hospital, regardless of what Mother thought was wrong with you."

Iris gently raked her fingers through his dark curls and looked at him with regret. "I'm fine, now, Barrett. Let's not dwell on it. If I'm sad, I can't be mad at you."

She made him smile.

"You're bent on being mad at me, then."

"I am. It's up to you to make me glad."

"Let's revisit the irony of the situation," he suggested, as a lazy grin reminded Iris to appreciate how handsome he was.

She thought about what he'd said to her about the irony of the situation the day he found her at the farm, and she asked if she could buy it back from him.

"You said that the irony was that I could have had the farm, that you would have given it to me."

He nodded and waited, wondering if this beautiful, frustrating woman would ever figure it out.

When she continued to look clueless, Barrett made a small sound of impatience.

"We're like a huge jigsaw puzzle, you and I, and all the pieces are blue!"

She looked so shocked at his outburst that he gave into a soft laugh.

"Iris, sweetheart, you are working on my last nerve."

"Well, then help me!" she snapped, causing him to laugh at her again.

"I see you're feeling better," he observed.

She had to smile at that. "Please, and thank you," she added belatedly.

Barrett's patience was wearing thin. He was just going to have to risk it all, and let the chips fall.

"You want me to help you understand what I meant by saying I would have given you the farm," he stated, in an attempt to just be clear, and she nodded.

He moved forward to sit as close to her as he could, and slipped his hand up into her hair before kissing her, not as he had kissed her before but slowly and deliberately, sensing her responses and catering to them, taking his time and leaving no doubt as to his intentions.

It was a long while before he rested his forehead against hers, as he had done once before, and they closed their eyes as the same heady rush coursed through both of them.

"If you wish to understand the irony of the situation, then marry me," he whispered.

Iris drew in her breath and let it out slowly, meeting his gaze and holding it with her own.

"Oh," she breathed faintly.

"Oh," he agreed, with a gentle smile.

Iris returned to her original confession. "I heard you."

"And I heard you."

She saw where this was headed and rescued them.

"I love you."

Barrett pulled her up from her pillows and wrapped her in his arms, looking into her eyes in a way that left her breathless.

"And I love you," he returned, giving her a little kiss.

"You didn't really ask me, though," she reminded him.

"No. Technically, I was simply letting you know what the irony of the situation was," he teased, smiling at her version of a displeased scowl.

"I'm asking you now," he said quietly, just when she began to think that he didn't intend to. "In fact, I'm begging you."

"Because you need a mechanic?" she asked dryly.

Barrett struggled not to laugh at that and she reluctantly smiled at him.

He lifted a strand of her beautiful hair out of her eyes and looked at her in a way he never had before.

"Please marry me," he whispered.

She nodded, more tears beginning to appear.

"You have to say yes," he instructed.

"Yes."

"I should warn you," he said after another long kiss. "I don't believe in long engagements."

"I know a minister," Iris reminded him.

Barrett looked around and found her phone, giving it to her, and holding up his own.

"You call Pastor Ben and I'll call the Webbs."

Chapter Twenty-Five

Iris stood watching with peaceful contentment resting in her pretty eyes, as their dream home began to emerge from its foundation by the lake. A new road had been made from the main highway to this location, and a beautiful rail fence flanked it on each side, as well as expanding from the entrance across the long frontage of the property.

The old road had been closed with a wide gate that would only be opened to allow various farm equipment to access the acreage and the back gate that Iris used to plant her foot on and ride while she pushed it open was no longer needed.

The farmhouse would soon be torn down. Her husband had asked Iris if she would be upset about that, and offered to leave it if it would be a difficult thing for her, but she confided to him that she wanted to live in a house that only the two of them had ever shared, and that the old farmhouse was the site of too many bleak memories and represented a past that she wanted to walk away from.

She had caused him to break into a pleased grin by telling him this, and it only served to propel him toward creating their forever home to sink their roots deep into, raise their family and watch the efforts of their labor grow and flourish.

Iris smiled to herself when she felt Barrett's strong arms reach around from behind her and pull her back against his chest. She flinched just a little when he nuzzled her neck with tender affection.

"What do you think, Mrs. Webb?" he asked in a low tone that had a lilt of happiness in it.

She covered his arms with her own and breathed in the warm late spring air.

"I think if I squint hard enough, I can see our entire future," she replied.

He dropped a kiss on her head and stood watching the progress of the construction crew with the same light of joy in his eyes that rested in his wife's.

After a quiet moment, he laughed quietly, nodding toward the lake as Nip apparently decided to beef up his résumé by trying to herd a flock of ducks.

"We may have to hire Nip a crew of cattle dogs to train," he mused, appreciating his efforts.

Barrett reached to catch Iris's hand and persuaded her to walk with him to the orchard that was now within view of their new home. They both were pleased with the second wind the orchard seemed to have caught once dead limbs had been pruned and care had been taken to keep the old trees healthy.

Iris stood looking up with a childlike smile of pleasure and Barrett watched her, as the sun lit up her beautiful hair and a subtle breeze played with the thin summer dress she had on.

He coaxed her to come closer and she seemed to know that he just needed a special moment with her. They stood resting against each other, closing their eyes and letting themselves get lost in their silent conversation.

"You do realize," Barrett pointed out softly, "that by marrying me, you ended up extending our contract."

She opened her eyes and gave him a puzzled look. "How do you figure that?"

A mischievous grin lit up his eyes. "Do you always sign your name to papers you don't bother to read?"

She looked at him suspiciously. "The only thing I signed was a marriage license."

"Did you happen to count the pages?" he asked, watching her stare at him in bewilderment.

"Why should I have counted the pages?" she demanded.

He shrugged and she gave his arm a little pop.

"What did you make me sign?" she persisted.

"I didn't make you sign anything, sweetheart. I just gave you a pen and you blazed a trail of ink, from one page to another. That's just how eager you were to marry me."

"What did you make me sign?" she repeated, viewing him with a bit of reservation.

"It's all very vague," he replied airily. "Something about always obeying me and never keeping anything from me, and something along the lines of committing to never walk away in the middle of an argument. The specifics escape me, now. But I'm sure we have a copy of it, somewhere. I'll try to find it, if I remember. Maybe."

Iris tilted her head and regarded him with a slow smile.

Barrett suspected he was looking at trouble but he thought he could take her, and decided he was up for it.

Also by Rhonda Hanson

The Father Series

Father's Choice
Father's Wings
Father's Song

A linked novel

Father's Friend

The Master Of Hawthorn Manor

The Adventures of Pahwoo and Her Friends

Grace Under Pressure Publishing
P.O. Box 337
Bell Buckle, TN 37020

graceunderpressure.com

Printed in the USA
CPSIA information can be obtained
at www.ICGtesting.com
JSHW010848010724
65665JS00005B/17